"Madeline, fr
through the s
you, very mu

"I..." she took a small step toward him, ...ned an inch toward her "...think..."

With a short leap she was back in his arms. She tipped her face up to him. With a smile she cupped her cold fingers on his cheeks and drew his head down.

"I like you, too, very much."

Her kiss was sweet, and it was steamy and ardent. It was his undoing. He was completely captured. How could a woman melt against him like that and not be his for all time?

She could not.

When she would have drawn away, he held her tighter. He felt it when she gave herself back to him and to the unrestrained fever that bound them to the moment.

Author Note

Thank you so much for picking up a copy of *Rescued by the Viscount's Ring*. It really does mean a great deal to me that you have chosen to spend time with Madeline Macooish and Rees Dalton.

If you read *The Earl's American Heiress* you will recall that Madeline ran away with a stranger. As you probably guessed, things did not end the way she expected them to. What she had thought would happen was that she would marry the man she chose, not the earl her grandfather had appointed her to wed.

Rather than finding love and independence, she finds herself boarding a ship bound for Great Britain, alone, penniless and in search of her family.

Her great act of independence leads smack into wedlock with a stranger. All she gains by running away is a guilty conscience...and of course Rees Dalton, eleventh earl of Glenbrook.

It does not take long for them to care deeply for each other. Making a lifetime commitment takes a bit longer.

This story deals with forgiveness, both needed and granted. Haven't we all been in the position of either needing it or granting it?

How much can be forgiven?

I'm certain you know...it's quite a lot when love is at the heart of things.

I hope you enjoy Madeline and Rees's journey to find it.

CAROL ARENS

—

Rescued by the Viscount's Ring

HARLEQUIN
HISTORICAL

HARLEQUIN®
HISTORICAL™

Recycling programs
for this product may
not exist in your area.

ISBN-13: 978-1-335-50531-6

Rescued by the Viscount's Ring

This edition published by arrangement with Harlequin Books S.A.

For questions and comments about the quality of this book,
please contact us at CustomerService@Harlequin.com.

Harlequin Enterprises ULC
22 Adelaide St. West, 40th Floor
Toronto, Ontario M5H 4E3, Canada
www.Harlequin.com

Printed in U.S.A.

Carol Arens delights in tossing fictional characters into hot water, watching them steam and then giving them a happily-ever-after. When she is not writing, she enjoys spending time with her family, beach camping or lounging about a mountain cabin. At home, she enjoys playing with her grandchildren and gardening. During rare spare moments, you will find her snuggled up with a good book. Carol enjoys hearing from readers at carolarens@yahoo.com or on Facebook.

Books by Carol Arens

Harlequin Historical

Dreaming of a Western Christmas
"Snowbound with the Cowboy"
Western Christmas Proposals
"The Sheriff's Christmas Proposal"
The Cowboy's Cinderella
Western Christmas Brides
"A Kiss from the Cowboy"
The Rancher's Inconvenient Bride
A Ranch to Call Home
A Texas Christmas Reunion
The Earl's American Heiress
Rescued by the Viscount's Ring

Visit the Author Profile page
at Harlequin.com for more titles.

For Avery Michelle De Cuir,

Your nurturing spirit and generous nature
are a blessing to all who love you...and there are
a lot of us, my sweet granddaughter.

Chapter One

New York Harbour—December 1889

Madeline Macooish was not one to use ugly language, even under her breath. Which did not mean she did not think of colourful words on occasion—on this occasion, to be precise.

No matter how she tried to outwit Bertrand Fenster, she could not. He trailed her like a pesky fly or a bad odour. Like a bout of hiccups that returned time after time.

Like a suitor intent on acquiring her grandfather's fortune, which, of course, was exactly what he was. She ought to have known better than to be led astray—far astray—by the deceitful smile of a scoundrel.

Feeling his greedy gaze on her back, she spun about, glare at the ready.

All she saw were masts bobbing at anchor, along with red funnels spewing smoke and steam towards the mass of grey clouds stretching from the mouth of the Hudson to the eastern horizon.

Oh, but he was here. She'd felt his lurking presence on and off ever since she parted company with him in Chicago a few months ago.

She ought to be used to it by now, to not feel threatened

by his secretive pursuit, but she would feel more at ease with an ocean between them.

Truly, what sort of false-hearted cad continued to trail his prey even when she had informed him, from the very beginning, no less, that she was no longer entitled to a fortune? Indeed, she had made it clear that in running off with him she had forfeited any money Grandfather would have given her.

And not because he would cut her off. No—he would never do that—but because she had betrayed him by running away and did not deserve one cent from that dear man.

Sadly, for all that she considered herself to be an excellent judge of character, she had fallen under the spell of the hoodwinker's charm, had believed him to be sincere when he vowed his eternal devotion.

It was her own fault that she was in this situation. Had she been more level-headed she would not have run off, but married the man Grandfather had intended her to. That union would not have been the love match she had always dreamed of, but neither would she have been missing her family as desperately as she did now.

She had to conclude that love was blind, as the saying went. However, looking back on things, she now realised it had not been love she had felt, but rather infatuation.

Luckily she had come to learn that Bertrand was a bit dim in spite of his winning facade and handsome face.

The deep bellow of a ship's horn thrummed over the harbour. Another answered.

Straightening her shoulders, Madeline gathered her smile and approached the ticket office. It was time to sail for Liverpool.

She had worked hard at odd jobs to earn the fare and had exactly enough money for a steerage ticket, but no more.

'Good day,' she said to the ticket master standing behind the window. 'I'd like to book passage on the first ship going to Liverpool.'

'That would be the *Edwina*, at dock right there across the road.' He nodded towards the large, modern-looking vessel. 'She's sailing on the hour.'

Truly, that was rather perfect. It was unlikely that Bertrand would have time to follow her even if he did have the funds to do so.

'Oh, that will do nicely.'

'Will that be steerage, miss?'

Her plain but clean gown should have made that obvious. In the past when she had travelled with Grandfather her frilly gowns made it clear that she travelled first class, no matter the mode of transportation. This was bound to be a far different trip than any she had taken before.

She nodded, smiling. She was going to find Grandfather, to beg his forgiveness for what she had done to him. If need be, she would cross the ocean, sleeping on the deck. She missed him more than she could ever have imagined.

'That will be thirty dollars.'

That much? Madeline gulped past the tight button on her collar. She withdrew the money from her purse, counted it out to the ticket master, knowing it would be two dollars short.

'Oh, dear.' She blinked at him, pressed her lips into a tight circle. 'I must have lost... Oh, I was certain I had the full fare only an hour ago.'

'There's the *Sea Minnow* sailing next week. She's a smaller vessel, but seaworthy. Her fare is only twenty-five.'

'Oh, but my situation is urgent.' She glanced over her shoulder, spotted Bertrand emerging from behind a stack of crates. 'Is there perhaps something cheaper than steerage on the *Edwina*?'

'I'm sorry, miss.' He shook his head. She believed he

did regret having to turn her away. He had a kind face and rather reminded her of Grandfather.

'Sir, I can't look back, but is there a tall, slim gentleman approaching?'

'A dashing-looking fellow with a bit of a swagger to his walk?'

'He's not a bit dashing, but, yes, that is him. His attentions towards me are not welcome.' Oh, good. The ticket master was frowning past her shoulder. 'I must get to my grandfather.'

'I don't know how I can help you other than to summon a police officer.'

'I can work off the two dollars once I'm on the ship.' How close was Bertrand now? Any moment she expected to feel his skinny-fingered hand clamp about her elbow. 'And my only luggage is this valise. I won't need anything stored.'

'Now that I see him closer, the fellow does look like a charlatan.'

'Oh, he is—and how much closer?'

Swiftly, he wrote out a ticket and slid it towards her. 'I've got a couple of dollars in my pocket.'

'You are too kind, sir.' She would have kissed his cheek, but there were bars across the window. Instead, she pressed her lips to her fingertips, then reached past the barrier and touched them to his cheek. 'Thank you.'

'Hurry now,' he urged. 'I'll tell him you are taking the *Sea Minnow.*'

In spinning about she noticed that his name was Fenwick Stewart. She tucked the name in her memory because, somehow, she would repay the kind gentleman ten times over.

Now, she need only board the ship without having her rejected suitor know it.

All of a sudden, a gust of cold wind hit her back. It blew

her skirts about and propelled her forward. She tucked her small valise securely into the crook of her arm. It would not do to lose the few possessions she had left in this world.

She dared a glance over her shoulder. Bertrand was at the ticket window. With his eyes off her for an instant, she ducked behind a stack of wood crates and crouched into a shadow. From here it would be a quick dash up the gangplank.

Footsteps tapped rapidly on the dock, coming in her direction. All at once, a young girl rounded the corner of her hiding place and crouched down. The poor child was crying, her face buried in her knees.

'Hello,' Madeline said because she could hardly ignore her presence. 'Are you hiding, too? This is a rather nice spot for it.'

'Please don't give me away, miss.'

'I'll try not to, but who are you hiding from?'

'Papa.'

This was tricky business. She could not keep the child's whereabouts a secret from her parent.

'I see. I'm hiding from a fortune hunter, just until I can get on the *Edwina*.'

As she suspected, that bit of information caught the child's attention. Hopefully the fact that they were both hiding would form a bond between them and give Madeline some indication of how to proceed with this turn of events.

'I'm supposed to get on the ship, too.'

Madeline scooted closer. 'We are both in a bit of a pickle, it seems. Why don't you want to go with your father?'

She hadn't said so—quite—but it seemed clear that she did not want to.

'I do.' She turned red-rimmed eyes up at her, dabbed her nose on her sleeve. 'But Mama isn't going to Liverpool and I want to stay here with her.'

That was understandable. Had Madeline been lucky enough to have a mother, she would have done anything to remain with her. While Grandfather had done a loving job of raising both her and her cousin, Clementine, she had always longed for her mother. It didn't matter that she had no clear memory of her.

'Why isn't your mother going with you?'

'There wasn't enough money for her ticket. Papa is going to send for her once he starts his new job in London. But I want to stay with Mama.'

'Clara Lee Adelbackmore!' a man's voice shouted.

'Clara!' a woman's voice echoed, but it sounded worried rather than stern.

'You must be Clara?'

'Yes, miss.'

'Your parents are frightened. They don't know you are only feet away. Surely they must be fearing all manner of horrid things to have happened to you.'

The same as Grandfather must be fearing for her. Shame for what she had done to that wonderful man made Madeline want to weep right along with Clara.

It would have been right and good to send Grandfather a wire letting him know she was safe, but she was not quite sure where to send it. He was no longer in Los Angeles, she did know that. London was where he might be. She could only guess that Clementine had been forced to marry the Earl of Fencroft in Madeline's place. As desperately as she needed Grandfather's forgiveness, she needed her cousin's, as well.

In this case, a wire would not do. The magnitude of her misdeed called for an apology in the flesh. Had the prodigal son sent a note to his father, well, it would not have been right.

'I'll come out of hiding after Papa sails with my brothers.'

'I doubt they will go, not with you missing. You should

go along with what your father and mother planned. They purchased a ticket for you. You must use it.'

'I won't go without Mama.'

Of course, they could all make the trip together. And Madeline had a perfectly valid ticket gripped in her fist.

She could give it to the girl's mother. It would mean remaining in New York until she earned enough money for another fare. It might take a very long time since she hadn't many skills and she would also need funds to live on.

She desperately needed this ticket and should not part with it. But standing by when a child and her mother were about to be separated and knowing she could prevent it— that was a bit too much guilt to carry.

Madeline's heart was far too heavy with regret as it was.

'Come along.' She stood up and reached her hand down to Clara. 'Your parents are growing quite frantic. In a moment it will be the police looking for you.'

She shook her head. Her hat slipped off her mop of dark-brown curls.

'It's all right,' she said with a smile which would appear sincere even though Madeline felt like weeping. 'Your mother can have my ticket.'

'But the fortune hunter!' She sprang to her feet. 'Won't he catch you?'

'No.' She straightened the girl's hat, adjusted the ribbons under the small, trembling chin. 'I'm a good bit smarter than he is.'

Rees Dalton stood beside the Captain of the *Edwina*, smelling like coal, soot and sweat while silently observing passengers coming aboard over the wide gangplank.

'Is there anything more specific you can tell me about what would constitute lax behaviour in the fire room, Captain Collier?' All activity aboard the ship he had recently purchased was of vital importance to him, but the furnace area was critical when it came to the safety of everyone on board. 'Anything at all that you might have forgotten to mention?'

'No, my lord.' The Captain rocked back slightly on the heels of his boots. 'Your attention down there is paramount. As I said before, if the work is done incorrectly it could cause an explosion. I've heard of such things happening.'

'While we are on board the ship, please remember to call me Rees, or Mr Dalton. I can hardly observe operations if my identity is discovered. I fear no one will act naturally in my presence.'

'Not to be presumptuous, sir—Rees, that is—but might you not have hired a man to see to the job? It is hardly suitable for a man of your position.'

Rees shook his head while watching a family across the dock near the ticket office. There were six of them holding on to each other and looking distressed.

'No. I cannot remain at my estate while the safety of passengers and crew aboard my ship is at issue. There are certain things a man must see to himself.' But, in fact, he had hired a few men to secretly inspect the less-urgent areas of the ship's operation. 'May I borrow your spyglass, Captain?'

Rees took the offered telescope and focused the lens on the family. A girl of about twelve years was crying inconsolably and her parents and siblings were not faring much better.

'It's a common sight, Mr Dalton.' The Captain tugged on his coat. The twin rows of polished brass buttons would be sparkling in the morning sunshine had there been any. 'Often it's too costly for all the family to make the crossing at one time. The father will go, then send for the rest when he is settled.'

'I see,' Rees muttered while scanning the dock for anything that might be out of place. 'Is there not a family fare to prevent such a thing?'

He supposed he ought to know, but he was only recently a ship owner. There was more he did not know about the way things worked than what he did.

'The previous owner didn't offer it.'

Perhaps he ought to have. Mr McClure had gone bankrupt. It's how Rees had been able to purchase the ship at a reasonable price.

From what he had learned of the situation, the man was more concerned with setting a record time for an Atlantic crossing than anything else. Apparently, there was fierce competition among ship owners to make the fastest crossing time.

McClure had put that before anything else. As a result, he had neglected the welfare of the passengers. Even the crew tended to be careless of their comfort. Word had spread and passengers booked more pleasant passage. Naturally the venture failed and he never did make the quickest time.

'Tell me again, Captain, what might go wrong within the fire room.'

He'd heard it all before, but it still bore repeating.

People entrusted their well-being into his hands. While he hired fellows to see to some things, it was for Rees to monitor the most important ones.

It would be unconscionable for him to remain in Glenbrook while there was the smallest chance that a careless accident might cause harm to his passengers.

So far his watching had confirmed that McClure did not hire the most capable of men.

'The heat needs to remain constant. Sudden cooling might damage a valve which could cause a furnace to explode. Watch for that, Lord Glenbrook, first of all.' The Captain plucked at one of his coat buttons.

Rees nodded while he continued to scan the dock with the spyglass.

All the way from Liverpool he'd been posing as a fireman, working right alongside labourers in the boiler room. He had a fairly good idea now what hell must be like. Heat, sweat, filth and aching muscles—it was barely a fit job for a human, common born or not. Although he had come to see that there was nothing common about the men he worked beside.

Even though his muscles ached and sweat drenched him most of the time, he would continue the business of shovelling coal.

While he scanned the telescope across the ticket office on the other side of the road, a movement caught his eye. He focused the lens on a stack of barrels.

Yes! Just there a man crouched, peeking out from behind a barrel. Evidently he did not want to be seen.

He appeared to be watching a woman standing at the ticket counter. The lady glanced over her shoulder. She could not see the fellow from her vantage point.

What could he want with her? Clearly something was not as it should be.

With her ticket in hand, the woman turned from the ticket booth. The smile she had given the ticket master lingered on her face. For an instant, Rees forgot he was looking for careless employees because he was certain he had just glimpsed the face of an angel. Fair hair blew in fine whips from under her hat and her wide blue eyes sparkled even in the gloom of the cloudy morning—but it was her smile that captivated him. All the sweetness and innocence of the world were reflected on her lips.

But wait! The man emerged from behind the barrels an instant before the lady hurried away.

Rees was by nature a protector and he knew when someone needed protecting.

While the man spoke to the ticket master, the angel ducked behind a pile of wood crates. Seconds later, the child who had been weeping so desperately dashed away from her family. She ran behind the crates where the woman was hiding.

He switched his focus back to the man standing at the ticket office. The fellow slammed his fist on the counter, then glanced about before he spun on his heel and walked away.

A spyglass was an interesting device. Captain Collier must have seen all manner of interesting happenings over the years.

He was about to hand the glass back when the woman and the child came out from behind the crates, hand in hand.

The child was no longer crying, but rather grinning broadly. With the lens focused so closely, he clearly understood what was happening. The angel not only returned the girl to her parents, but pressed the ticket she had just purchased into the mother's hand.

After a few quick hugs, the family hurried up the gangplank, laughing and looking joyful.

The lady who had just given up her ticket stood where she was, glancing about, her winglike brows pressed in thought.

What would she do now? Clearly she was not a lady of means who could simply purchase a new ticket.

A prosperous-looking family began to embark. So excited were they about boarding the great ship with her whistle blowing and her red stacks steaming, they took little note that the angel had joined them. She walked slightly behind, head bent and giving the appearance of being a servant to them.

He followed their progress with the glass. The family passed the fellow collecting tickets and stepped aboard.

Smiling, with wisps of blonde hair streaking across her cheeks, the angel followed, but was prevented from boarding when the ticket collector blocked her way with his outthrust arm.

She had no ticket, after all. The employee was only doing his duty in forbidding her.

Still, he must have steel for a heart, being able to withstand her smiles as she gestured after the family who had no idea she had tried to filter in with them.

She made a motion with her hand, searched through her purse as if she should have a ticket, but where was it?

In the face of her pleading the employee stood firm.

'Another one attempting to stow away,' the Captain commented with a resigned sigh. 'Although I've never seen a woman try it. I'll send for someone to remove her.'

'Allow her to board.'

'I beg your pardon, Lord Glenbrook? The woman is as good as a thief.'

'I must ask again that you call me Mr Dalton.' Rees handed back the spyglass. 'Escort the woman aboard.'

'But—'

'You will allow her to board.'

Rees groaned when the Captain presented a respectful dip of his head, then went off to do Rees's bidding. What sort of captain showed deference to a labouring fireman? At this rate his identity would be revealed before they left port.

It was imperative that no one discover who he was. Disguised as a humble fireman he would be able to learn who in the furnace room was reliable and who might be putting his passengers at risk by negligent behaviour.

As difficult a thing it was, not being forthright about who he was, it would remain so. People had given him their fares, entrusted their safety into his care. No matter the discomfort he endured as Mr Dalton, fireman, he would deliver them safely across the Atlantic.

He remained where he was, watching while the woman boarded the ship with the Captain. He couldn't see it from here without the glass, but he knew the smile she was bestowing on Collier would feel like one of those visions when the sun burst through clouds, casting its light in brilliant rays upon the earth.

Even if the Captain didn't recognise it as such, it was the way Rees saw it and this was his ship. If he wanted to allow the woman passage, she would have it.

He only wondered if he would cross paths with her during the voyage.

It was better that he didn't. Miss Bethany Mosemore waited for him in Glenbrook. Unless he could find a way out of it, she was going to become his wife. He had only recently discovered what a great mistake their union would be.

Madeline's stomach growled rather loudly in complaint of missing both breakfast and the midday meal.

The main thing to keep in mind was that she had somehow managed to board the ship. She could only count her blessings for it.

Since that mysterious good fortune had befallen her, perhaps she would also find something to eat.

But where? This was a huge ship. She could search half the day and not find the steerage dining room.

It would shorten the process if she asked someone, but who?

Everyone seemed to be in a rush. Her fellow passengers were absorbed in the task of settling into their quarters. The ones who were not leaned over the rail, watching while the ship pulled away from the dock.

Asking a crew member for directions to the dining

room was out of the question. Those busy people buzzed about, each of them occupied in getting the ship underway.

She could hardly put the state of her appetite ahead of that.

'You will simply have to wait,' she muttered, listening to the growling protest her stomach raised.

'Is there something I can do to assist you, miss?' asked a masculine voice from behind her—close behind her.

In fact, half a mile would be too close behind her. The man's voice had a resonance to it that made her heart beat faster. She did not want her heart to beat faster.

Had she learned nothing from Bertrand Fenster?

Well, ignoring the fellow would be rude and in fact she did need help. With any luck—and she'd had a bit of it so far—the fellow did not look the way his voice indicated he would.

Perhaps when she turned about she would find an elderly, grandfatherly gentleman offering aid.

Comforted by the hope, she pivoted about.

Luck had quite clearly deserted her, leaving her to gaze into the bluest eyes she had ever seen, abandoning her to stare at a smile that quirked with laughter and—and never mind what else it quirked with. She would not have her head turned by a quirk again.

'I imagine you are hungry,' he stated.

How could he possibly imagine such a thing? And why was he looking at her with an air of familiarity?

'Somewhat hungry,' she admitted because he wore a crewman's uniform and would be able to direct her to the closest place to obtain a meal.

'The dining room is that way…' He lifted his arm and pointed past her shoulder. 'Just three doors down. If I'm not mistaken, there is scent of fresh bread to lead the way.'

Perhaps there was, but there was also the masculine

scent of this man which was suddenly more appealing than bread.

But bread, yes, she was hungry. 'Thank you, sir.'

She nodded, then turned, feeling the slight vibration of the ship under her shoes as she walked towards the dining room.

Pausing with her hand on the doorknob, she glanced over her shoulder because could a man really be that handsome?

Oh, well, yes, he could.

Chapter Two

'I, Madeline Claire Macooish,' she groaned, while wrapping her arms about her belly, 'being of sound mind—'

Or perhaps not. Had she been that she would be wed to the Earl of Fencroft and not huddled under a lifeboat tarp, dying.

'Do bequeath all my worldly goods…' Of which she had none since her small valise had vanished when she set it down in the steerage dining room while pretending that she had as much right to eat there as anyone else.

What she hadn't known was that poorer-class passengers tended to bring meals with them. Not that she had a dime to purchase what leftovers they might have.

Luckily, a sweet young man, Edward, had shared his bread with her.

Oh, she had been more than grateful at the time for the food and for the company, but now twelve hours later she was certain she would not eat for the rest of her life, of which there was not much left.

Earlier today, she had thought herself lucky when the Captain of the ship told the ticket master that she be allowed to board.

In the moment she had decided it was more strange

than lucky. Given that she was clearly a stowaway, it was beyond belief that he would spare her a word or a glance.

Once, when she and Clementine were young, Grandfather had taken them to Paris with him on one of his business trips. She clearly recalled dining with the Captain of the ship. Grandfather had warned them to be on their best behaviour because it was a great honour to dine with the Captain.

So why had this important personage permitted her to come aboard? It certainly was not because she had charmed him. Of course, she tried her best, but the fellow was adamant in his resentment of escorting her up the gangplank.

Indeed, he had left her standing at the rail, gripping it tight while the ship heaved up and down.

Better that she did not think of that motion now.

In the end, the Captain had given no answer to her question of where she was to stay. He'd simply grunted and walked away.

It was all too curious to consider in the moment.

Well, she had told herself she would do whatever it took to get to Grandfather and Clementine, even if it meant sleeping on deck. Of course, she had thought that before it began to rain and before the rolling waves tossed the ship in a way that made her stomach flip inside out.

When she first spotted the lifeboat covered by a tarp and hanging on a pair of hooks, it seemed a sweet haven. It took only an hour for her to feel the effects of the rocking which felt worse than standing on the deck had.

Looking for a new shelter would have been a brilliant idea, except that it was raining. And what a cold piercing rain it was.

On the brighter side of the situation—something she always strove to look for—the lifeboat was only feet from the ship's rail. It made her frequent trips to vomit over the edge easier.

Of course, that had been hours ago when this journey was still an adventure. All this time later, no matter how she tried, she could not summon her venturesome spirit.

This was no way to die—curled in a wet, shivering ball—no longer having the strength of will or body to go to the rail. If only she had had the good sense not to cross the Atlantic in December.

How long did it take to expire from seasickness and exposure? Too long, no doubt.

But the worst of it was, if she died she would not have the chance to beg Grandfather's forgiveness, or feel his great strong arms wrap her up and hear him tell her all was well. That nothing mattered except for her coming safely to him.

Instead of Grandfather slaughtering the fatted calf and calling for a great celebration, he would be arranging her funeral.

What she ought to do was get out of the lifeboat, seek help. The thought of the grief he and Clementine would suffer made her heart hurt worse than her belly.

She was the worst granddaughter ever born. She had been given so much, been loved so dearly, and what had she done?

Cast it away for some grand romantic lark, believed the lies of a man who assured her he adored her even without her fortune.

Truly, she had always believed she was smarter than that. She was not going to slip the veil like this. No! She was going to fight.

As she sat up, her stomach heaved. She was dizzy to the point that if she tried to stand she would surely faint. Even if she managed to make it to the rail and pull herself along seeking help, she would no doubt topple over the side. There would be no body for Grandfather to bury and he would wonder what had happened to her for the rest of his life.

Perhaps she would try again in a little while. She curled into herself, trying to imagine that her clothes were not wet, that she was not encrusted in an icicle. No, rather that she was wrapped in a blanket that had been warmed by a fire. That she held a cup of hot tea in her hand which warmed her from the inside out.

Perhaps if she could trick herself into being warm, she would wake in the morning to find the sun shining and her stomach adjusted to the rolling of the ship.

Yes, in the morning she would be stronger, things would be better—perhaps even adventurous. She would find Grandfather and Clementine and prove somehow how desperately sorry she was for betraying them.

Only a fool, or the owner of a ship that had been cursed with some incompetent employees, would leave his cabin at two in the morning during a bitterly cold Atlantic storm.

Rees doubted he would find anyone neglecting their work at this hour and in this weather, but it could not be discounted.

Which was why he was huddled into his heavy coat and walking the deck, looking for any little thing that might seem out of order.

Better a fool than remiss. Living with the knowledge that something had happened because of his negligence was not a thing he could bear. This was his ship. He was responsible for the lives entrusted to his care.

The problem was, being so new to owning a steamer, he didn't know exactly what 'something' out of place might look like.

He'd simply have to go by his instincts on it. Ordinarily his instincts were reliable.

Rain pelted his face while he walked past the lifeboats, checking them one by one to make sure they were secure. At least he thought it was rain. It felt more like icy pinpricks assaulting his skin.

As wicked as this storm seemed, Captain Collier had assured him that the *Edwina* was secure, that she had been through worse and with ease.

Still, it could not hurt to make sure the lifeboats were intact.

He might own a ship whose reputation had taken a blow, but, because it had, the *Edwina* had been a great financial bargain.

In Rees's opinion, it was important to invest Glenbrook's wealth in various places. He knew some in society looked down upon 'being in trade', so to speak, but when it came to the welfare of those dependent upon the estate, it hardly mattered what society might think.

If hard times came, and they would, his people would be protected.

And as far as wagging tongues went, he was only a viscount. Gossip over him would not be nearly as ripe as for a duke or an earl.

He stopped suddenly, staring at the row of lifeboats. Something was not quite right here. All of the boats were swaying, but one of them in a different rhythm than the others. It appeared to be carrying a weight that the others did not.

This mysterious weight might shed some light on what he was seeking. Perhaps someone who would rather laze about than perform their duties was hiding inside.

He dashed towards the lifeboat, not an easy thing to do on a wet, rolling deck. Every instinct told him he would find someone whose employment would be terminated when he tossed back the tarp.

He gripped the canvas, yanked it open.

'What—?' His fist went slack, but his heart squeezed at the sight of a woman curled in the bottom of the boat.

Not just any woman, but the angelic beauty he had ordered the Captain to escort on board.

What could have happened to her since he last saw her going into the dining room?

'Collier!' he shouted, knowing he would not be heard, but needing a release for his anger. Had the Captain not found her proper shelter and left her to fend for herself?

'Miss?' He touched her shoulder, giving it a slight shake.

She did not do as much as twitch. Her skin looked thin and far too white, her lips tinged blue.

Reaching over the side of the lifeboat, he scooped his arms underneath her and lifted her out.

Her head rolled back. One arm fell limp at her side. She was heavy, but he suspected the weight had to do with yards of drenched cloth.

'It's all right,' he whispered while easing her head up against his shoulder. 'I've got you.'

The proper thing to do would be to rouse some woman from sleep and ask her assistance.

But then, proper hardly mattered in a life-and-death situation, and instinct warned him that her situation was desperate. His quarters were all the way up on the next deck, but the room would still be warm from the fire he had only recently banked. It would not take much to get a good blaze going.

'Hold on, angel.' Her lips were near enough to his ear that he ought to have felt warmth pulsing from them, but did not.

Without a second to be spent rousing a helpful woman or finding a proper room, he ran. His feet nearly slipped out from under him a time or two when the deck jerked unexpectedly.

* * *

It seemed an hour, but could only have been minutes before he carried her into his room and kicked the door closed behind him.

The space was warm, but not nearly warm enough.

What to do first? Building up the fire was urgent, but so was getting her out of her wet clothes. No matter how hot the flames, heat would not penetrate her icy garments.

Since he could not lay her down on the bed without soaking the mattress, he went down on his knees in front of the stove. He gathered her close with one arm, opened the stove door with the other. He stirred the coals with a poker. A few weak flames came to life. He added fuel, gave a great sigh of relief when the fire blazed.

If his fingers felt half-numb with cold, he did not want to imagine her condition. Her very bones must be chilled. He feared she was slipping away even as he held her.

This might well be the only gown she owned, but he ripped it from her without a care for the fabric. There was not a second to be lost in fumbling with buttons.

He stripped the clothes from her, then tossed them to the corner of the room—perhaps they could be mended, but he had not been careful, only fast.

Rising, he held her tight and brought her up with him. Carefully, he laid her down on the bed, then covered her with a sheet. Gathering the two blankets heaped at the foot of the bed, he laid them over the stove to warm them up.

'Hurry up, damn you,' he muttered to the flames and the wool, as if cursing at them would speed the heating.

There! One was hot, so he ripped away the sheet and tucked the blanket all around her.

If only she would moan or shiver, if only her eyes would move beneath her pale lids.

As soon as the second blanket was heated through, he traded it for the one he had just put on her.

On and on he went like this. He had no idea how long he repeated the process, but it seemed a very long time.

At last she made a tiny sound—a quiet groan.

'Come on, angel. Listen to my voice, come towards it.'

What he ought to do was summon the physician he kept on staff, but it would mean leaving the lady alone.

It was still too risky for that. She needed warmth, constant and steady heat to bring her around.

Rees was warm. The exertion of caring for the lady had him sweating.

Body to body provided the best and most constant source of heat.

Because his clothing was still damp, he stripped down to his small clothes. He tucked a new warm blanket about and under her so that when they touched, it would not quite be skin to skin.

It wasn't proper to be this close to her, but neither was it proper to let her die.

Easing on to the cot, he lay down beside her and hugged her close.

Even through the wool blanket the shock of her cold skin against his chest nearly made him recoil. Instead he hugged her tighter, briskly rubbing her arms.

While he did his best to protect her modesty, when it came down to it, they were sharing a bed with no vows spoken to sanctify it.

There would be repercussions for this, but with a life at stake, *her* life—for some reason, he had been drawn to her from the first when he spied her through the glass— he would deal with whatever came after.

'Think about a blazing fire,' he whispered close to her ear. 'Summertime and warm breezes.'

Perhaps the suggestion of heat would somehow help. 'Do you enjoy picnics in the sunshine? Walking in the park with it beating down on your head?'

After a time, he thought that her arm did not feel as icy as it had. Maybe her lips were losing the blue tint. He touched them with his thumb, hoping to add some heat and see them grow pinker.

There was not much he could do other than wait and see what happened. Hopefully by dawn he would be able to leave her long enough to bring tea and the doctor.

He did not allow himself to drift off to sleep in the event she woke, or in the event she did not.

The latter did not bear thinking.

This stranger in his arms was going to become his wife, just as soon as she was coherent enough to see the need and agree to it.

Honour dictated it to be so.

How would she react to the news? What kind of life would they have, for that matter?

He could not even imagine since he knew nothing about her other than that she was willing to give away her passage to a desperate mother. She must be selfless, or at the very least exceptionally kind.

There were men of his station who would know less of their brides than that.

And there was something he did know about her, knew quite intimately. Something he would not allow himself to dwell upon until they were properly wed.

All this was going to be a stunning surprise to her. One moment she had taken refuge in a lifeboat and the next—well, she would be wedding a man she'd never met.

Entering a marriage she had no choice in was bound to be distressing, but nothing about this could be helped. The pair of them were sharing his bed. The fact that she was not in any way consenting to it did not change the outcome for either of them.

He slid his open palm over the blanket, hoping to heat

the wool even further. He was acquainted with the form of her limbs far better than he had a right to be.

When a man knew the shape of the arch of a woman's foot and the curve of her calf—if he'd memorised the way her hip curved under the blanket—he was quite obliged to marry her.

By no misbehaviour on her part—or on his, to be honest—this lovely lady had been compromised even though his intention in lying down with her had not been seduction, but to save her life.

For all that it mattered.

The reality was, here they were. People were going to know it. Salacious tales had a life all their own. Rather mysteriously, Rees had always believed, gossip seemed to just know things.

He would not shirk his duty towards the woman sharing his bed.

And it could not be denied that marriage to this stranger would be a great boon to him.

When he returned home already wed, his engagement to Bethany Mosemore would be voided.

He would not be forced to ruin his brother's life by marrying the woman Wilson loved. Of course, he would not have been put in the position of doing so had his brother and Bethany not kept their feelings for each other a secret.

There would be a great scandal over it all once he returned home, but better that than his family in despair.

For all that he knew nearly nothing about the woman he embraced, something—a gut feeling—told him she would be a better match for him than Miss Mosemore would be even if she were not in love with his brother.

And, of equal importance, a better mother to his twin daughters.

Had this angel not emerged from behind the crates

holding that little girl's hand? That had to mean she liked children.

It could mean nothing else.

Voices.

Madeline heard conversation that she did not believe was from her imagination. The vague, quiet voices coming to her in the moment were feminine.

But there had been another voice, one from her imagination that had been masculine. In her dreams it had spoken to her of heat—had described sunshine and roaring fires in great hearths. That voice, as she recalled the fantasy, had felt hot where it brushed her cheek.

As dreams went, it was quite—odd! Deliciously, scandalously odd.

The last lucid thought she could recall before this still-dreamlike moment was that she was dying and would never be able to tell Grandfather how bitterly sorry she was for betraying him as she had.

And now here she was, warm as toast while listening to voices whispering over her.

Soft flannel caressed her skin. Odd that, since she did not recall being in possession of soft flannel—or in possession of anything come to that.

'It's a wonder she survived,' uttered a man's voice. The speaker seemed to be sitting beside the bed. He was holding her hand.

She tried to open her eyes to see who it was, but her lids felt sealed.

Was he speaking of her? Probably, since she had not expected to and nothing was really making any sense in the moment.

'I'd like to know how you pulled her through. What technique did you use?'

'I simply warmed her as best I could. That's the whole of it.'

Funny, that last voice sounded familiar even though there was no reason for it to. She knew no one aboard the ship except for the family using her ticket and the young man who had shared his lunch.

The thought of the bread she'd eaten made her stomach turn in an unpleasant way.

It was true that she'd met the Captain, but he hadn't spoken to her enough that she would recognise his voice. And there was the man who had directed her to the dining room. His voice had been—

'But she hasn't come round yet?' The hand that squeezed hers had a gentle, caring touch.

'No, not as much as lifted an eyelid.'

Now would be the time to lift it, if she was able. In that moment she could not as much as moan.

Whose voice was that? Familiar and yet not. Oddly, it calmed her, warmed her. She desperately wanted to know whom it belonged to.

'I believe, Dr Raymond, it is time to remove the lady to more suitable quarters,' a woman's voice said and not without censure.

Oh, dear, what unsuitable place was she currently occupying?

Wherever it was, she was still aboard the ship. Her queasy stomach was not mistaken in that.

'Not yet,' said the man holding her hand—Dr Raymond it had to be. 'She's done well here and I recommend she not be moved.'

Thank the good Lord. Moving anywhere in the moment seemed quite beyond her. Perhaps when she could manage to lift an eyelid, then she might be moved to more 'suitable' quarters.

For now she wanted to drift back to sleep. To hide awhile from seasickness and maybe listen again to that other comforting voice.

As confused as she was about things, Madeline thought the voice belonged to the person who must have rescued her from the lifeboat. Perhaps this was his room and that was why the woman rightly thought it was unsuitable for her to be here.

But where was the poor fellow sleeping? She prayed it was not in a life raft.

As soon as she recovered, and she now thought she might, she would find Grandfather and, once he forgave her, she would ask to have the generous fellow compensated for giving up his space.

Growing drowsy without ever having fully woken, she heard the women's voices again. They seemed distant and displeased, although she could not tell why. Broken words came to her while she drifted down.

Common—not to be trusted, was it? Or trussed-up? Not a gentleman or a janitor.

Nothing made a bit of sense except falling asleep. The last thing she had any awareness of was of her hand being held.

Funny, how the texture of the hand holding hers changed. It was rougher now than before—the length of the fingers longer and the breadth of the palm wider.

'Sleep now, angel.' Ah, that comforting voice again. But perhaps she was already asleep and this was all a part of the dream. 'We will discuss things in the morning. It will all be set right tomorrow.'

Bread. It was the last thing she saw before drifting off, or deeper. A loaf floated on the air between where she stood on deck and the entrance to the steerage dining room.

* * *

It was slightly after daybreak but hard to recognise the dawn because of dark clouds pressing the sea.

Walking towards the Captain's office, Rees swore the grey sky leached into the ocean, made them look like one dreary expanse where there was no visible horizon.

He rapped smartly on the door, hoping the man was alone. It would not be easy to explain why a fellow from the fire room had left the furnaces to visit the ship's Captain.

The door opened, letting out a whoosh of welcome heat and the scent of rich, dark coffee.

'Good day, my lord.' Captain Collier stood to one side by way of inviting him in. 'Is something amiss? You look rather stormy.'

And why would he not look stormy? A man of his employ had left a helpless woman to the elements!

'I am rather—more than rather.'

'You've heard of the empty vessel, I assume. I only just discovered it myself.'

'What vessel?'

The Captain indicated an empty chair with a nod of his head while pouring another cup of coffee, then handing it to Rees.

'One of the men you hired to keep a lookout found an empty flask near the fire room. He asked around about it, but no one admitted knowing anything about it.'

'They would not, I imagine.' Rees stood up. The delicious bitterness of the coffee turned suddenly sour and he set the mug on the table. 'Perhaps in the past drinking while on duty was overlooked. It will not be now.'

'It might not have been a crew member. A passenger, perhaps, who wandered below decks so as not to be seen imbibing? I suggest we find the woman who tried to sneak on board.' Collier pursed his mouth so tightly that his

heavy grey moustache covered his bottom lip. 'A stowaway is always the first we must suspect.'

'The one you abandoned to fend for herself with an Atlantic storm brewing?'

'Abandoned?' Collier also rose. 'I hardly did that. As
pretty as she is, I imagine she found a place to sleep.'

'She did, in fact—with me.'

'I see. Well, you can trust that your private affair will
not spread beyond this room. Just beware, my lord, a pretty
face is the last to be suspected of wrongdoing.'

Heat pulsed in Rees's chest, rolled in an angry flush
up his neck.

'I find it odd that she sought you out,' Collier continued, tugging at his ear and apparently unaware of Rees's
ire. 'I would venture that she knows who you are and—'

'She did not seek me. I found her near death from exposure in a lifeboat.' Rees clenched his fists behind his
back. The last thing he needed to do was pummel the only
Captain he had to man this ship.

At this, the Captain did have the good grace to look
stunned.

'I—I thought...' The Captain sat down on his chair with
a thud. 'Why would she think that was a proper place?'

'Why did you not find her one, Captain? As a soul
aboard this ship she was your responsibility!'

He gulped several times. 'I hope—that is—did she survive?'

'Her death will not be on your conscience. I cannot say
the same for her future happiness.'

'What do you mean?'

'I mean that you will report to my cabin at nine o'clock
this evening to officiate my marriage to her.'

'But, Lord Glenbrook! The woman is a commoner. I
cannot help but wonder if she has sought you out for your
title. Perhaps it is the reason she stowed away.'

He had assumed his Captain to be a smart fellow, but had he not heard a word of this conversation?

'I hope you are more observant than it appears, Captain. Did you not notice earlier that the woman was being pursued by a man before she boarded? That even with that she gave away her ticket to someone else?'

The Captain stared dumbly at the wall past Rees's shoulder, then the ceiling.

'I'll expect you promptly at nine.'

Rees stepped outside, took a deep breath of cold salty air before heading down to the belly of the ship.

What he ought to do was go back to his cabin, inform the lady of her destiny, but he still had a full day's work in the boiler room.

If someone was drinking on their shift they might be inattentive to what they were doing. An accident could happen—an explosion would cripple the ship, cripple it in the middle of the ocean.

Perhaps he ought to turn about and go to his cabin. He did owe his future bride a warning of what was to come.

But he also owed her, and everyone else, a safe ship to cross the Atlantic on.

Besides, he doubted that the poor girl was recovered enough to accept the situation anyway.

He also doubted she would regard their nuptials as the divine deliverance it seemed to him.

Tonight would be soon enough to confront her with her future.

Chapter Three

Rees entered his modest cabin after an exhausting day of shovelling coal into the furnaces in the boiler room. Could it really be after six in the evening already?

It appeared that the woman had not stirred on the bed since he'd checked on her a few hours ago. Nearly sixteen hours had gone by since he'd found her. Surely she ought to be waking up.

Not this very moment, though. If she awoke and saw him looking like a tortured soul escaped from Hades she would likely scream.

If his eyes looked the way they felt they would be the colour of a beet. He didn't need to look in the oval mirror hanging on the wall to know his skin was black with ash and streaked with sweat.

As much as he looked as though he had just burst from perdition, he smelled like it, too.

Ah, but the lady looked peaceful, her hair spread across the pillow, aglow with the brushing he had given it before dawn this morning.

It had been an incredibly improper thing to do—pleasant, yes, but not the act of a proper gentleman.

Still, her hair needed care more than propriety needed

to be observed. What was one more act of scandalous behaviour after what he'd already done?

He could not help but stare down at her for a moment. It was the oddest sensation to feel that she was his—and yet he had not introduced himself to her.

Her cheeks had gained a bit of colour, so had her lips, yet her brow was puckered in delicate lines, as if she were troubled by something in her sleep.

Whatever it was, it could not be as disturbing as the news she would get when she did wake up.

As Glenbrook he had been issuing orders for all of his adult life. He said what was to be done and people did it.

This situation was vastly different. This lovely woman's future had been decided while she was unaware. Surely, though, she was sensible enough to understand that she had no choice but to accept his proposal of marriage.

For a moment his heart felt as though it had stopped. He could not actually be sure she was not already married.

But of course she could not be. She did not wear a wedding band. There was no indentation on her finger to indicate that she had done so in the past.

Quietly, he crossed the short distance between the bed and the wall where a mirror hung over the water basin placed on a crude stand. He slid the box of Cuban cigars he had purchased for Wilson further away from the water basin.

He bent, splashed water on his face, then winced at the cool temperature. Had he been at home, his valet would have made sure the water was hot, the towels fresh and clean. Glancing about, he noticed there were no towels.

Here aboard ship he was simply Mr Dalton. If he needed anything, he saw to it himself. Of course, that was before he found the woman. Recently he had spent the better portion of his time dealing with her needs and not his own.

He would like to say the closeness they had shared was

pleasant, but the truth was, they had not shared it. She had been completely oblivious to the fact that he had watched each breath she took, holding his own until he saw her take another one.

No, he could not describe the experience as being pleasant.

Cold water tingled his scalp when he washed his hair. Black rivulets streaked the basin. He ought to shave, but the fellows he laboured with did not. Since he needed to appear to be one of them, he would make do with keeping the hair on his chin clean.

Behind him, he heard bed springs squeak when the lady turned over. Hopefully that meant she would soon awake.

In spite of the fact that she had come to him unexpectedly, she was an answer to prayer. The fact that she looked like an angel tumbled to earth was no coincidence to his way of thinking.

He drew his sweaty shirt off over his head, tossing it into a corner.

Perhaps, with this turn of good fortune, the image of shock on his brother's face when he had learned over breakfast that his beloved was slated to wed Rees would be put to rest. It was unfortunate that the discovery had been made the day before the *Edwina* sailed. There had been no time to attempt to put things to rights, or even inform Wilson he would find a way to do it. Hearts had been left broken.

Even had there been time, it would be a difficult thing to accomplish. There really was no gentle way of setting aside a wedding in the works.

Especially this one. Lord Langerby had been more eager than most of the doting guardians courting his favour for his niece to become Lady Glenbrook.

Although to call the man doting would be wrong. In Rees's opinion, he did not care much for Bethany. Perhaps he meant to use her new social position to advance himself in some way.

Whatever his reason, it was now dashed.

Even as confident as he was that, in the end, this would come out right for his brother, Wilson's stricken expression haunted him.

Sometimes if he hummed a jaunty tune it helped in some odd way to blur the vision.

'Drunken Sailor' it was, then. He hummed the tune while he scrubbed his beard.

While he circled soap on his chin, he relived what had happened that same morning he'd announced his betrothal to the family.

It would be accurate to say that his own shock at discovering his brother's feelings had been as great as Wilson's had been at discovering the engagement.

Rees had been walking in the garden, seeking a moment of respite from his many obligations and puzzling over why Wilson had looked so distraught at breakfast. Suddenly he realised he was not alone.

His brother and his fiancée were hidden in an alcove, but he was able to hear their conversation clearly.

Wilson wanted to make a run for Gretna Green. But Bethany, for all her professions of devotion, was not willing to defy her uncle.

Apparently, the poor girl would rather live in wedded misery with Rees than go against the man's wishes. He had thought Milton Langerby to be a disagreeable sort, but he must be even more unpleasant than appearances suggested.

Any man who would force a woman— All of a sudden, he had to look away from the mirror because, in a sense, he was that man even though the situations were vastly different.

Weren't they?

At the time of his betrothal arrangement to Miss Mosemore, he had not considered that she had accepted him against her will.

Most women wanted to be his Viscountess. There was no reason to believe she was any different.

For his part, he was willing to marry because he knew he must produce an heir and his small daughters needed a mother. Bethany seemed as well-suited as any other well-bred lady. Indeed, she appeared to have a sweet and biddable nature.

Of course, knowing what he now did made it completely impossible to wed and bed the woman his brother loved.

Until the moment he crawled into bed with a cold, lovely stranger, he'd had no idea how he would manage to extricate himself from the arrangement with Milton Langerby.

What a gratifying thing it was going to be to take Miss—well, he did not know her name—home and present her as his wife.

To see the look of relief on his brother's face when he discovered his life was not ruined would be a great joy.

'Hello,' he heard the voice of salvation whisper softly from the bed.

Madeline's bones did not ache. She heard singing. Both of those things might mean that she had passed to the great beyond.

Except that she doubted a heavenly being would be singing about what was to be done with a drunken sailor. A cherubic voice would not sound earthy and masculine like this one did.

Add to that the fact that the queasiness in her stomach was returning.

It all indicated that she still inhabited her mortal body, as unlikely as that seemed.

The last she remembered clearly, it had been the middle of the night. She had thought about getting out of the lifeboat and seeking help, but she hadn't had the strength to do it.

That was right! She'd feared if she tried she would fall overboard and decided she would rather die where her body could be found.

As to how she got from there to here? It was a complete mystery, a blank in her memory. And exactly where was here? She could not imagine.

She'd had dreams of women's voices and men's, of bone-deep cold and sudden heat. The recollections of them were foggy. That was how it went with dreams—true as anything while in process, but afterwards they made no sense at all.

There were only three things she did know for verified fact. First, she was warm. Second, she would soon need to vomit. And third, she was intensely curious to discover who was singing.

She turned over on—on a bed? She now knew four things. Someone had put her into bed.

With a great deal of effort she opened one eye, then the other. Looking through a narrow slit, she saw— *Oh— oh, my!* All of a sudden, her eyes had no trouble popping wide open.

Her vision sharpened on a man's naked back. His finely toned muscles flexed and pulled while he lathered soap in his beard.

This was not heaven, she knew that, but then again, how did one explain the image? She'd never seen anything like it on earth.

What was going on here?

Why was she in a room with a half-clothed man?

There was but one way to find out.

'Hello.' Her voice cracked on the word. She sat up, but found it to be a great mistake.

The man pivoted at the waist, gazing down at her.

She recognised him! For as brief as their meeting on deck had been, she would never forget his eyes or the way he looked at her as if he knew her—which was absurd.

For half a second his amazing eyes widened, looking surprised. 'You are an American!'

'Yes—and I'm going to be sick.'

He snagged up a pot from the floor, then held it in front of her. Rather than thanking him, she nodded briskly because—oh—this was horrible.

While she gave in to what her stomach dictated, he gathered her hair in his fist and drew it back from her face. He patted her back, whispering comforting words.

She could only imagine how furiously she would be blushing if it were not for the fact that she was clammy and no doubt pale as paste.

Only two people had ever seen her in this condition: Grandfather and Clementine—her intimate family.

She was no more intimate with this man than she was the Man in the Moon.

After her insides settled, the fellow handed her a towel.

'Thank you,' she gasped.

Interesting how social niceties prevailed even in moments of severe humiliation.

'Feeling better?' he asked, squatting down beside the bed and taking the bowl from her hands.

'Much.' Her trembling hands would reveal she was lying, but the answer did sound more pleasant than if she had admitted to feeling wretched.

'I'll take care of this and be right back.' He stood up, strode the half-dozen steps required to reach the door.

'Oh, thank you again,' she said, as would be expected in any situation. Grandfather would be glad to know she hadn't forgotten the manners he'd taught her even though she had misplaced good judgement.

For pity's sake! Politeness was one thing, curiosity quite another.

'Who are you? What are you doing in—in my room?' Even as she claimed the territory, she was not certain it was hers.

'I'll explain it all.' He waved the pot. 'As soon as I get back. It will only be a moment.'

She watched him sling a coat over his bare back, then go out the door. The vision of his flexing muscles lingered in her mind even after the door had been closed for a full minute.

Staring, whether in memory or in the moment, was rude, but was not shaving in another person's quarters even more inconsiderate?

Then again, would it be considered inconsiderate when the person whose privacy was invaded did not particularly mind?

And what was wrong with her that she did not?

With great care she eased back on to the pillow. Just because she had somehow survived the elements was no reason to believe she would survive being seasick. If only the blamed boat would stop heaving—oh, she ought not to even think that word!

In slipping back under the sheets she felt soft fabric slide over her ribs. Lifting the blanket, she peered under.

A man's red flannel shirt covered her. Or nearly. It was gathered about her hips. When she stood up it would not even decently cover her knees.

It was a lucky thing she would not be standing. Just thinking of it made her pull the blanket over her head.

What she ought to be thinking of was the man. Why he was in her room—or why she was in his?

Probably the latter, since having sneaked on board, she'd have no quarters of her own.

She heard the door open, then close. Footsteps crossed the floor.

'I've brought a pot of tea. The steward says it will help with seasickness.'

It could not possibly, but it had been kind of him to go to the trouble.

Who was this man? Why was he being so attentive to a complete stranger?

'You must not let yourself become dehydrated.'

He was right. If she intended to survive this, she was going to have to emerge from the covers and give the tea a try.

A part of her wished not to. The effort would be too great.

But she also knew she had been given a second chance to live and for Grandfather's sake she must try.

She slid the blanket down, eased up on her elbows.

'Here, let me help.' He braced his arm behind her shoulders to steady her, then placed the cup in her hands.

Her fingers trembled. His big rough hand slid under hers to steady the mug.

Surely he was behaving in too forward a way. Funny— no, not funny as much as downright odd—that he seemed so at ease about touching her. And with such familiarity.

'Good,' he coaxed. 'Just a little more.'

'Where am I?' No matter how sick she was, this was important to know.

'On board the SS *Edwina*. You are in my cabin.'

He eased her back on to the pillow, took the mug from her fingers and placed it on the stovetop to keep warm.

'We'll try again in a few minutes.'

'Who are you?' Besides someone with compelling eyes. Someone who gazed at her as if he knew her every little secret. Which no doubt included the fact that she wore no undergarments under this red shirt. Even with the top button done up to her chin, she felt exposed.

'Rees Dalton. I work aboard ship in the boiler room.'

Which would explain his finely developed muscles. The ones she could not help but peek at, since his coat was sagging open. Even being on the brink of death again, there were some things a woman noticed.

Even in her still-befuddled condition she wondered why he did not put on a shirt.

Could she be wearing his only spare? A labouring man would not be expected to have a vast wardrobe.

'You'll have questions.' He sat back on his heels and looked at her. The pair of deep auburn curls looping across his forehead did not quite hide the lines of a subtle frown. 'I have a few, as well. I'll begin by asking your name.'

'Madeline Claire Macooish.'

'Pretty,' he said with a nod and a smile that came from his eyes as much as his mouth. 'Madeline.'

It was true, she'd always been grateful to her parents for it. Although, Macooish wasn't beautiful as much as humorous, which in her opinion gave the name balance.

Not right this moment, though. Nothing was balanced. Especially the ship. It swayed back and forth, dived up and down.

She nodded at the compliment to her name because she did not dare to speak for fear of what might come out.

'Are you unwell, Madeline?'

'Quite unwell. I fear I will never recover from this.' And yet she did manage to notice how nice his voice sounded when he said her name and to note how improper it was for him to do so even if he did think it was pretty.

The Queen's name was lovely, but one would not address her as Victoria.

A firm rap on the door prevented her from pointing it out.

'You will recover,' he announced, then patted the top of her head in a rather doting manner.

It was beyond odd that his attitude towards her seemed familiar, as though they had been friends for a very long time, yet she could recall only the briefest encounter with him.

She had the strangest feeling that her infirmity had stolen a part of her memory.

Crossing to the door, he drew it open.

Glancing that way, she saw the ship's Captain. It was dark outside. His silhouette looked surrounded by stars.

It was a magical sight, really. One her cousin, Clementine, would write poetic words about had she been the one to witness it. She missed her best friend desperately and only hoped she would have the chance to beg her forgiveness.

'I've come to perform the wedding ceremony, my lor—' The Captain tugged on his coat buttons, cleared his throat. 'Mr Dalton.'

'Wait outside a moment.'

So many things made no sense. Who was getting married? And also puzzling was the tone of Mr Dalton's voice. It sounded as though he was issuing an order—to the Captain of the *Edwina*!

She could not imagine a situation where a fellow who worked below decks would address the Captain of an ocean liner in such a high-blown manner.

Yet the Captain did not seem to take offence, but did as he was told.

She thought she was wide awake, but maybe she had slipped back into a state where reality and dreams mingled.

But, no. The ship swayed. Seasickness remained a very real beast.

'Is there to be a wedding?' She shoved a hank of hair away from her face. Her fingers slid through the strands smoothly when they ought to have caught on massive knots. Well, that was odd. 'I'm sorry if I have disrupted your plans.'

'Ah…' He reached for a cigar box on the washstand, flipped open the lid, then drew out a cigar.

He clasped his hands behind his back, looking down at her. Lines crinkled the corners of his eyes. His lips pressed together in a firm line while he nodded his head oh, so subtly.

What was the man about?

All of a sudden, he squatted down beside the bed. He clenched his hands between his knees, holding her attention with an intent blue-eyed gaze.

'How do I say this?' His lips twitched, but subtly.

Whatever it was, it seemed to have him tongue-tied.

'I've found that if one forms words on one's tongue, then huffs out a breath, it usually works.'

He nodded, stared down at his fists, at the cigar he rolled between his fingers, then back at her.

Rees Dalton was uncommonly handsome. Truly, he nearly made her forget the state of her stomach. Nearly, but not altogether.

'Captain Collier is here to perform a wedding.'

'He said as much—but here? When?'

If his fiancée came in and found Madeline in her intended's bed, thigh-deep in his shirt, there would be no marriage.

She held out her hand. 'Help me up and I'll get out of your way.'

Where she would get out of the way to was the issue. Certainly not to a lifeboat.

'May I borrow your coat?' If she intended to survive seasickness and find Grandfather—which she most certainly did intend to do—she would need to keep warmish until she found shelter.

What had become of her clothing? No doubt some kind woman aboard ship had removed it and taken it away to be laundered.

'We are two days away from land. It's dark and frigid outside. Where do you intend to go?'

'I'm sure I'll find—' Actually, she was not sure of anything, only hopeful. 'In any event, I cannot be here when your intended comes.'

'Just huff out the words, you say?'

'It works every time.'

Huff.

'Captain Collier has come to marry us.'

Madeline Macooish glanced about, as if there were a secret corner of the small room that might be hiding a different bride.

'Us…' he repeated softly. He skimmed her hair with the backs of his fingers, gently as if he were luring a distrustful kitten closer. 'You and me.'

She swatted his hand. She tried to give him what she must think was a severe look by arching her brows. She could not know that the expression only made her look puzzled in a very endearing way.

For the first time, he really noticed the colour of her eyes. He thought they were an exact match to his own shade of blue. Cornflower, his mother was fond of saying.

What would his mother think of the scandal that would erupt when he came home married, leaving poor Miss Mosemore shamed?

There would need to be some financial settlement made in order to pacify her uncle. Somehow he would make sure the money went to Bethany and not Langerby. That way she and Wilson would have the funds to begin their life together before her uncle settled her on someone else.

Damn it! He would deliver them to Gretna Green in his own carriage if it came to it.

Once he explained to his mother how things were between Wilson and Bethany, he felt certain she would be the first to insist upon the trip.

All would work out for the best in the end. It would, as long as he could convince Miss Macooish of the need for them to marry.

Circumstances being what they were, she really could not choose otherwise. Still, he judged, by the expression on her face, that it was going to take some doing to convince her of the necessity.

'Mr Dalton, I believe you have gone mad.'

'No, Miss Macooish. I assure you I am sane. But there are certain facts which must be faced.'

All of a sudden, she looked rather green, glancing at the pot, then back at him.

'What facts might those be? I am quite unaware of what has happened to me since I took shelter in the lifeboat, but I doubt I have lost the right to free choice.'

How to explain that, yes, she actually had?

'You nearly died.'

'True, and I still might.' She nudged the pot with her bare toe.

'You won't. I will not allow it.'

She shook her head, rolling those angelic blue eyes. Lamplight shimmered in her hair. For half a second he forgot what he was about.

Ever since he'd become Glenbrook, he'd had no expectation that his bride would be freely chosen. Nor had he ever hoped she would be so lovely. And a penniless American? How could he have dreamed that?

'That is comforting, of course, but you have not explained why you believe we must marry.'

'You are right. I'm sorry.' He reached for her hand, but she yanked it away, shoving it under the blanket. He was accustomed to touching her by now. He must remember that she was not. 'I'm the one who found you while I was out walking late at night. You'd taken shelter in a lifeboat.'

Luckily she did not ask why he would be taking the air at that time and during a frigid storm. He felt it important to keep his identity a secret for the good of all aboard ship. The fewer people who knew the better. It was bad enough that the Captain gave him away at every turn. As for his bride? How could he know whether she was good at keeping secrets or not?

'I thought, at first, you might be dead already. If it had been a few more moments…?' He did not want to frighten her, but it was urgent that she saw how desperate the situation had been in order for her to understand the necessity for what he had done. 'I carried you back to my room. Perhaps I should have found you quarters with an unmarried woman, but there was not time for it. Warming you up was the most urgent thing.'

'I think I remember voices,' she murmured, tipping her head to one side, looking as if she were trying to summon them from shadow to light.

'The doctor was here, also two women. You'd have heard my voice along with them.'

'It's all a fog, but it appears I have you to thank for my life.'

Her hand crept slowly out from under the covers. She held it out as if offering a formal handshake. He caressed her fingers instead. The scent of the cigar wafted between them. She had no idea of the degree of intimacy he had shared with her, but perhaps shared was not quite the right of it.

She yanked her hand away, tucked it back under the covers.

'As grateful as I am, I hardly think I need to marry you because of it.'

'Out of gratitude, I agree you do not. But you do need to marry me out of necessity. Without a husband, what will become of you? Where will you go?'

'Somewhere…' She shrugged, glanced about the modest cabin. '…else.'

'There is no place else. You know that or you would not have sought shelter in the lifeboat.'

'Looking back, I realise it was not the wisest choice, but still—'

'We have spent hours together with no chaperon. People know this. Already they are talking.'

He should not be enjoying the way her cheeks turned pink, the way her eyes blinked wide in dismay. But how could he not? She looked as pretty and delicate as a porcelain doll. Indeed, just like the ones his small twin daughters dragged about with them.

'And might I point out that if you leave this room, it will be in my shirt and nothing else. You haven't even a gown to your name.'

'You might point it out, if you wish to be so ungentlemanly. But where arc my clothes?'

'Ruined beyond repair.'

'Surely a bit of water hasn't done that much damage.'

No, but ripping her out of them had.

'You have no funds, I assume.' He knew she hadn't—otherwise she would have purchased another ticket after giving hers away.

Her silence and the downward sweep of her gaze affirmed this was true. 'I'll get by.'

'Will you? Tell me how. Without money, without even a stitch to put on, you are helpless. Not to mention that you are sick and need care. I cannot in good conscience allow you to leave this room.'

'You, sir, cannot prevent it.' She flung the cover aside and stood up. She closed her eyes against the dizziness that tried to bring her to her knees.

The ship lurched. She began to fall but he caught her, held her steady.

'You will remain with me. Surely you see the need?' Her fingers dug into his arms while she fought to stay upright.

'Yes, I do see the need to stay here, but not to be married.'

He eased her back to the mattress, then sat down beside her.

'You have been sleeping in my bed. I have tended to your needs and we have been quite alone.'

'I hardly see how—' Her expression said she saw it quite clearly. While words might have stalled on her tongue, she was clearly looking for a way out of this predicament.

'Do you know how I warmed you?'

She shook her head. Again, the movement catching the lamplight in her hair made it appear most enchanting. Even without knowing a thing about her, she somehow touched him—made him want to wrap her up and keep her safe.

'I held you close in the bed, shared my warmth, wrapped you up in it.' There was no gentler way to say it. 'I assure you, marriages have been forced for much less.'

'I do not recall the event. You might be making it up.'

'Am I making up the birthmark shaped like a heart on your hip? That knowledge alone forces me to marry you. Why would I make it up?'

'Because—well, truly—I have no idea why.'

'Think of it, Madeline. You are a woman alone with

no money and no place to go. I offer my protection and my name.'

And his title, but he would need to wait and reveal that to her once he knew her to be discreet.

'I can't understand why you would want this!' She hugged her middle, so he reached for the pot. She pushed it away. 'The one and only thing you know of me is my name.'

'I know that you are an American,' he said, then let the silence stretch.

Clearly her mind filled in the image he did not describe because a slow flush crept up her neck. 'A bit more, perhaps, but still—'

'I have my reasons for wanting this marriage that are not about common decency.' He would admit that much. It was only fair. She sat upon the mattress, her shoulders hunched. 'I'll explain them to you later. But I swear, even if those reasons did not exist, I am bound to offer you marriage and you are obligated to accept.'

'I can't.'

'Are you already married, then?'

'No, but—'

A knock pounded on the door. Collier was becoming impatient standing out in the cold.

'We will make our vows, but right now I give you an additional one, just between us.' He could not in good conscience refuse to offer it, although it was not what he wanted or how a marriage commitment was intended to be made. 'If, at the end of three months, you do not wish to remain married to me, I will give you an annulment.'

'You swear it?'

He nodded in spite of his firm belief that marriage vows were a sacred thing and intended for a lifetime, whether made to a stranger or to one's true love.

Catching her hand, he brought it to his lips and swiped a kiss across the backs of her fingers.

'I vow it. But who knows? Perhaps we will be sublimely happy.'

'Stranger things might have happened.' The frown cutting a line in her brow said she did not really think so. 'If I agree, will you help me find my grandfather?'

'He is missing?'

'Not in the way it sounds—it's just—I need to get to him.'

He would take her anywhere she wished to go. He did own a ship after all. Not that he could let her know that yet.

'I promise to find him for you.'

She glanced down at the red flannel shirt that was miles too large, plucked at the sleeve, then sighed.

'After three months you will annul the marriage?'

'I will, yes.'

'How do I know I can trust you to do it? You might not.'

'I am a man of my word.'

'For all that I have no way of knowing that, I suppose I have no choice but to accept that you are.' She closed her eyes, pressed her fingers to the sides of her head. They were trembling.

All at once, she blinked, looking at him with resignation. Funny how with that, he thought he saw the barest hint of a smile at the corners of her lips. Or perhaps he imagined it.

'At least you are not a peer of the realm,' she mumbled.

'Would it matter if I was?'

'Apparently not. It seems I am to go through with this regardless of social standing. But I'm glad you are not.'

'But why—?'

'Mr Dalton!' the Captain called. 'I'll catch my death out here!'

'I guess you ought to let him in,' she said, then tried to stand, but wobbled precariously.

'Don't get up.' He caught her elbow to ease her back to the mattress, then sat down beside her.

'You are a bossy sort. Has no one ever told you?'

Not to his face they hadn't. With the exception of his mother, naturally. She mentioned it on occasion.

'I'll try my best to be agreeable.' He liked to think that trait came to him naturally, but he could understand why it might not look that way to Miss Macooish.

'I'm known for being so. It's my shining virtue. Always pleasant as a sunny day.' Did she realise she was scowling while she said so?

Done with waiting, the Captain opened the door and stepped inside. His beard had begun to frost over.

'There are many things still to learn about each other, but they will have to wait,' he murmured.

'Not many things, Mr Dalton—everything.'

Everything and more. There were two precious little girls who were going to be overjoyed to have a mother. He prayed that the annulment he had promised would not break their hearts.

Hopefully this marriage was not going to be some grand mistake.

Not that he could have made another choice in the matter, but wasn't it an odd twist that in saving Miss Macooish's life, he had also taken it from her?

Slowly, he drew the band from the cigar, watched lamplight warm the red-and-gold etching of a bull pawing at the ground.

Well, then, for better or for worse.

Even though Madeline had spent the day curled in a miserable ball more asleep than awake, her mind had cleared of the odd fog blending dream and reality.

She had recited wedding vows with a stranger. No matter how she wished to believe that had been part of the fog, she had been quite lucid by then.

'I, Madeline Claire Macooish, take thee, Rees Dalton, as my lawfully wedded husband.' She had stated the words quite clearly.

'To have and to hold'—what an interesting thought that was. Rees Dalton was an exceptionally handsome man. She thought it would be a fine thing to hold him.

It would, if she did not have to consider the annulment, which she most certainly did have to consider, no matter that the vows also had to do with being together until death parted them.

Madeline lay utterly still, fearful that the slightest move might cause her to reach for the blasted pot.

There was something wrong with this ship. She had sailed on others and not been seasick. Hopefully it was due to the storm and not the normal condition of the vessel cutting a path over the ocean.

There was no way she would survive the crossing if that were the case. Even though Rees Dalton insisted she would, and even with his valiant effort to get her to eat and drink, she had her doubts.

She would try, of course. Getting back to Grandfather and Clementine gave her purpose. Made her breathe when she wanted to stop, to sit upright even if she only flopped back on to the bed again.

Would he—her husband—still be with her when she fell into Grandfather's arms and begged for the love she had heartlessly discarded?

And how would Grandfather react when he learned she had married a common working man? He had groomed her to wed an earl, after all. He'd spent countless hours and huge sums of money on lessons of proper, ladylike behaviour with the expectation of her becoming the Countess of Fencroft.

She knew titles, which outranked which and who was to be called what. She knew how to smile when she wanted to frown, to speak with politeness when she wanted to tell the truth. She knew what gown, hat and gloves to wear for every social occasion.

Her education had been extensive. Her behaviour was quite polished when required to be. No one would guess she and Clementine had grown up as free as hummingbirds in the warm and sunny little town of Los Angeles.

It was impossible to predict what Grandfather's reaction to her marriage would be when she did not even know what her reaction was.

She lifted her arm, held her hand in front of her face.

There it was on her finger, the cigar band proclaiming that she was, in fact, a married woman.

Who was this man she had married? She knew only a few things about him.

He was Rees Dalton and he worked aboard ship.

Also, and any woman with eyes would know this, he was an exceptionally handsome man. Who had eyes that colour of blue and a gaze so penetrating that it looked into you as much as at you?

No one she had ever met.

Of course his hair begged for touching. It was neither straight nor pincushion curly, but fell past his collar in loopy waves.

The man did confuse her. For all that he acted in charge of everyone, he was a labourer. Even though he had the vocabulary and self-assured stance of someone who ought to be dressed in a finely tailored suit, he wore a sweaty scarf around his neck and smelled of coal and ash.

Ordinarily, she had no trouble figuring people out, as long as one did not count Bertrand Fenster. She had quite lost her mind over him, the second-most handsome man she had ever met.

The man she was now married to—at least for a time— was a puzzle. One she was interested in solving. Perhaps she was feeling a bit better because of late she had not been interested in anything beyond the blasted enamel pot with the sickening image of a vine slithering about it.

The doorknob turned.

She closed her eyes. If Rees Dalton thought she was awake, he would try to force her to drink some wicked-tasting tea, or eat a hunk of crusty bread.

She listened to his footsteps crossing the floor to the water basin, heard the rasp of his hands and smelled the clean scent of soap while he washed.

'Madeline.' His accent sounded British with a dash of Scots to salt it. Her own bland cadence was far less interesting to listen to. 'I know you are not asleep.'

She tried to snore, but the sound came out an embarrassing snort.

Caught out, she opened her eyes, eased up to her elbows.

'How are you feeling this afternoon?'

Afternoon? Lying abed in a room with no windows had made her lose track of time passing. All the moments melded.

'Wretched.'

He looked down at her through the mirror, smiling. He would smile since he was not the one with the mutinous belly.

'I see you have not used the pot since I left this morning.'

'Only because I'm too weak to reach it,' she complained, then instantly regretted the words. Now he would insist more forcefully that she eat the bread he was reaching for.

He knelt beside her, lifting the crusty slice to her mouth. He nodded, which was a more encouraging way of telling her to eat than last time when he had outright insisted.

'If you eat it, I'll take you outside to see the sunset. The storm is passing and, with the lingering clouds, it ought to be a beautiful sight.'

'As lovely as that would be—' and it would if she had the strength to stand. This illness had left her weak, and skinny. Bones poked in places that used to be nicely rounded. '—I don't feel it right to parade on deck in your shirt.'

Because he held the bread under her nose, she took a nibble. It did not taste as vile as it had last time.

There might be a chance she would survive this after all.

'Yes…well…' He glanced about in confusion, which was interesting. As of yet she had not seen that expression on his face.

Somehow, she managed to finish the bread.

Rees pressed the mug of tea into her hands. Oh, good, her hands were not shaking. Before now, he had needed to steady the cup.

For all his high-handed manner, she did believe he had a nurturing heart.

He'd proved it time and again by not complaining about sleeping on the floor after what was clearly a hard day's work in the fire room.

Not once had he grumbled about it—or anything else.

Quite the opposite, he had shown nothing but gentle compassion in tending her in her illness. He smiled in the face of her frowns. Really, who could resist returning the gesture even when she was suffused in—well, she would rather think of how lovely it was when he brushed her hair. He had quite a gentle touch.

After hearing what he had done to save her life, she

knew he was quite right when he insisted they must marry. She could hardly resent him for the necessity.

Not if she wished to walk about on deck without being stared upon as a fallen woman. She had no idea what people back home thought of her for running off. She suspected that Grandfather would have done what he could to keep her reputation intact, especially since he had devoted his life to making it shine with respectability.

Over the past few months it had been difficult being a woman getting by on her own. Satisfying in its way, but all things considered, she appreciated having a man—a husband—to watch out for her.

And not just any man. There was something about him that made her just—just wish she was not such a weakling when it came to resisting a compelling smile.

What, she could only wonder while looking over the rim of the mug at his encouraging smile, had the cost of their marriage been to him? Surely he had not gone on his late-night stroll seeking a wife.

In the grand scheme of things, three months was not such a long time. She would use it to get to know Rees Dalton. One more friend could only be a good thing.

A friend—not a husband in the true sense. That was something she did not even dare to daydream of.

While she sipped the tea, he removed his coat from the wall, slinging it over his arm.

Of course, there was no reason he should miss the sunset. She would not be envious, no, she—

'Finished?' He took the mug, then set it on the table across from the bed. 'Give me your arm.'

What could he possibly want with her arm?

When she did not give it, he caught her wrist, slid the jacket sleeve over it, then did the same with her other arm. Next he wrapped a blanket around her legs.

It felt wrong for him to see her bare knees, but hadn't

he done more than look at them? And he was her husband now, so really there should be no shame in it, except that they were going to annul the vows, so that did change everything.

She would need to keep that thought in mind next time she got lost in his gaze.

'Let's go,' he said.

Oh, and his lips… She would absolutely have to remember there were only three months of marriage between them when she watched him smile like—never mind.

He slid his arms under her and lifted her from the bed, then carried her outside the short distance to the ship's rail.

The very air had a rosy glow to it and she knew the sunset would be unlike any she had ever seen. The same was true of Rees Dalton's grin. It hovered somewhere between playful and assertive—with a bit of mischief creeping in.

So close, with her arms looped about his neck, she was doing a wickedly awful job of ignoring how he made her feel so warm—so lovely.

He laughed, just under his breath, then turned her chin gently but firmly towards the horizon.

'Oh, my!' What else could she say?

Of all the sunsets she had ever witnessed—and there had been many exquisite ones to give thanks for—this one was…

'It's like a ruby that caught on fire,' she murmured in awe of the crimson blaze pulsing in the sky.

'As though it slipped into the ocean,' he added. His voice reflected the very amazement suffusing her. 'As if it is burning under the water.'

'Yes, just so.'

There were no better words to describe the display, so she did not try. Watching took her complete attention, nearly complete anyway. She was very aware of how strong the arms holding her were, how firm and muscled the chest she leaned against was.

'Do you think it's a sign?' Rees whispered. Did he, like she did, think that speaking loudly would profane the moment? 'Seeing this together and only one day wed?'

'I think it's a sign that the Creator has a magnificent hand.'

'Indeed. But do you believe He limits it to the sky? Perhaps He has a hand in our lives, as well.'

Did he mean 'our' as in humankind? Or did he mean 'our' as in Rees and Madeline Dalton?

Nothing could make her look away from the full glory of the sunset—except one thing.

She felt Rees's gaze settle upon her. There was nothing to do but to answer the draw, to turn and look back at him.

How was it possible for her to look into those blue eyes and actually feel his thoughts? She was nearly certain he had not referred to the sunset alone.

'I imagine,' she whispered, 'we will not know that until we become better acquainted.'

He nodded, gave her the smile that said so many things at once, then lowered his head and kissed her very tenderly on the mouth.

'There,' he said. 'We have a start.'

The fire room was fiendishly hot. Rees figured he ought to be used to it by now, but even the act of breathing was misery.

He stripped off his shirt, tucked it into his trousers, then jammed his hat further down his forehead. While it would be cooler without the hat, it did serve to absorb the constant drip of sweat coming down his forehead. Even with it, his eyes would be red and burning by the end of his shift.

He glanced down the row of his fellow firemen. One of them sang while he worked; another one cursed.

Rees was a silent worker, occupying his time with thoughts, some random and some worth dwelling upon.

He wondered about these men, what their lives were like beyond this dark, stuffy chamber. One thing he knew: life would be easier for them once he returned home and made sure to double their pay.

He would also hire another water boy. For there to be only one to douse the men with buckets of water was not nearly enough.

The previous owner of the *Edwina* had neglected some important matters. What price could be put on the well-being of the crew? In his mind it equalled that of the safety of the passengers.

Glancing down the line, he noticed that one man, the fellow who was cursing, had slowed the pace of his shovel. It was crucial for the engines to remain at a constant temperature. Any sudden cooling could lead to disaster.

Luckily, the fellow beside the sluggard noticed and shouted for him to keep pace.

While they worked, Rees kept watch on the man. Something about him just felt off. He did not share the camaraderie evident with the rest of the crew.

Newly hired? Perhaps the reason was as innocent as that. Or was he keeping a secret about his sobriety?

The men working down here—or anywhere on the ship, as far as that went—must be reliable at all times.

With the discovery of the empty flask so nearby, he felt it important to be cautious. Carelessness, no matter the cause, could cause a great deal of damage to the ship.

Not that the vague knowledge helped much. It would take watching and luck to find what he sought.

Thinking of luck, he turned his thoughts to the new Lady Glenbrook. He had the feeling he had indeed got lucky in his marriage. He knew nearly nothing about her, but one thing he did know was that Madeline was kind.

He had not known even that much about his first wife when they married. Margaret had come from Scotland and he'd only met her the week before the wedding. With all the hustle involving the ceremony, they had not had a private conversation until the wedding night.

For all that their marriage was short, he had been content with it.

He had every hope that he would be with this one, as well. And not only for his own sake, but for the sakes of his little girls.

He thought Madeline would prove to be a good mother to them. More so than Miss Mosemore would have been. That lady had never seemed at ease with his children.

But Miss—no, Lady Glenbrook now had kept a family of strangers together at great cost to herself. This selflessness indicated that she had a tender heart.

Surely this could only bode well for Victoria Rose and Emily Lark.

How to go about telling Madeline about them, though? By rights he ought to have revealed their existence before reciting vows.

It was a rather large thing to find oneself suddenly married, but to find oneself a mother, as well?

Even though she could not have reasonably refused his proposal, he kept quiet about them.

For the sake of his brother's future, which meant the future happiness of the entire family, he'd needed to wed this lady.

Now that he had, he must tell her about his daughters.

Once he did, he would need to convince her to remain wed to him! While he had offered her the annulment, he hoped she would not want it.

Marriage was a sacred and binding union, no matter how one went into it.

From the corner of his eye he spotted the cursing man stop working altogether to lean indulgently on his shovel. During the time he'd been down here in the fire room—the pit, as he thought of it—he'd never seen anyone do that.

'Keep to it, man!' his neighbour shouted while not changing the rhythm of his shovel. 'Got to keep the temperature constant if you don't want to blow us all up.'

The man scowled, but went back to work. With a sideward glance, Rees watched to see if his hand would stray to his pocket, to a hidden flask.

With an hour left to his shift, he let his mind drift back to a more pleasant subject.

That being last night's sunset. The sight of the sky and the sea ablaze in crimson had been breathtaking, but not as breathtaking as watching his bride's face. She'd been in awe of the beauty, the same as he had, but then she'd turned her gaze upon him.

Had he been walloped in the gut with a mallet, the effect would not have been as startling.

He wanted to hold her, cling to the instant when her eyes locked on his. What had passed between them had been intense.

It was the strangest sensation. He could not recall one like it. When she talked about them getting to know one another, he felt he already knew her.

Possibly because her life had been in his hands, quite literally, for a time, but he felt it wasn't that.

It was more a knowing—a sense of rightness. Oddly enough, he thought that whatever the singular sensation was, she was feeling it, as well.

Or maybe it had been due to the sunset, to magic ripe in the air which made even the most unlikely thing seem possible.

Yes, it was unlikely that the beautiful stranger he had wed would want him beyond the three months—but it was not impossible.

Given that Madeline was sitting upright on the edge of the bed without feeling faint, she thought it likely that she was going to survive.

And if she was going to survive it was only natural to wonder about her future.

It was certainly nothing like what she had imagined when she purchased her fare on the SS *Edwina.*

Had it really been only days ago? Everything had been so logical then. She'd had a straightforward goal. Use the money she had worked half the summer to earn and then purchase her fare to England, where she would look for Grandfather and Clementine.

It had been far too long since she had seen them. Her heart ached with the need to hug Grandfather tight and laugh for no good reason with Clementine.

Surely the Earl of Fencroft would not be hard to locate, especially now that Rees had promised to help.

From all Grandfather had had to say about the Earl, he was active in society. Locating him ought to be a simple thing to do. Then, once she found him, she would find her family.

She would, as long as Grandfather had done what she expected him to do and brought Clementine to wed the Earl in her stead. Given that he was devoted to the cause of having his granddaughter wed an English nobleman, it was more than likely that they were in London.

Perhaps she would even find them in time to prevent Clementine having to marry where she did not wish. It was Madeline who loved balls and festive parties. Clementine would happily spend her days teaching school.

All of a sudden, she gasped out loud.

What was she thinking? She could not marry Lord Fencroft in Clementine's place. She was already married! It would be beyond scandalous to seek a quick annulment and then enter an even quicker marriage.

She simply could not.

It was still so natural to think of herself as a free and independent woman. Everything had happened so quickly, her mind was in a whirl.

She ought to have thought more of the consequences to her cousin before she ran away with a scoundrel. There were a great many things she ought to have thought of.

But since she had not, here she was married to a stranger. A handsome and intriguing stranger, who—for some reason—did not feel all that unfamiliar.

Of course, she had heard of kindred spirits and the like; everyone had. The same as they had heard of pixies and fairy dust.

Love at first sight could not be trusted; she had learned that hard lesson. What she sensed with Rees was not that. It was different in a way she could not quite figure out.

What she did know was that he had swept into her life like a whirlwind and changed it. For three months only, but would those ninety days change her whole life?

Naturally she was left to wonder what had changed for Rees when he saved her life.

Would he break a loved one's heart with the news of his marriage? Would his lady wait for the annulment? No doubt she would not—what woman would stand for having her beloved married to someone else, no matter the necessity for it?

When all was said and done, she was grateful to be alive and seriously indebted to Rees Dalton.

Also, she was greatly fascinated by him. He was handsome, but there was more to him than that. Many men were handsome, but she sensed that with Rees, handsome went beyond a pleasant-looking face.

There were fellows who would have left her a ruined woman, gone on with their lives and perhaps rightly so.

Oh, but to Madeline, honour was a very handsome trait. Clearly it went soul deep in Mr Dalton. Having been deceived by a cad, she appreciated his integrity all the more.

To her dying day she would hold dear last night's sunset and the kiss. For all that the kiss had been brief, it had been—what?

Exciting? Certainly that. She had felt the frisson to her toes and back.

Unexpected? Yes, but oddly natural—as if—oh, she was not quite sure what.

An invitation? Clearly that. He wanted to know her more intimately than he already did. She should not want that. It would only make matters more difficult when they parted ways.

And yet she did want it. There was a secret place in her heart where she saw herself crossing her fingers, wishing on clover and pixie dust, that there was no sweetheart who would be crushed at the news of his sudden marriage.

She would have to try very hard not to let that impulsive side of her nature get the upper hand. For most of her life it had only led to fun—until the day it led to Bertrand Fenster.

From now on she would act with logic, think logical thoughts. She would be proper and— She touched the sleeve of the red flannel shirt, breathed in the scent of the man it belonged to. The man she belonged to.

It was going to take some doing to put away dreamy images of the sunset—the kiss.

The doorknob turned.

'How are you feeling?'

Rees came into the cabin, smiling. His amazingly blue

eyes crinkled at the corners. Warmth washed all through her because it seemed he saw past the surface of her, all the way to her soul.

She wondered if he looked at everyone that way or was it unique to her?

Oh, good glory! What was she to do?

She had never, ever been a logical person. What insanity made her think she could become one today?

'Better.' She had to return his smile. There was no way not to. It sprang from her heart naturally.

His mouth tweaked up on one side and he winked. She thought so, anyway, but he used both eyes, so she was not sure. Whatever, it was endearing.

She ought not to feel endeared to him, but the injudicious girl in her heart that she tried to keep repressed picked up her skirt and was dancing a merry jig. What was wrong with her? Had she no common sense?

A three-month marriage was all this was. A temporary alliance.

'Here, this is for you.'

He handed her a package wrapped in brown paper and tied with twine. How had she not noticed it tucked under his arm when he came in?

His big, masculine presence in this small room had overcome her, that was why.

She reminded herself to be logical. Yes, diligent in her pursuit of sound judgement.

She untied the scratchy twine and opened the paper.

'Oh! It's wonderful! Where on earth did you get it?'

There must be a store aboard ship where one could purchase a soft wool gown and pretty little boots to match.

'I met a woman with an extra one.'

'It looks brand new.'

'Lightly used, I imagine.' He sat down beside her on

the bed since there really was no place else to sit in the small space. 'But the shoes are new.'

'I wonder if they will fit.' She ran her fingers over the wool. It was a wonder that he had found a woman in steerage with such a fine garment—and that she had been willing to part with it.

'It will, as soon as you have gained some weight back.'

That might be a while. She was only now beginning to feel like eating.

'How did you know my size?' she said, lifting the garment up and thinking it would be perfect.

'I've good reason to know it.' This time his odd wink made her blush, or maybe not the wink, but his intimate knowledge of her size and shape, of the way it made his eyes spark before and after the wink. 'Mrs Dalton.'

'I'll keep a tab of what you spend and when we find my grandfather I will pay you back everything.' Every single penny.

'You will not.' It was a wonder how a frown could look compelling rather than stern. She was far too fascinated by it. 'Now, put it on and we will go to the dining room.'

Put it on here? With only inches between them? He might be her husband in name, but—oh, more than that, given what had passed between them. But she did not recall the event, so how could she simply take off his shirt and put on the gown?

'I cannot. I've no underclothes.'

'I'm sorry. I didn't think. I'll bring dinner in.' He shrugged one shoulder. 'No matter. I like the way my shirt looks on you. I won't mind seeing it for a little while longer.'

Madeline knew when she was being flirted with. She had been repelling such advances since she was sixteen years old, for mercy's sake.

Oddly, she did not feel like repelling this one, for all that it was the very one she ought to.

She did believe in marriage being sacred and binding. That was why she must resist this sham union so that when the real one came to be, she could give all of herself to it. Tender reminders of this one would only cast a shadow on her lifelong love.

A lifelong love who would be more—well, more everything—than this man was?

As it was, she feared she was going to remember the sunset kiss at inappropriate times.

'I'm sure you want it back,' she said. Mischief lurked in the corners of his smile, so evidently he was not at all anxious for the shirt's return. 'And I will feel much less an invalid when I am properly dressed.'

'Yes.' He tugged playfully on her shirt collar, then stood up. 'I imagine you will.'

With that, he went out the door.

He might or might not come back with food. Since he hadn't taken the time to clean up, she wondered if he would even be permitted into the dining room. Even steerage had cleanliness standards.

Rees Dalton had the look of a man working hard all day long—and the scent of one.

She really, truly, needed to stop dwelling on the way he smelled.

It would take great concentration since she had never met anyone with such a manly scent. All the fellows she had ever met had been gentlemen.

Men of leisure, or of business, they were far different. With their smooth hands and finely tailored clothing, they smelled like Eau de Cologne Russe, which was used by women as well as men, so it hardly made one's heart beat oddly.

She stared at the closed door, sighing.

The man she had married made her heart beat oddly.

Rees was gone longer than he expected to be.

While his order to Captain Collier to arrange for two first-class meals was well met, his instruction to procure finely tailored ladies' undergarments was not.

It was not as though Rees could do it himself—not without jeopardising his disguise as a common man.

But, damn it, he would not give his wife less than the best.

An attitude which was not without risk. She had recognised the worth of the wool gown he had given her. Had she worked as a seamstress, perhaps? Or a lady's maid?

If she agreed to remain with him, share his life after the three months, there would be much she would need to learn about society and its ways.

Playing the role of Viscountess was something most women spent their whole lives being educated for. He wondered if she would even be willing to learn.

He prayed so. He had offered the annulment because he needed her to agree to the marriage. To his mind, the vows he had spoken were not merely words. The intention was for a lifetime, every syllable bound in honour.

Even if that belief did not go bone deep in him, there was another reason he needed to avoid the annulment.

His sweet little girls. They wanted and deserved a mother. He could hardly allow them to become attached to Madeline only to have her leave. A mother was someone who stood by one's side one's whole life no matter the trouble they got themselves into.

There was also the matter of Wilson and Bethany Mosemore to be attended to. It was imperative that they be married while Rees still was. Langerby was an unpleasant old coot and might find a way to cause mischief if Rees was suddenly unmarried again.

Those three issues were important. But there was another.

When he'd held Madeline on the deck at sunset, all wrapped in the blanket, something inside him had—surged—that was the best he could explain it. His heart had taken a sudden leap, both the heart that pumped his blood and the one that swelled his soul.

He could not explain why it should be so since he barely knew her. The mother of his children had never caused that reaction in him, or if she had it was to a much milder degree.

There was much he did not know when it came to his new wife, but the one thing he did know was that not only did he need to keep her—he wanted to.

With dinner and package in hand he entered his cramped quarters to find her standing at the wash basin scrubbing her face with a wet towel. Her legs would be shapely once she gained some of the weight she had lost.

She glanced over her shoulder at him. The part of her face not covered by the cloth flushed bright pink. He could not tell whether she was smiling or grimacing behind it.

Once he got to know her better, her expressions would become second nature to him, but for now he was left to wonder.

'I've brought dinner and…' He nodded at the crudely wrapped package tucked under his arm. '…the rest of what you need.'

'Oh, well, thank you.' She slid it from under his arm gingerly with two fingers, as if she thought the contents might explode.

The Captain, still red-faced when he'd handed them over to Rees, had purchased them from a newly wedded

countess on her honeymoon. She'd had no trouble parting
with the garments since she possessed a larger trousseau
than she could possibly wear. Also the Captain had told
him that Lady Ambry had been touched by the story of
a new bride with nothing to wear. Indeed, the kind lady
had even included a nightgown and slippers.

All the way back from the Captain's quarters Rees
had been trying to work out how to explain how he had
obtained the 'above-his-station' garments. But again, he
would give his bride nothing less than what she was due
as Lady Glenbrook.

For all that she did not know who she was.

'Thank you.'

'You can change while I wash my hands. Then we will
eat.'

She went still, clutched the package to her chest while
glancing about with a frown dipping her delicate brows.

Of course she would be shy about dressing in the same
space as him.

'It's all right.' He picked up a towel and draped it over
the mirror. 'I will not look back until you say to.'

She nodded, her lips pressed in a tight, tense-looking
line.

Scrubbing his face, he listened to the sounds behind
him: ripping paper, her gasp of surprise and the shifting
of delicate cloth. Oddly, this was one of the most intimate
moments he had ever spent with a woman.

The fact that she trusted him enough to keep his word,
to not turn to peek, made his heart swell and give a hopeful little dance.

Then again, it could be that it was not trust as much as
the fact that she had no choice in the matter.

Damn it, he was choosing to believe she trusted him.

'They are very nice, although I can scarce believe I am

discussing undergarments with a man—I hope they did not cost you a month's wages.'

'I have a bit of money saved.' More than a bit—he just could not admit how much at this point. 'Those were left behind in the ship's lost-items closet, so they did not come at a dear price.'

While he did not turn to look at her, he fully enjoyed listening to the sounds of dressing going on behind him, seeing it in his mind's eye. He had never promised to close that eye—as if he could.

First came the slide of his flannel shirt, scraping over soft skin, then the soft thump when it hit the mattress.

She would be standing behind him with nothing on. He had to dig his fingers into the cloth rag. It was a good thing she did not know how hard an internal battle he was fighting.

He needed her to trust him if there was any hope of her remaining Lady Glenbrook. Of course, the fact that he had not been truthful about who he was would complicate things. He could not keep the truth from her for ever—or even another couple of weeks.

Instinct told him he could probably trust her with the knowledge, but for a while longer he thought it best to remain Rees Dalton, seaman. Better he wait with the news until he knew why she did not wish to be wed to a peer.

He heard her feet shuffle, the soft glide of fabric up her leg when she stepped into the drawers.

His knees nearly buckled at her sigh of pleasure. The effect on him was more intense because she tried to conceal it.

Truly, if he had it to do over again, he would wait on deck while she changed.

'"What shall we do with the drunken sailor?"' he sang softly, because if he heard that lovely sigh again it might be his undoing. '"Early in the morning!"'

'"Hooray and up she rises."' Her voice joined his. '"Early in the morning."'

Then she laughed and it undid him more than the sigh had.

He was a lost man. He liked his wife and he feared her in a sense because he had a suspicion she was the kind of woman a man could fall in love with and in a very short time.

The fact that they were married, would spend a great deal of intimate time together, increased the likelihood.

It was odd to feel such deep affection before one was actually acquainted with one's wife. He had not felt such tenderness for Margaret until six months into the marriage. But then, she had been a very private person and had taken a long time, along with a great deal of consideration, before she opened herself to him.

He did not recall an instance when they had sung together.

'You may take the towel off the mirror now.'

He did, seeing her smiling face reflected behind his. Lord help him, his grin appeared utterly besotted.

Was he not more sensible than to fall headlong into the unknown?

Apparently not. He had the oddest sensation of tumbling through space and time.

'Thank you, Mr Dalton. Somehow clothes make me feel human again and a bit hungry.'

'Will you call me Rees? Mr Dalton seems rather stiff.'

'I hoped you would let me. It is a very nice name. Rees.'

'I've called you Madeline already. May I continue? It's very lovely.'

'Of course. I would like to think we will become friends. Using our Christian names will help make it so, I think.'

She sat down on the bed, then patted the spot beside her. 'Shall we eat our dinner, Rees?'

Sitting hip to hip on a small bed with Margaret and sharing a meal was another thing he had never done. If he had, it might not have taken so long to get to know her.

That was one mistake he would not make again. He would take every moment he could to learn about his new wife. With Margaret, he had expected to have a lifetime to do so, but a tragic childbirth changed it all very suddenly.

With Madeline, he understood from the beginning that he only had a few months.

'It's good to see your appetite improving.'

'I can truly say that I have never tasted a better egg in my life.'

'It's only boiled. I thought it might be easier on your stomach.'

He could hardly tell her it was a first-class egg so perhaps it made a difference. If he could say that, she would probably laugh and then he would laugh with her.

Laughing with this woman was something he thought he would enjoy for a lifetime. Too bad he had made that blamed promise.

'Are you always so thoughtful? I think you have done far and away more than you needed to do for me. There are men who would not.'

He noticed the shadow that crossed her eyes, the very slight dimming of her smile.

'Are you speaking of the fellow who was following you before you boarded the ship?'

'Bertrand? How could you possibly know about him?'

'I'll confess, when I pointed you towards the dining room, it was not the first time I had noticed you.'

'Really, when was?'

She looked so puzzled that he wanted to use his thumb to smooth away the frown line creasing her forehead.

Instead he popped the egg into his mouth whole.

After he gathered his thoughts during a long chew, determined that the truth was the best way to proceed, he said, 'I was watching through a spyglass when you were boarding. I saw a man crouching behind a barrel and staring at you. I assume he was Bertrand?'

'Yes—Bertrand Fenster—and a more depraved fellow you will not meet. I will say, had I known you were watching it would have been a relief. Not that you could have helped me at all, you being on the ship and me on the dock—but still, it would have.' She tipped her head to the side, considered him with those cornflower-blue eyes. 'How is it you came to be on deck with a spyglass, Rees? I would expect you would be needed below to get the ship moving. You shovel coal into the furnace, isn't that so? You are a fireman?'

'Yes.' It was not quite a lie because in the moment it was his occupation. It did trouble him to keep the full truth from her, but for now it might be best.

Each hour that he spent with her made him believe she was discreet, someone who knew how to keep a secret. But if he was wrong in his assessment, he would no longer be able to work in secret. Lord Glenbrook would never learn all that Mr Dalton would be privy to.

The men he had hired to help him might learn something, but in the end, it was his responsibility to see to the success of his new business. It might be his shining trait of character, the ability to take charge of a situation and see it to a good outcome.

He never really understood why his mother saw his self-assurance as overbearing.

As much as he would like to be honest with Madeline, part of the truth would have to do for now.

'I was taking the air before my shift.'

'I've seen how hard you work. Truly, saying thank you

for all you have done to help me sounds vastly inadequate. But I do thank you. I am most grateful for it all.'

On the same note, saying 'You're welcome' would sound equally inadequate. The woman had no idea the good turn she had done his family.

When he returned home already married, there would be a scandal to be faced. Better that, though, than a family plunged into misery.

It hardly seemed fair to put Madeline at the centre of the storm and her having no knowledge of it, but there was nothing to be done but forge forward.

When he felt the moment was right, he would reveal it all.

'I could hardly do otherwise than to help you.' Finished with his meal, he set the plate on the floor. Madeline had finished a moment before, so he took hers, too. 'There's something I've been wondering about—dozens of things, actually—but why was that fellow following you?'

'Would you mind walking on deck for a bit? I know you must be tired after working all day, but all of a sudden, the room seems stuffy and I could use a small stroll.'

'It's cold out. Are you certain you are up to it?' He wrapped a blanket about her shoulders. He could not help but wonder if she needed the stroll or if she did not wish to discuss the man.

Chances were she did not wish to speak of him. In his experience, a change of location often deflected a topic.

He opened the door and she went out before him.

She did not object when he cupped her arm, but rather leaned into him for support. She could not know how it made him feel gallant—and, well, heroic.

It was nice that she left her hair unbound. It slid over one shoulder in a shimmering cascade.

And just like that, the point he had thought of a moment ago involving distraction was proved.

The breeze lifted a strand of pretty hair, blowing it across her cheek and lips. Her sweet half-smile turned him soft inside, shoving thoughts of Bertrand Fenster to the shadows of his mind.

Damn it, even there in the shadows the man troubled him.

Chapter Four

Madeline was unsure of many things this evening and positive of one thing. Out here on the vast Atlantic, it was always cold and windy.

What a lucky thing she had Rees to steady her. While she'd recovered from hypothermia and for the most part seasickness, she remained weak.

Honestly, if she were not clutching the arm of this man she'd married, she might be carried away by a gust of wind. He would watch her sail right over the rail in her new wool gown, never to be seen again.

Rees must have recognised the possibility because he kept her several feet back from the edge.

With darkness fallen there were only a few people out on deck.

One elderly man sat on a lounge, his feet up and blankets tucked about his legs. With a cup of coffee cradled in his hands he gazed at the stars. Madeline could not be sure from this distance, but she believed he was smiling in awe at the mysterious universe twinkling overhead.

Clementine might find words to describe the awesome sight.

Madeline was at a loss for words. All she could do was sigh and feel overwhelmed, awestruck and so very small.

'You must be used to this by now,' she murmured. 'Have you been working aboard ships for a long time?'

'No. Only from Liverpool to New York and now back again. This is my first voyage.' He swept his free arm up, palm open towards the sky. 'I'm not sure this is something I could ever get used to seeing.'

'I imagine not.'

It had to be her imagination that stars reflected on the surface of the water. They were so far away how could it possibly be?

'What have you seen, Madeline? What have you seen in your life that is so amazing you would never tire of looking at it?'

Well, no, she could hardly tell him the first thing that came to her mind. Luckily, it was dark outside, or he might have seen her blushing. But truly, seeing him standing at the mirror when she had first come to herself had been a sight she would always recall. She had never seen a man look so—never mind. She was done with following her heart at a whim. She would not allow common sense to abandon her again.

Although, clearly Rees was an honourable man.

It would be wrong to simmer him in the same kettle as Bertrand. As far as she could discern, Rees wanted nothing but to care for her, for a time.

'That would be sunset last night,' she said, giving a more appropriate answer than the one her wily heart had conjured. 'I expect I will never see another one quite like it.'

But he had been there with her, shared that vision. She thought he wanted to learn something about her, not so much what she had seen. Having known him for such a short time, she was not sure how much she was willing to reveal.

And yet they were, in a sense, a legal sense no less, married.

It was only natural for him to want to know about her.

Truth to tell, she wanted to know about him. A small voice in her mind told her this might not be wise, given they only had a short time together. It might be all right, though, as long as she did not consider him any more than a friend.

A friend—yes. Forget the sneaky voice trying to convince her she wanted more than that.

Friendship was vastly satisfying, was it not?

Bertrand Fenster had to be on Rees's mind. His question had to be leading back to that sore subject. She would need a moment more to decide how much to tell him. Bertrand went to the heart of why she had run away from home and she was not certain she wanted anyone to know that.

She did not want to know that! It was not an easy thing to face one's faults. But quite clearly she was a runner. She had run away from Grandfather; she had run away from Bertrand.

It shocked her to her core to realise she would rather run from a problem than face it. Until this moment she had not known that about herself.

'Also the Pacific Ocean on a clear sunny day,' she said, running from the truth he was after. What a coward she was. She closed her eyes while she spoke. After all, he did have a way of looking at her that made her feel—seen. 'Malibu, to be precise. When you stand with your feet in the sand it makes them feel so warm and delightful. Then all at once cool water rushes up and tickles your ankles. It's the strangest sensation because when you are not looking at it, but rather at the horizon, it makes you feel as if you are moving even though you are standing perfectly still.'

It was one of the things she and Clementine enjoyed doing together. What she would not give to be standing beside her cousin while they flung wet sand at each other with their toes.

She opened her eyes to find Rees gazing at her.

'I'd like to see it one day.' With her, did he mean? Or just see it?

An image came to mind of the two of them, standing shoulder to hip on the shore and gazing out at for ever. As pleasant as the picture was, she had best not imagine it too deeply—want it even in fantasy.

Naturally he could not mean with her since three months was not nearly enough time to go to California, have a proper visit and then return to England.

Besides, he had employment which he could not simply walk away from. Going home was the last thing she wanted in the moment. She needed to find her family.

'Why did you say you were glad I was not an earl?'

She swatted him playfully on the arm. 'You aren't, are you?'

'Certainly not.' His attention shifted suddenly to a man standing near the rail and several yards down from where they stood. 'Why would you think so?'

'You seem well spoken for someone who is not. As if your schooling came from—I'm sorry. I don't mean to make it sound as if a fireman could not be well educated.'

'Let's say I were an earl… Why would you object?'

There was just no way to avoid telling him about Bertrand and her foolish decision to run away with him.

'Do you mind if we sit somewhere? The answer is not a simple one and I'm getting weary of standing.'

He did not answer immediately because his gaze shifted once again to the man beside the rail. The fellow withdrew a large flask from his pocket. He unscrewed the cap. The ship lurched suddenly. Some of his beverage spilled on his shirt.

'Shall we go back to our room?' Rees asked.

This was the first time she had thought of the tiny space as their room. It was his by rights. She had no claim to it.

'Is there someplace else?' It felt good to be out and about. She would not mind seeing people. For all that she enjoyed Rees Dalton's company, she liked being in the company of others, socialising and getting to know them.

'Shall we see if the dining room is open?'

'That would be lovely, thank you.'

All of a sudden, he swept her up and carried her past the man at the rail. The scent of alcohol came rather strongly from him.

Rees stopped suddenly.

'Is there something wrong?' she asked because he was looking at the man quite harshly.

'No. He's just a fellow I work with.' He carried her towards a staircase, then up the treads. 'I thought to have a bit of a word with him, but then thought he was enjoying his solitude.'

'I can walk,' she said in order not to appear an invalid. Thankfully, Rees seemed to know better. Walking any distance, especially upstairs, was a bit beyond her.

'Would you not want my wealth if I were a peer?' he asked, going back to the conversation.

'Would you want mine if I were an heiress?'

'I'd have married you either way. Circumstances, the right and wrong of our situation, would not have been altered by money or social status.'

Coming to the door of the steerage dining room, he set her down.

Apparently, he knew her well enough to realise she would want to go inside under her own power.

The thought gave her pause because how could he possibly? Was intimacy growing between them so quickly?

For an instant their gazes caught and held. She covered the moment of awareness by pretending to gain her balance.

He held the door open and she walked inside, feeling short of breath and half-confused as to why. She was weak, yes—but what was that link drawing them closer and making it seem the most natural thing in the world?

Well, breathless was breathless and she was grateful that Rees stood so close behind her. The knowledge that, if needed, his arm would be there to steady her felt—right. Yes, that was the exact word to describe what she felt.

Also startled—and yet at ease.

The sensation was peculiar in the extreme.

It was warm and dim inside the dining room with only a few people socialising at the long table.

One of them was the young man who had shared his bread with her on that first day. She smiled at him. His return smile looked confused.

Was it that her appearance was so altered by sickness that he appeared stunned? Or was it because she had told him she was travelling alone and now she was with a man?

'Hello, Edward,' she said, pausing for a moment as she and Rees made their way to the far end of the table. 'May I present my husband, Rees Dalton?'

Better to just say so rather than have him wonder if she had fallen into sin.

The young man extended his hand to Rees, but spoke to Madeline. 'That's good news. Some people have been flapping their fat tongues and saying that you—'

'If you would not mind setting them straight, Edward?' Rees stated.

Her new husband did have a superior manner about him. Edward was his social equal, so it seemed odd. The fact that Rees was older might explain it, though.

Still, she had never met anyone quite like Rees Dalton. All things considered, she imagined he would make a rather fine earl.

'Mrs Dalton and I would appreciate it.'

'It will be my good pleasure, sir.' He nodded at Rees, his expression serious. 'I wish you a quick recovery, Mrs Dalton. Looks as though you were more sick than people thought.'

'Please don't worry. My husband is diligent in caring for me.' He was. She was not sure that even Grandfather had enough money to repay him for his effort.

If Grandfather forgave her, that was. If he did not, what would she do? The horrible thought caused a lump to swell in her throat. Unless there was a distraction to divert her mind, she was going to weep out loud.

'Can you manage a bit of cheese and bread?' Rees asked, drawing her neatly back from visions of life without her family—of scrubbing floors and mending socks, of a lonely little room with only mice for company.

She nodded. 'I need to try.'

He crossed the room and made a purchase from a woman who sat at a table selling loaves.

The food looked delicious and horrid all at the same time. She smiled when she nibbled on the cheese because the taste was a vast improvement over the egg she had eaten only an hour ago.

'You want to know about Bertrand Fenster and why I do not wish to wed an earl,' she said. Here was one thing she could stop running from, at least.

'Not that as much as I want to know about you.'

'I'm afraid you will learn the worst of me first.'

He tucked a strand of hair behind her ear, grazing her cheek with his knuckles in the act. It felt a great comfort, somehow.

'Not so, Madeline. The first thing I learned of you is

that you gave your passage away to keep a family together.
I know you have a kind heart.'

'What I also have is an impulsive heart. A heart that
does not necessarily think things through before acting
on a course.' Had she finished the bread already? 'It is
my shining character imperfection, I fear. As Bertrand is
a good example.'

'Whatever you tell me, I will not judge you for it.'

'Oh, well, you have not married a fallen woman. Not in
the way you must be thinking. Yes, I did run away from
home with Bertrand, but I never—well, you need not fear
on that account.'

'So, you are virtuous and kind. Two very good traits
as far as I am concerned.'

'Do you consider being defiant a virtue? Because I was.
You see, my grandfather, who had never, ever done anything that was not in my best interest, arranged a marriage
for me and I—' Oh, she was going to seem a horrid person.

'And you did not wish it?'

'Of course not. I wished to make my own choice. And
there was Bertrand offering one to me. In the moment he
seemed so dashing and heroic. I'm embarrassed to say
so, but I foolishly thought I was madly in love with him.
Hmmph, by the time the train was halfway through New
Mexico I knew he had lured me away on purpose and I,
the fool, had fallen for his scheme.'

'You are a beautiful woman, Madeline. Any man would
want you.'

'But it wasn't me he wanted.' Not at all. 'And the fellow
I was contracted to marry—it wasn't me he wanted either.'

'Those men were fools.'

'Bertrand was greedy, not a fool. And the other man—'
This was risky to admit. Right now, Rees thought she was
simply a poor woman in need. Once he knew the truth
about her, he might try to hold on to her when the three

months were up. If on the very odd chance that did happen, she did not want to wonder if it was because of her money. '—was an earl and facing financial ruin. He and everyone who depends upon him would be destitute, except that Grandfather agreed to give me to him.'

His intense gaze settled upon her. She could nearly feel him sifting her words, her thoughts even.

'My grandfather is a very wealthy man.' Hopefully Rees was not congratulating himself on becoming one, as well. 'I had no wish to become one of those American heiresses whom everyone resents and envies in the same breath.'

His expression went blank all of a sudden. She was rather adept at reading people, but she could not breach the wall he put up between them.

'So, you see, had you been a peer of the realm, I would find myself back at the beginning, after all I had done to try to make a free choice for nothing. I might just as well have gone along with Grandfather in the first place and saved a lot of heartache for everyone.'

Apparently, he had nothing to say to that because he stared at her until the silence became uncomfortable.

'Now you know about me. The worst of me,' she said, trying to breach the wall, but his vacant expression made it a slippery thing that she could not grasp. 'I'd like to know about you.'

'It's late. I've got an extra shift tonight.'

Funny, he hadn't mentioned it before, hadn't acted as though that was the case.

No, she thought it more likely that he wanted to get away from her. He no longer cared to share quarters with a woman of such a clearly selfish character.

Rees had not been assigned a second shift. He'd given it to himself.

Even had he wanted to continue his conversation with

Madeline, which he did not, he would have needed to get to the fire room.

One of his fellows might be working drunk. A sip or two of an evening was not unacceptable. Then again, if he brought the flask into the fire room… Damn it, that was a flammable substance.

Captain Collier had said the worst damage to the ship might come by way of fire.

He was not certain the man was working the late shift, or if he would be inebriated, but he could hardly bed down in the cabin without knowing for sure.

All the man would need to do was bend over and the flask fall from his pocket and into the oven.

The resulting flare-up could end in disaster. Rees had studied enough to know the sudden increase in temperature might ruin the steam tubes. The damage it could cause to the ship did not bear thinking of. It might even cause a deadly explosion.

While the ship did have masts, the sails that went with them had become obsolete. The thought of this vessel with so many souls aboard being stranded in the middle of the ocean made him feel ill.

Rees stepped inside the boiler room, recoiling from the sudden heat. Glancing about, he saw men shovelling in a constant rhythm. Sweat looked like blood on their skin from the reflection of flames in the ovens.

The man he sought was not present. Which did not mean he would not come.

'What're you doing here, Dalton? This ain't your shift.'

'Couldn't sleep.'

If the fireman had heard about Rees's recent marriage, it was a relief that he did not make some ribald joke about being gone from his bride.

Rees would have had to return the joke in kind, but his

mind was far too preoccupied to come up with anything even half-funny.

'Go to your berth, Reggie. I'll fill your place.'

He shook his head. 'Billy's not feeling well. You can take his spot.'

Rees went to the third furnace down and sent Billy away. He settled into the work even though his muscles screamed in protest.

He ignored his body's need for rest because even if the man he was looking for did not show up tonight, Rees would rather be here than in the cabin with Madeline.

She had opened her heart to him, revealed to him what she thought to be her great disgrace.

No doubt she expected him to do the same.

What was he to say?

Admit that he was no better than Bertrand Fenster? That scallywag had completely misrepresented his motives in courting her.

While Rees had not done that completely, he had done it in part. There was quite a bit more to him wanting to marry her than what common morality demanded. He ought to have had the courage to tell her all of it from the beginning.

Why had he not? There was the bit about Wilson and Bethany, also his feelings about marriage being a sacred union, but had it been more than that?

From the first time he spotted an angel through the spyglass, he'd felt something for her. That something still simmered in his chest.

After her confession, after revealing her greatest secret, he believed she could be trusted to not reveal his.

But had he waited too long to tell it? Surely once she knew she would want the annulment sooner than the three months.

He found he did not want it at all. Life with this woman would be—well, fun was what it would be—joyful.

Yes, and would she not make a wonderful mother for his twins?

His mother had asked him to bring home a governess for the girls. What would she think when he brought Madeline instead?

If he brought her instead.

When the truth came out, as it had to in one way or another, she would be within her rights to cancel the three-month agreement and seek annulment right away.

The thought broke his heart, because even if it were not for his brother's sake, or his children's, he did not wish to lose her.

Ever since she had awoken in his bed, blinked those wide blue eyes and said hello, he'd felt joy, an eagerness for life beginning to fill the void in his heart that Margaret's death had left.

He needed to shovel harder, faster in order to deal with the guilt eating at him, but he kept to the steady rhythm that the boilers required.

In a few days they would arrive in Liverpool. Once they docked, his carriage would be waiting. He could hardly deny who he was when the family crest was blazoned on the door. He could not pretend to be a commoner when his driver addressed him as Lord Glenbrook.

He would need to tell her about his children before the moment they came running up to him crying, 'Daddy! Daddy!'

That she was their new mother—only mother, really, since they had no memory of another—was not something to discover by surprise.

The fact that he had not already admitted the truth was not all his fault. One hardly delivered that news to someone when she was deathly ill.

But tomorrow—tomorrow he would tell her everything.

* * *

It had to be close to dawn. Where could Rees be? He worked far too hard.

All manner of things could happen to a person who overtaxed himself. Happen to her person, to put a fine point on it.

She sat up suddenly, blinking. Her sleepy mind had appointed him as her person and she thought it was not simply because she legally bore his name.

What could it mean—her person? She was not sure, except she was not going to lie here and worry about whether he had fallen asleep and tumbled into the furnace or into the ocean.

After dressing quickly, she dashed—as well as she could dash—outside to find him.

And there he was, leaning on the ship's rail and gazing out at the sunrise.

She felt foolish all of a sudden. Rees was a grown man and capable of looking after himself. He had been doing it his whole life without her aid.

'Rees Dalton,' she said quietly because somehow anything louder in this moment, where darkness gave way to daylight, seemed wrong. 'Come inside and go to bed.'

He did not respond by as much as moving or turning his head.

She came to him, touched his elbow. 'Rees?'

He started, gripping the rail tight.

Oh! He had fallen asleep standing up. A second later and he probably would have tumbled into the ocean.

She had arrived just in time to rescue him!

Some inner sense must have woken her to his danger and just in time.

What could that mean, inner sense? Naturally it was coincidence and nothing more.

He looked at her, blinking once before his gaze sharpened on her face.

'Madeline, what are you doing out here?'

'What on earth? You've been hurt!'

Half a smile tipped his mouth. 'You were worried about me.'

She touched his brow where a decent-sized lump swelled in a glorious display of purple and blue.

'You were about to go over the rail, did you know that?'

'I wouldn't have.' He shook his head. Morning rays caught his hair, made it glimmer, except for the spot with a dash of blood dried on it.

'I don't know how you can be so sure. You were standing here asleep.'

'It was a very long night.'

'You work too hard.' She slipped her arm around his back to urge him towards the door. Even through his flannel shirt, the one she was so familiar with, she felt muscles rippling under her fingertips. They were firm, warm, and she liked touching them far too much.

She would need to be careful to make every effort to resist touching him in the future. Mustn't she?

Going inside, she led him to the bed.

'Lie down,' she ordered because he looked as if he were about to take his place on the floor.

'Where will you sit?'

'On top of you if that is what it takes to get you to lie down.'

Judging by the big grin slowly spreading on his face, she realised those were words better thought than spoken aloud.

'How did that happen?' she asked while she filled a bowl with water from the basin.

He gave a great yawn when he sat down on the mattress.

She brought the bowl and a clean rag, then sat beside him.

'I didn't watch where I was going and ran into a shovel.' He shrugged while she gently dabbed dirt from around the bruise. 'It happens all the time.'

'Does it? Who does it happen all the time to?' Very gently she wiped coal residue, sweat and a drop of blood from his face.

'Not the same person,' he said with a lopsided grin.

His lips, so nicely formed and flashing in humour, were dirty, too. She could hand him the cloth or   'You,' she said, while dabbing his bottom lip with the rag, 'were injured because you grew careless from working too many hours.'

She smoothed away the dirt from his upper lip, taking her time and admiring how finely shaped it was.

'You must take time off.' She spoke this last firmly because, really, he must.

'Such an assertive wife, dictating what her husband may or may not do.'

'Apparently someone must,' she answered while getting the very last smear of grime from the corner of his mouth.

'I believe I'm going to kiss you.'

'No, you are not.'

'Am I not?' He lifted his hand as if to cup her cheek.

'Definitely not. Now hold still while I wash the blood from your hair.'

'I did not know there was blood.'

She stood up. 'That is because you are too exhausted to know it. I'm going to dump the dirty water. I want to see you asleep on the bed when I get back.'

'I like having a wife.' Looking up, he nodded once with neither a smile nor a frown, but with an expression that somehow touched her as surely as a kiss would have. 'I'm glad to be married to you, Madeline.'

'And now you are delirious. Go to sleep.'

Once outside, she emptied the water into the sea. She stood for a moment, watching the drops catch the sunlight and fall through the air.

What he said made her feel as though she was falling through the air. She only hoped that at the end of this she would not be splattered like the drops when they hit the ocean's surface.

It might happen because she rather thought she enjoyed being married to him, as well.

She did not know a great deal about him, it was true. But she knew enough.

Aside from the obvious fact that he was so handsome any woman would lose her wits over him, he was kind and honourable. If she never learned more than that about him, her heart would be soft towards Rees Dalton.

How frightening it was that her feelings for him were growing so quickly.

'Good morning, new day. I wonder what you will bring.'

With that, she went back inside.

Rees was already asleep, but upon his pallet on the floor.

Oh, just there she'd missed a bit of ash when she washed his face. It smudged his cheekbone, so she knelt down and stroked it away with two fingers.

'Rees?'

One blue eye slowly opened, looked up at her.

'Get on the bed.'

'No point in it. I'm only here for an hour. Got to get up for my regular shift.'

'I think not.'

He closed his eye, adjusting his wide shoulders on the blankets, and from one breath to the next fell deeply asleep.

Looking at him, she could only sigh. Some things were irresistible, such as the hank of auburn hair crossing his eyebrow and touching the corner of the swelling bruise. Lightly, slowly, she swept it up to where it belonged, then stopped. It did look rather fetching the way it was. The strands sifting through her fingers felt sleek and lovely.

Yes, sometimes a woman just had to sigh.

And sometimes she had to act on behalf of the man she well—cared for. There was no point in denying that she did.

That being the case, she was not going to wake him in an hour.

She would need to let someone know he would not work a third shift in a row. Other than Edward, there was but one soul she knew aboard ship.

The Captain. Collier, was that not his name?

Hopefully the man was an early riser. If not, he would be awoken by pounding on his door—or at least insistent tapping.

After a night's sleep she was feeling a bit restored. Her errand might be a bit of a challenge, but she was certain she could manage.

As lofty as his position aboard ship was, Captain Collier might not care for the welfare of a common fireman.

Not at first, but he would after she explained how devoted Rees was to his job.

There were not many people up at this early hour, so no one noticed a steerage passenger opening the gate to the upper deck.

Madeline felt no remorse for the breach. Had the crew cared about the division of the classes, they would have locked the gate.

But they hadn't, so up the stairs she went to look for the Captain.

Up she went, slowly, having to catch her breath a time or two. She ignored the unpleasant sensation and pressed on.

Overcoming the lingering weakness was something she

needed to do quickly if she was to find her own way once they reached Liverpool. She would need to be strong while she, with Rees's help, searched for Grandfather.

It should not be overly difficult to find him. Once they located Lord Fencroft, they would probably find both Grandfather and Clementine.

She directed her thoughts heavenwards. 'Please don't let my cousin be desperately unhappy.'

Madeline could not bear to think it. The very last person who would find fulfilment as a countess would be Clementine.

Reaching the upper deck, Madeline glanced about. Long rays of morning sunshine streaked across the deck.

If she were the Captain, where would she be this time of morning? Breakfast, perhaps? Or going about his duties?

Since she had no idea what those duties were or where they might take place, she decided to follow her nose to the delicious scents wafting out of an open door.

This had to be the first-class dining saloon. She knew this room would be laden with tables of food. Upper-class passengers were not required to bring their own meals as was largely the case in steerage.

She paused beside the door for a moment. While her gown was plain, it was finely made of very expensive wool. Perhaps she would not be recognised as a steerage passenger.

No matter if she was. Rees was not going to work his shift and she would not be prevented from telling the Captain he would have to find someone else to do it. If she was confronted, she would simply smile and do her best to make a friend of an adversary.

With one foot inside the room, she stopped. Only feet away she spotted a plate of strawberries.

This was December. How on earth?

As if in a trance, she was drawn to the juicy, red display. With each step she gave thanks that her appetite was returning so quickly.

Luckily, she was the only diner up at this early hour. Everyone in steerage could sneak into the room with no one the wiser, except for the fact that food would be missing. That would be noticed.

She reached for a berry, had it nearly to her lips, could smell the sweet tang when— 'Good morning, Mrs Dalton. It is good to see that you are recovering.'

She popped the berry into her mouth before she could be told to leave.

'Captain Collier,' she stated in the authoritative tone a first-class lady would use, but gave a sweet smile to soften it. 'How lovely to see you this morning. In fact, I was looking for you.'

'Yes.' He twisted a button on his jacket while staring at the high shine of his boots. 'I ought to have been the one searching you out.'

'Well, here we are together.' His demeanour towards her was far more congenial than the first time she had encountered him. 'What a stroke of good luck.'

'I feel I must apologise for leaving you to fend for yourself that first day.' He looked up. He was not such a difficult man to read. His gaze did not shift away from her. He did not try to hide the shame shadowing his expression. 'As Captain of the boat, I was responsible for your welfare, and I failed miserably.'

'I accept your apology, Captain Collier.' Even if she did not, she would have to appear to since she was about to tell him to find someone to take Rees's place. But the man was sincere and so was she. 'We all make mistakes.'

She was hardly one to 'cast the first stone'.

'I thank you, Lady—Mrs Dalton, I mean, of course.' He shook his head at the misspoken word. No doubt he was accustomed to speaking with ladies who actually bore that title. It was an honest mistake. 'I do not deserve your forgiveness. You might have died because of my callousness towards your situation. Rest assured that I have learned a bitter lesson and will not make the error in the future.'

Good, his newly found resolution to help the common man would serve her well when she made her request... demand, rather, on Rees's behalf.

'You said that you were seeking me, Mrs Dalton?'

She nodded and answered only after savouring another berry.

'I have come on behalf of my husband.' Was that bacon being carried in? Surely the enticing aroma could be nothing else. 'He requires his shift off today.'

'Is he ill?' The Captain nodded towards the platter being carried in. The attendant set it on the table beside where they stood.

'No, but he will be if he keeps up as he has.' She closed her eyes when she bit into the thin slice of meat. How could she not? Some things were meant to be savoured. 'He worked his regular shift yesterday, then with only a short time between worked another. He meant to work another, but I didn't wake him.'

All at once, the Captain's eyes sharpened on her and a frown cut his brow. 'Did he say why he felt compelled to spend so much time in the furnace room?'

She shook her head. How odd that the Captain took such interest in Rees's devotion to work. 'He did not.'

'I suppose he has an important reason.' The Captain pursed his lips, scrunching his brow in a frown.

'Perhaps he did. But he will not be working today. You must find someone to take his place.'

'Indeed. Make sure he does not overtax himself. I will get someone to stand in.'

'Thank you, Captain.' She smiled, the gesture quite sincere.

She imagined he was not accustomed to having steerage passengers ask for favours.

'It is the least I can do, Lady—Mrs Dalton.'

Hopefully the Captain was better at manning the ship than he was speaking. How many times a day did he use a wrong word? she had to wonder.

Of course, there were worse things than speaking a mistaken word.

Madeline had done much worse and was in no position to judge anyone.

Rees could smell bacon and maple syrup. He smiled even though he was only dreaming the scent.

His belly grumbled and woke him.

The door was wide open. Bright mid-morning sunshine flooded the cabin.

He'd overslept! Missed hours of his shift!

Stiff from sleeping on the floor, he came to his feet, slowly working out the achiness that had settled in his joints.

'Madeline?' Where had she got to?

'Here I am.' Her face popped into view just beyond the doorframe. He was certain he would never get used to how engaging her smile was, how her blue eyes sparkled in good humour.

'What are you doing out there?'

'Sitting in a chair and enjoying the air. It's what one does on a sunny day, is it not?'

'Not in December.'

'It is cold, but still there is sunshine and it's been a while since I've enjoyed it.'

'Come back inside and close the door.'

'All right.' She shut the door behind her, but her grin made it feel as though the sun had come in with her. 'Are you feeling rested?'

Rested enough. 'Is that really—where did you get bacon and syrup?'

'In the first-class dining room. Look, we have strawberries, as well.'

'How did you manage to get up there?'

'The crew does not bother to lock the gate between decks. Naturally I did not admit that to Captain Collier, so I'm sure, if I put on my best manners, I can bring us dinner, as well.'

'You spoke to Captain Collier?'

'Of course I did. Since you were sleeping, you could not tell him you would not be working your shift today.'

'Not work my shift? I must.' He snatched a slice of bacon and chewed it while he shoved his stocking feet into his boots.

The *Edwina* seemed to be moving at her normal speed. There was nothing to indicate anything was wrong. Apparently, luck was on his side—for now.

'You do not. The Captain sent someone in your place.' She shook her head, but even her frown made him feel alight inside.

'Now, sit down and eat.' She pointed to the bed.

He did and patted the empty space beside him.

Nothing seemed wrong. He did not even know that something would go wrong. Carrying a flask was not necessarily a criminal act.

Forgoing a few lovely moments with his wife might be.

She set the plate on his lap, then settled on the mattress beside him. This cabin was not intended to house more than one person, but he did not mind sharing the space.

The food had grown cold while he slept, but it did not matter. Sitting so close to her made him feel warm enough to make up for it. This kind of heat was far more delicious than sizzling bacon was.

'If you dip the bacon in the syrup it will taste heavenly,' she said.

'What about the strawberry—should I dip it, too?'

'No! Don't!' She caught his hand. Her laughter was the nicest thing he had heard since he'd last been with his daughters. 'You'll ruin the strawberries and the syrup.'

'Ah, well. I'll accept your judgement since you risked sneaking to the upper decks to get them.'

'It wasn't all that much of a challenge since I did not have to pick the gate lock.'

'Would you have known how to?'

'No. But I'd have found a way around it easily enough.'

'How? A lock is a serious obstacle.'

She blinked at him, her wide blue eyes so innocent looking. Her comely smile made him want to do anything she asked of him and more—far more.

'I'd find someone to do it for me. I've been known to charm my way past an obstacle.'

'Truly?' Of her ability to do so, he had no doubt.

'Yes, I've been trained in the art of friendliness.'

'There is a great deal I do not know about my wife.'

'And even more that I do not know about you.'

He had given her a chance to call him husband, set the bait for her answer, but she hadn't taken it.

And why should she? In her mind he was only her husband for three months. He didn't have much time to get her to change her mind.

And if he did not manage to change her mind? It did not bear thinking. He wanted her. What he really needed to do was change her heart, not her mind.

'What would you like to know?' he asked.

'Everything. What is your full name? Where do you live? Do you come from a large family or a small one? What is your greatest virtue and your greatest flaw—although, I think I already know them.'

'Do you?' He swiped bacon in syrup. 'And you are right about this. Can't recall when I've tasted anything better.'

'Clotted cream with the berries would have been heaven, but I didn't see any.'

On his mental list of things he was going to change aboard ship he would add that: clotted cream.

He lifted a berry to her lips and watched in fascination when she bit into it, then nearly groaned when a drop of juice trickled down her chin. He caught it with his thumb, but his mind pictured kissing it away.

'Rees Joseph Dalton,' he said, but his mind added the Eleventh Viscount Glenbrook in quite an accusing way. 'My biggest fault, then. Tell me, what is it?'

She tipped her head to one side, then the other, studying him with that sugar-and-spice smile. He could only wonder if her lips were naturally that shade of pink or was it the stain of the berries?

'If you truly want to know, you tend to be bossy. You assume everyone will do your bidding.'

'My mother would say you are a good judge of character.'

'A woman in my position must be.' Her face was ever changing, he decided while looking at her attempt to frown by slanting her brows. This was not the first time he'd found the gesture enchanting. 'Many people, both gentlemen and ladies, seek my friendship because of my grandfather's money. I've been deciphering who is genuine and who is not since I was seven years old.'

'I did not seek you out because of your wealth, Madeline.'

'And a lucky thing, too. I forfeited all that when I chose Bertrand over my family. You know better than anyone I am as poor as a church mouse.'

'We will find your grandfather. I've no doubt he will be waiting for you with open arms.'

'I don't know. He did not deserve what I did to him. I was selfish and unloving.'

'I imagine you could charm him into forgiving you.'

She shook her head. 'It doesn't work on Grandfather. Believe me, I've been trying since I was a babe.'

'I suspect he was helplessly smitten, it's just that he didn't let on. But he will forgive you because he loves you.'

'You are a kind man, Rees Dalton.' To his great surprise she leaned towards him and kissed his cheek. The scent of strawberries on her lips was nearly his undoing. He was not likely to win her affection by pouncing upon her. Oh, but he wanted to. 'And honourable. Those are your greatest qualities, I think.'

Honourable? He was a wretch. He felt the shame deep in his bones.

Ah, but it was a very good thing he had not pounced. When she discovered all he kept from her, she was bound to resent him—and that was if he was lucky. Chances were she would do more than resent him. She would flee with all haste.

'Have you been married before?' she asked. 'I have not.'

'Yes. My first wife died in childbirth nearly three years ago.'

'I am very sorry, Rees. It must have been a terrible blow.'

He nodded, seeing Margaret's face come to him through the fog of time. But those bleak days seemed far distant from his life now, so when he saw her, she was smiling.

'But I do have my children, twin girls.'

He would have liked to ease the twins into the conversation gently rather than blurting out the news as he just had. But it would naturally be her next question.

'What a great blessing they must be.'

'Beguiling little lassies, for certain. They enchant me every day.'

'It has to be difficult to be away from them for such long periods of time.' She tapped her fingers on her lips while studying his face. 'Who cares for them?'

'My mother.' This was true. Others on the staff saw to them as well, but for the most part it was his mother who did the coddling.

'You are lucky to have her, my friend.'

Friend, not husband. He should not feel so disappointed by her words, their marriage being as new as it was, yet he did.

'I count her among my blessings every day.'

'My memories from when I was sick are vague.' She propped her elbows on her knees, made a cradle of her hands and rested her chin on them. 'But I do remember that there was a reason you wanted this marriage, rather than it being the decent thing to do.'

Here was where matters became tricky. He would have to tell her about the situation with his brother and yet choose his words with care.

Each hour he spent with her made him—desperate, yes, quite that, for her to stay. Three months was not going to be nearly enough time with Madeline.

How could he have ever thought it would be?

He had not—he had never wanted a time limit. While in the beginning he had been guided by notions of the way marriage ought to be, vows made were vows kept and all that...theory.

Now that he had kissed her at sunset, had woken from his bed on the floor in the night and watched her sleep, now that she had tended his wound with those gentle fingers, things had changed.

Ever since she breached the upper deck and confronted the Captain in order to give him a few more hours of sleep, affection had sent theory on its merry way.

For some reason, the fact that she had brought him

strawberries and bacon, and taught him the pleasure of dipping that bacon in syrup, touched him deeply.

As small a thing as that was, it was big—huge, really. It gave him hope that a bond was building between them. Perhaps an intimacy he very much wanted to explore— over the course of many years.

Which, in the moment, left him treading a perilous path between truth and deception.

He owed her the truth, but feared he had left it for too long. She would leave him. The light so recently burst to life in his soul would go out. He had lived in darkness for too long.

Here they were together. The time was right and yet the words dried in his mouth.

Chapter Five

In spite of the effort Madeline had gone to in order for Rees to have the day away from his job, he had gone to the furnace room.

She could add this to her list of things she knew about him—he was devoted to his work. What other man was that devoted to a difficult career?

Over the course of the afternoon, she had done a fair amount of thinking.

What else was there to do during the hours that he was away?

Now, several hours later, she watched him wash at the basin, thinking again about the conclusions she had come to. Or half-thought about them.

Logic took a bit of a holiday while she watched the bare muscles of his back stretch and flex. Perhaps she should not indulge in the pleasure, but he was her husband even if it was for such a brief time.

The reason he was her husband, the one he had told her was to his benefit, had become more clear. He needed a mother for his children. At least she thought that was the reason.

Even though it was the most logical motive for a widower to want a wife, it seemed odd. If he had thought she would become a mother to his children, he had done so knowing it would be temporary.

A circumstance which put her in a difficult situation. A mother who went on her merry way after only three months was no mother at all. The children would end up heartbroken. But perhaps their bond with Rees's mother was strong and she filled the role as both mother and grandmother.

If there was a reason other than for his children that he had married her, she had not been able to figure out what it was.

'Shall we go for a walk on deck?' he asked.

All afternoon she had been listening to the wind rattle the door. It was bound to be cold out but— 'Yes, that would be lovely.'

Outside the sun cast long, late afternoon shadows on the deck. For all that sunshine glittered on the water and gave the illusion of warmth, it was a bone chill out there.

With only the one coat between them, he placed it across her shoulders, smiling in that way he had of making her want to stare at his mouth.

How could she not when their gazes connected, held, for longer than mere friendliness accounted for? That intimate look passed between them more and more frequently.

His fingers lingered long on the task of tugging the coat about her throat. Funny that her reaction was that it was not long enough. Funnier that she felt the tug on her heart more than her collar.

Mentally, she gave herself a good shake. There was a reason he had offered her only a short marriage. He was not looking for a real union any more than she was.

And yet—there was no 'and yet'. His tender touch meant nothing. Nor did the way his gaze lingered on her in the most intimate of expressions.

He was a decent man doing a decent thing. Having

compromised her in the act of saving her life, he did what was proper. She must be careful not to read any more into it than that.

Sadly, she was known for following her heart more than common sense.

If, for some reason, this stroll was leading to a kiss— and she really had no reason to think so other than what she read in his smile—well, it might lead there but she was going to summon the wisdom to refuse—again.

Her heart had led her astray with an unworthy man once before. Even though Rees was worthy, she would not let her heart pick unwisely again.

Unless, her small but insistent inner voice suggested, she already had. She turned a blind ear—or answering thought—to it.

Yes, she might look like fluff, but inside she was steel— or at worst tin. What she would not do was give in to a kiss and forsake the inner strength she had learned over the past few months of getting by on her own.

Admittedly, he had not offered a kiss. It had been her own imagination wandering. But still, she would not.

Wind whipped along the deck, pelting them in the back and quickening their steps. It was even colder out than she had expected it to be.

Rees's arm came about her, drawing her close and warming her. She hadn't said a thing about feeling shivery, yet he'd known.

The intimate connection felt so tenuously between them only a short time ago was growing stronger. She knew it without him saying so, without her confirming it. It was just there, the awareness of it pulsing between them.

A part of her welcomed it, but another part greatly feared it. And wisely so. She did not dare to make another mistake she would end up running from.

'Let's go inside,' he murmured.

'That is an excellent idea. Did you know that when the sun shines in Los Angeles it is almost always warm?' Not so here in the middle of the Atlantic Ocean, where wind blew off the water and dampened one's clothing, making it smell like salt and fish.

She suppressed a shiver.

'Come.' He swept her up in his arms as if she weighed nothing at all, then carried her towards a staircase.

His strides were long and determined, his arms, cupping her thighs, firm. The whole of it made her heart flutter. The fluff in her character was delighted.

'Where are we going?'

'You said the gate to first class was not locked.'

'It isn't, but we won't get away with it this time.'

He opened the gate, carried her up the steps. The only sign of exertion he showed was that his breathing came faster. She felt his chest expand against her side.

'I look too low-born?'

'Too virile.'

'The gentlemen up here do not?'

'They look important—to their own minds, anyway.'

'But you think they are not?' His mouth quirked with the question and of course it made her heart beat oddly.

For a man who ought to be gasping for breath, but was only half-winded, he had a lot of questions.

'You and your fellows are the ones who keep this ship moving. I imagine that, somewhere, the owner is busy at a game of whist, drinking a glass of sherry without a thought of how his investment is faring.'

'You think that?' Lines in his forehead arched, formed a peak which made him look amused, of all things.

'I've met many wealthy investors.' Fended them off more times than she could recall. 'Most haven't a care about what their funds are doing, not as long as they continue to increase.'

Delicious aromas wafted out of the open dining-saloon door. From several feet away she noticed a welcoming orange glow. It suffused the room with the promise of a toasty warm fire in the hearth.

'Do you think they will notice I'm from the lower deck?' He winked.

'Beyond a doubt.' He wore the clothes of a man who worked below and the scent of coal lingered on him.

'I wonder if they will care.'

'Set me down, Rees.'

He did, but slowly as if he did not want to stop touching her. When her toes met the floor, she was even slower stepping out of his arms.

What was happening to her? Certainly not the same thing as had happened with Bertrand. Oh, no, this was far different. Her heart fluttered for Rees in a far different way than it ever had for the fortune hunter.

Perhaps because he was, in fact, her husband.

Did that temporary bond make the attachment less risky? Only time would tell.

She walked ahead of him and peered inside. Drat, there were a couple of dozen first-class diners inside.

Looking back at Rees, she saw that he was shivering.

Beyond the doorway was food and warmth. She was going to do her best to make sure they partook of both.

It would be helpful if she wore pearls and lace.

'Follow me,' she instructed with a quick glance back at him.

Rees grinned, nodding. He seemed confident of her success. In her mind she was only half-sure she could gain them entrance.

She straightened her back, lifted her chin. With a very upper-class smile she stepped inside.

Someone gasped.

It took only an instant for the head waiter, dressed in an

expensive-looking tuxedo, to march forward. The scowl on his face did not deter her smile in the least.

Grandfather's expensive lessons in behaving as a proper lady of society would not go to waste.

'A table near the fireplace, good sir.' She knew how to make her eyes twinkle and did so without shame. She was rewarded by seeing the fellow's gentlemanly nature respond. He was not quite smiling, but he was close to it. 'And a table close to mine—for my servant.'

'I do have a table for you, miss. However, your man will have to dine in steerage.'

'I'm sure that's impossible.' She touched her throat, allowed her lips to tremble a bit under her smile. 'My travelling companion has fallen ill. I have no one else but this man to act as chaperon.'

'Surely there must be a woman to accompany you to dinner.'

'I would not reveal this to just anyone, but am I right in thinking I can trust you?'

'You may count on my discretion, Miss—?'

'Macooish.' Grandfather was not without influence in certain circles. It could not hurt to display the family name. 'Well, the fact is, I am exceptionally timid. This fellow has been employed by my grandfather for many years. Grandfather will trust my safety to no one else.'

She shrugged her shoulders, noticing the other diners begin to stare and whisper behind their hands. 'Won't you help me, sir? I have only been to the dining room once since we left New York. Truly, I am nearly weak with hunger. If you seat us near the fire, you will be my hero for ever.'

It was true, he would. It would take a kindly heart to ignore the displeasure of the other diners and come to her aid.

'Come this way, then.' His face reflected the compas-

sion she had first sensed in him. 'There is a table close
to yours, but in the shadows. Perhaps no one will object.
But may I ask, why is he dressed as though he works in
the furnace room?'

'Well, he does. I allow him to earn extra money where
he can.'

'Most commendable, miss.' He pulled out a chair for
her. Rees sat close to the fireplace in deep shadow. They
would not be able to speak to one another, but at least they
would eat fine food and keep warm. 'I'll send a waiter
over directly.'

'What is your name, sir?'

'Mr Peabody.' He gave a half-bow and went to find
her a waiter.

She would have to remember his name along with the
others who had been kind to her. If Grandfather forgave
her, he would want to reward them.

Moments later she was eating an exquisite meal made
all the more delicious because of what she had been
through. She even sipped crisp champagne, twirling the
smooth stem of the goblet in her fingers.

She glanced behind her, saw Rees with a decent meal,
but not as fine as hers and no spirits to go with it.

He did look warm and satisfied, though.

She dabbed her mouth with her napkin and would have
motioned for him to take her home—back to the cabin,
that was. In truth, she had no home, but at that moment
a small orchestra came in, sat down and began to play.

It had been too long since she had heard such lovely
music.

There was a dance floor close at hand, but so far no one
was dancing. She wished they were because she adored
dancing. If she could not participate, she would enjoy
watching others do so.

Closing her eyes, she swayed to the music, let the melody wash through her. She had believed she would never feel this lightness of being again—this place where melody carried one out of one's body to float and twirl as if in a starry mist.

Oh, but here she was, eyes closed and the sweet, longing melody causing her toes to dance within her shoes.

A calloused hand covered hers, stilled the drumming of her fingers on the tablecloth.

'Come.' With a hand under her elbow Rees lifted her out of the chair.

Instead of escorting her to the door, he led her to the dance floor.

'What are you doing?' She knew what. She just could not believe it.

'Dancing with my wife.'

He caught her waist in one big hand, then swept her into a waltz.

Her face must have revealed her surprise, her utter and complete shock.

'Where I grew up, people used to waltz. I watched how it was done. Do you have the strength for it?'

Even if she did not, she was going to do it.

'This is going to cause a great scandal.'

He winked. 'We'd best enjoy it while we can.'

She did. Oh, how she did. Aria, chorus and lullaby swirled in her blood. Waltz, polka, prance and caper gave life to her steps.

Head dizzy and heart alight with—not love, no, but something suspiciously akin to it, she spun where Rees led.

For as brief as the moment was before they were told to leave, she revelled in it.

Drank it in to the depth of her soul. There had never been a dance she'd enjoyed more. A moment more exciting.

She focused her gaze on Rees's face so as not to notice

the frowns being cast their way. As a distraction it worked supremely well.

All of a sudden, scowling faces meant nothing. Rees's face meant—*everything* was the word that came unbidden into her mind. But how could that be?

Everything was a rather huge thought.

Had she learned nothing about giving her heart too quickly?

Perhaps not, because she found herself wanting to dance with him like this for ever.

Of course, for ever was not given to her. Within moments they were escorted outside, where the wind blew and cold penetrated.

It had grown dark while they had been inside.

She handed Rees his coat because it was his, after all.

He shrugged into it, then pulled her against his chest, wrapping her up with him.

All at once, the dance was no longer her most exciting moment.

This was.

He backed her towards the railing. She matched the rhythm of his steps and somehow it felt as though they were still dancing.

The last thing Rees felt for what he had done was regret, or shame.

His wife had wanted to dance. He had wanted to dance with her.

'I'd do it again,' he admitted. The joy he'd seen shining on her face while he carefully spun her about in front of the chagrined diners lingered on her face.

He had to admit it appeared outrageous, a common labourer, his only adornment the red-checked handkerchief tied about his neck, and the lady gowned in fine, if modest, wool behaving as social equals on the dance floor.

Rees Dalton might bear a title, but he was far from being his wife's equal. Indeed, she ranked far above him in every way that counted.

Her kind heart, her sweet and generous spirit, quite simply made her his angel.

'So would I. It has been too long since I danced with such a light heart. I think it is because I was able to get lost in the moment without having to try to outwit my partner. Most men I've danced with hadn't much interest in the fun of it. Only in how they might entrap me. Or, more rightly, Grandfather.'

'Whereas I have already entrapped you.'

She glanced away, focusing her attention on the black crests stirring the surface of the water. Perhaps he ought not to have said that even though it was in jest.

'Ah, Madeline,' he whispered against her hair while pulling her tight against him under the coat. She resisted for only a fraction of a second, so he continued to snuggle. 'I do not like to think of you without a light heart. Unless I'm wrong, and I know by now I am not, it is the way you are by nature when nothing else gets in the way.'

'It's true. My cousin and I have shared some delightfully scandalous times. Nothing wicked, mind you, and mostly no one knew about them.'

'The same can't be said of the last half-hour. Everyone knows. I hope you were not embarrassed by me.'

'I don't recall you stepping on my toe or tripping over my skirt. In fact, you were quite accomplished for someone who learned by watching others.'

'My mother says I have a natural talent for physical endeavours.'

She had said that, but it was in relation to climbing trees. Dancing had taken endless hours of practice.

'If you mean because I am a lady, well, an heiress more aptly, and you are a commoner—no—I'm an American lady. It is not the same thing as being a British lady of title. We are born as common as anyone.'

Madeline Claire Macooish was as far from common as a woman could get.

'Shall we walk on?' he said.

It would be a good idea since, standing here, all he could think of was kissing her.

'I imagine we ought to go downstairs to steerage. We've raised enough eyebrows for tonight,' she suggested.

'It's nicer up here.' He shifted her so that she was walking beside him, but still under the coat. He made sure not to let go of her waist. 'Besides, come morning, conversation about us will be the spice in their breakfast.'

'I wish I could hear it,' she answered with a laugh.

They walked past the lifeboats. Although not the same ones Madeline had sought shelter in, Rees could not even glance at them for remembering how she had been so near death. How fragile her hold on life had been.

No matter the price to his heart, and there would be one, he did not regret what he had done to rip her from the arms of the Grim Reaper.

'How much longer until we reach Liverpool?' she asked. 'I've lost count of the days.'

'Two only.'

'I've never been there.'

'It's not unlike New York. Lots of hustle, bustle and commerce.'

'Is it where you live?'

'I have a place there.' He did not admit it was a town house with a dozen servants to see to its care. This sweet moment was not the right time for the full truth.

He could only wonder if there would be one. The thought of her looking at him as a liar was becoming harder to consider. And yet the longer he waited the worse it would be.

'Will there be room for me? I would not want to crowd your family. Perhaps I can find a hotel until—'

He stopped. They had reached the bow of the ship. The great expanse of water stretching away before them became one with the darkness.

'You will stay with me.' He turned her in the coat, gripped her by the shoulders. 'As common as I appear, I am able to care for you.'

'All I'm saying is that you needn't. You didn't choose me, after all. I just usurped your life.'

'I may not have chosen—' He touched her cheek, traced the shape of her chin then tipped it up. 'But—'

But now, now he was going to kiss her.

She pressed her palms against his chest, backed out of the warmth of his coat. Wind caught the lapels. The fabric snapped like a billowing flag.

'I can't allow you to steal a kiss, Rees.' She pressed her fingers over her mouth, tapped them on her lips. 'It would be as though I learned nothing at all.'

'What I hope you have learned is that I am not a man like Fenster.'

Even though she stood within arm's reach, he kept his hands at his sides, his fingers curled into tense balls. He would not take advantage of her like that weasel did.

'Why did you marry me, Rees? You did not have to do it. I would have survived the scandal eventually.'

'You had no one else.' But why did it have to be him? she must be thinking. Why not give her to the care of a kindly fellow passenger, an honourable matron? Now was the time to reveal the truth about his brother, but he could not.

Not when another truth was the one pressing to be told.

'Madeline, from the first time I saw you through the spyglass, I—honestly I liked you—very much.'

'I…' She took a small step towards him. He leaned an inch towards her. '…think…'

With a short leap she was back in his arms. She tipped her face up to him. With a smile she cupped her cold fingers on his cheeks and drew his head down.

'I like you, too, very much.'

Her kiss was sweet; it was steamy and ardent. It was his undoing. He was completely captured. How could a woman melt against him like that and not be his for all time?

She could not.

When she would have drawn away, he held her tighter. He felt it when she gave herself back to him and to the unrestrained fever that bound them to the moment.

In the end, he did let her go. But he held on to the elation gripping him.

Somehow he had to convince her three months was far too soon to walk away from what was growing between them.

Perhaps it might not be so difficult considering what had just happened.

'Did you not just say I couldn't kiss you?' He felt like a rooster crowing in joy at the promise of a new dawn. No doubt his grin looked as cocky as a strutting fowl's.

'I said that.' She nodded, staring all the while at his lips, biting hers. 'And you did not kiss me. I kissed you.'

'And I'll never be the same for it.'

She turned in his arms, gazed silently out at the great ocean. He caught the coat lapels, then wrapped them up, cocoon-like.

What could she be feeling about his admission?

'Will you be the same, Madeline?' He had to ask. His heart was scratching at a wall he had never climbed. He had to know if there was any chance she would be on the other side of it.

'I don't want to be the same.' She reached up and squeezed his hand where it rested on her shoulder.

That was something to build on. He wondered if she felt him grinning against her hair.

In the wee hours of the morning Madeline stared at the ceiling. She listened to the sound of Rees's even breathing while he slept on the floor next to the cot.

She had admitted to him that she did not want things to be the same.

No matter how many times she changed position on the mattress, transferred her gaze from the door to the ceiling and back again, she could not figure out precisely what she meant by saying so.

Of course, she did mean those words.

Kissing Rees was something she would never regret. In a sense, doing so had been healing, oddly freeing and binding all in one incredible moment.

Perhaps she had meant that she, at the heart of her, did not want to be the same.

For all that she had believed herself in love with that weasel Fenster, she had never returned his kiss with any ardency.

Perhaps because he gave her no choice, but had taken what he wanted, made a conquest of her.

Oh, but Rees—he had given her a choice. To kiss him or to reject him, it was for her to decide.

Did he have any idea that by doing so he had freed her from the shame of allowing Bertrand to steal her emotions?

She thought that, yes, he might have, but only to a degree. How could he possibly understand that when he had let her go and not pressed her favour, her heart had shifted?

He could not know that, yet again, he was her hero. This husband of hers had taken away her shame and changed

her sense of being used into a sense of being respected—
cherished even.

The fact that he gave her a choice would mean the world
to her for ever.

Yes—for ever. What she still did not understand was
what this meant for her future.

Or if it meant nothing.

If it meant nothing, was that what she wanted? She had
certainly thought so until a few hours ago.

She turned on her side, gazing down on the face of
her husband.

Oh, but she did like him—intensely. Was there a word
for what she was so quickly feeling for him? She tried a
few out while looking down at him.

Friendship? Yes, that. Affinity? Also, yes. Brotherhood
or sisterhood? No, not that, not by a long mile.

She was quite taken with how handsome he was, but
to like him for that quality alone would be foolish and
dangerous.

While watching him sleep was fascinating, it was the
man behind those closed lids who intrigued her.

Years from now, after going their separate ways, she
would recall the way his lips tended to quirk in humour,
how when he teased her his eyes twinkled. On some distant day she would find herself staring off at the horizon,
wondering where he was. At night she would toss about
on her mattress, wishing she was tossing on it with him.

When she went on her way as they had agreed she
would do, she doubted she would ever come across a man
she trusted half as much.

Certainly not if she was back in the sphere of Grandfather's social acquaintances. Every fortune-hunting dandy
would be trailing her skirt again.

Trusting a man, she had learned in a bitter way, meant
everything.

But she did trust Rees. Because she did, it had made it possible to get lost in the scent and the feel of his kiss, to become absorbed in it.

There was so much more to him than being handsome, strong, manly and whatever it was about him that made her long to stretch out on the floor beside him and lie within the circle of his strong arms.

There was all that, but in addition she adored his sense of honour. A nicely formed face was wasted on a man without integrity.

Tender feelings for him were developing too fast for her peace of mind. Something inside, the quiet whispering voice, was continuing to make suggestions having to do with 'for ever'.

Honestly, Rees had not offered her three months because he wanted her for ever.

Perhaps he thought she would not fit in with the simpler way he lived, not now that he knew how she had been raised in wealth.

If he did think it, he was wrong.

In this moment, she was completely content to be in this small cabin with him. Being in a larger one would have him lying further away.

At some point during her contemplation of his face he woke up. All of a sudden, she was looking into his eyes, warming to his smile.

'Can't sleep?' he asked.

'No.'

'Me either.'

'Really? You have been giving an excellent impression of it for hours now.'

'Must have been having dreams that made me feel awake.'

He eased up on his elbows, shaking his head. Auburn

hair scraped his high cheekbones. He peered at her through the locks that dangled down his forehead.

Even in the dim light she saw his eyes twinkling at her. It was hard to imagine that eyes could be that shade of blue.

The voice in her head proffered that she would prefer to spend her life looking into them rather than remembering how nice it had been.

'What were you dreaming about?'

'Coffee, maybe? Want some?'

'What time is it? I wonder.'

'There's a couple of hours before my shift, I think.'

He got up from the floor, trying to disguise his groan. He lit the fire in the stove, then began to make coffee.

The room became suffused in an amber glow.

'I don't feel right about taking over your bed. I ought to sleep on the floor.'

He arched a brow, levelled her with a stare that told her there was no point in discussing the situation.

'Perhaps we—?'

He handed her a steaming mug, then sat on the mattress beside her.

'Perhaps we what?' he asked.

'Ah, well, we are married, after all.' She could not believe she was about to suggest this, but it seemed words spilled from her mouth with a will of their own. Which was absurd; one had to be consenting to the words one spoke. She might be a fool but— 'It would not be unusual to share the bed.'

His gaze fastened upon her, sharp and warm all at once. She had never seen anything quite like the way he was looking at her.

'We might be crowded, but surely it will be better than on the floor. There is no need for you to wake up sore.'

She sipped her coffee even though it was too hot because

she had to do something. His steady gaze made her feel odd. 'It's only for a few more nights, after all. Surely we can accommodate each other for that long.'

He cleared his throat, took a long swallow of coffee which had to have burned going down.

'Would you like some water?' she asked because he'd begun to cough.

Shaking his head, he set the mug on the floor.

'Tell me more about your grandfather.'

If he wanted to change the course of the conversation, she would be happy to talk about the man who stood in her father's place.

'His name is James—Macooish, of course. He is wonderful. And brave. He's loving and kind. He believes he is right in every situation—he is rather like you in that, I think.'

The similarity had not occurred to her before now. All of a sudden—all right—not so all of a sudden, she wanted to snuggle up beside Rees, feel his arm go around her and draw her close.

She was homesick for her family. Her heart tripped and squeezed in the instant it occurred to her that this man was now her family, too. They belonged to each other for several more weeks.

'I believe I will like him.'

'Everyone does.' For many people, liking him had nothing to do with his fortune. They knew him to be a good man. 'My parents died in a flash flood when I was very small. So did Clementine's. The only reason we did not die with them was that Grandfather would not allow it. As young as I was, I still remember how he held tight to us even though the water surged around us. And not just ordinary water. It was full of rocks and branches, anything that got washed downstream.

'Debris hit Grandfather, but not me or Clemmie because

he curled himself around us. I heard him crying out every time he was hit by something. I can still hear him groaning with the effort to hold on to us.'

'He sounds an extraordinary man.'

Once again Madeline thought Rees spoke more like a gentleman than a labourer.

'Yes, and stubborn. He'd set his mind not to lose us along with the rest of the family. The three of us were all who were left. In the days after, Grandfather could have given up in grief, but he didn't. He just kept on holding on to me and my cousin as though we were still in that flood, drying our tears and hiding his own. He raised us as lovingly as our parents would have.'

'And through it all, he managed to earn his fortune. I admire him for going through what he did, for raising you and still carrying on.'

'He was used to carrying on. He was born out of wedlock. His mother tried her best, but poverty was all he knew as a child. He refused to have the same thing happen to us, so he became rich in order to prevent it.'

'I see,' he said, but how could he possibly? But perhaps he had been through something of the same. Pregnancy outside of wedlock was hardly uncommon.

Heaven knew how many times Grandfather had cautioned her and Clemmie to guard their virtue.

No doubt Grandfather believed she had ignored his warning. That she was completely and utterly fallen.

'Not quite. You see, Grandfather earned a fortune, but lost it, only to earn it again. He didn't trust money alone to keep us safe. That is why he groomed me to marry the Earl of Fencroft. He was convinced that only a title would guarantee our security. He was certain that Lord Fencroft and I would make a brilliant match.'

'But you were not convinced.' He gave that look—the

one that saw past her eyes clear to her thoughts. Had she really only known him such a short while?

'I was not. Instead I believed a man who lied horribly to me and misrepresented his intentions in the worst way a man can.'

'Do you regret it now? Not Fenster, I don't mean, but not going along with your grandfather's plan?'

She shrugged. 'I don't think so. I could hardly let my future be dictated.'

'It is not uncommon for a woman in British society. Marriages are contracted for many reasons. Happiness might or might not follow the vows.'

'I don't know, Rees. I imagine I could not have been worse off than I was with Bertrand. And I would have had the security of my wedding vows.'

'Yes.' He nodded. 'Well, you have them now.'

'But only for three—'

He touched her lips with one large, rough finger. 'For as long as you wish.'

Chapter Six

'But we agreed.' Her voice sounded a bare whisper.

'So we did, my angel. And I won't go back on my word.'

If he had known in the beginning how much he would come to care for Madeline, he would not have presented the option. At the time, this marriage had to do with behaving in the morally responsible way with regards to a woman he had shared his room with and, by so doing, compromised her. In no less a way it was for the sake of keeping his family from being torn apart.

Damn it, things had gone far beyond that now. He would say he was falling in love with Madeline Dalton, but that would indicate there were degrees to that state of being.

One either was or was not in love. There was no falling, only fallen.

He was fallen. Completely and irrevocably fallen. The short time he'd taken to come to the conclusion was irrelevant. He might not know every little fact about her, what she adored and what she detested, but he knew her—loved her.

'Oh, good,' she said, her gaze sliding away.

Clearly, she did not feel the same for him as he did her. It ought to be a relief that she didn't. If she did not love him, she would not be crushed by his deception when he finally admitted the truth.

He would be the devastated one. His secret sat upon his heart like a cold stone.

Right now, Madeline thought he was honourable—truthful.

She would not once they docked in Liverpool. The fact that he was Viscount Glenbrook would become evident as soon as they stepped off the boat. There was something about a family crest on the carriage door that tended to give one's identity away.

The only conceivable way he saw for her to forgive him was to tell her all of it right now.

Huff it out.

She tipped her head to one side, smiling. He loved that gesture because her eyes twinkled. The generosity of her sweet spirit warmed him thoroughly.

'Let's just wait—see what happens.' She leaned forward, kissed his lips quickly. 'It's more that I still feel a need to make my own choice in how my life goes rather than that I want to be without you.'

Stunned by the admission, he returned the kiss tenfold. Revealing who he was right now was unthinkable.

He needed time to win her heart completely.

Soon, though—very soon.

'I like you, Rees.' Her breathless statement cut him to the quick. 'I like you very much.'

'Marriages have been founded on less.'

And dashed on less than what he hid from her.

But what if he found her grandfather? Might she be more willing to forgive him?

The fact was, he had met a fellow named Macooish not so long ago—in Scotland when he'd purchased his ship. His name might have been James—or John. He could not be sure. He did recall the man's face. He was strong and sharp minded for an older gentleman.

And he did have blue eyes.

What Madeline wanted most in the world was to be reunited with her grandfather. Rees had promised to help find him.

If he managed to do it, things might go strongly in his favour.

Luck, in fact, might be on his side. He had heard from someone that the Earl of Fencroft had married. Not the Earl that Madeline had been slated for—no, that poor fellow had passed away.

It was his brother, the new Earl, who had married. Now Rees wished he paid more attention to what went on in London. Or to Derbyshire gossip, as far as that went. Mostly he felt happier not knowing all the news and scandal that went with it.

He did know that the new Earl had wed—but to a British lady or an American heiress? He did not know that.

He could ask his mother, but she shunned the gossip of London more adroitly than he did. They shared the opinion that it was all stuffy nonsense. Did anyone in Derbyshire really care who wore what in the wrong way or who shunned whom for whatever absurd reason?

But in the end, his search for Madeline's family might not be as difficult as it now seemed. As luck would have it, the Fencroft estate was close to Green Knoll Manor. At one point their fences connected.

It would not do to reveal his hopes just now. There was every possibility that the search would not lead to Madeline's family, and he would not get her hopes up only to have them dashed.

For now, he would keep his thoughts to himself, just until he knew for certain.

In the event that Macooish was in residence at Fencroft Manor, it would be a great and happy surprise for Madeline.

He could think of no other wedding gift that would mean more to her.

It might be the very act that convinced her to remain with him beyond the cursed three-month agreement.

Yes, he would surprise her with the greatest gift he could give.

But between now and then he needed to tell her who he was.

Just not now. How could he possibly with her kiss still hot on his lips and her smile lodging itself deep in his heart?

No matter how he reminded himself that his continued silence only decreased her chances of forgiving him, he used his mouth to kiss her again.

He was a doomed man and deserved to be.

Still, miracles did happen, and he was going to carry on as if one would.

Was there not a saying that love conquered all?

Did not the Good Book preach forgiveness? He was sure he recalled a bit about love enduring all things.

All he could do was carry on in hopes of the saying being true.

In that spirit, he allowed the kiss to go on for a long, heated moment. When it ended he indulged in another, then another.

Then one once more for good measure.

He was going to need all the good measure he could get in order to make things come out right.

Madeline emerged from the cabin in search of sunshine and lunch.

Company, too, if she could find some. Rees had left to work his shift as soon as the sun came up. Now that she was feeling better, it was difficult to remain inside the little space for hours on end.

Except when her new husband was with her, then it was delightful. But now she needed company.

Rees had given her a bit of money to purchase food from the woman who sold bread and cheese in the dining saloon. Hopefully there would be something else she could buy. Now that her appetite had returned, she longed for the fare in first class.

Not that she would set foot in that place again. Even the promise of lush red berries could not lure her back there.

If she wanted friendly company, it was best to eat what might be had in the steerage dining room.

Out on the open deck she leaned into the wind, Rees's big coat clamped tight around her. Even wrapped in heavy wool she was chilled by the time she entered the dining room.

Oh, good. The vendor was in her customary spot. In addition to cheese and bread, she was selling some sort of stew. Madeline would eat lunch here, then take food back to the cabin for dinner. Rees was always tired and hungry when he came back from the fire room.

Had Madeline been a countess, she would make sure a servant delivered a variety of his favourite foods to him. Life operated differently when one was a commoner. It was the wife's duty to provide a meal with her own two hands.

She fell short in that area. Beyond buttering toast and serving tea, she was inept.

If she decided to stay with Rees, she would need to learn to cook and to sew. Oh, and to clean.

She purchased her food, then sat down at the end of the table closest to the stove.

Taking a bite of stew, Madeline closed her eyes to better savour the flavours warming her tongue. Would she be able to learn how to combine meat, potatoes and other vegetables in order to make them come together like this?

It took special skill to turn basic ingredients into a comforting meal.

She would do her best to learn—in the event that she wanted to remain married.

A few days ago, she would not have considered it. Now, with each passing hour, it was harder to imagine not seeing Rees Dalton rise in the morning and settle on the floor at night.

Grandfather might be disappointed in her choice. Unless Clementine had wed Lord Fencroft and fulfilled his dreams of his family secure with a title. In that case he might not care that Rees worked in the fire room of a ship. As long as one of his granddaughters had married well, he would be blissfully content.

Finished with the stew, she took a bite of bread and chewed it slowly. She could not imagine she would ever learn the secret to making bread. That task seemed rather mysterious.

Luckily, one could purchase bread easily enough. But there was something to be considered that was much more serious than knowing how to prepare food.

Two little girls, to be exact.

Madeline knew nothing about being a mother. In her social sphere she hadn't had much contact with children. She thought them to be lovely and precious, but how did one go about raising them?

She would be skilled at hiring a governess, but she doubted Rees's income would allow for that. Perhaps his mother would instruct her on the care of small girls.

If it came to that.

If it did not, the situation became far more difficult. Children were engaging little people. She could scarcely imagine being a part of their lives for a short time and then going on her merry way and leaving their fragile hearts bruised.

It would not be her merry way either. Her heart would be wounded, too. Leaving Rees would be hard enough without having to say goodbye to his daughters.

Even though she had never met them, she feared she would become instantly attached.

'Good afternoon, Mrs Dalton,' said a high-pitched voice.

Madeline snapped her attention back to the dining room to find the young girl from the dock sitting beside her on the bench.

'Good afternoon,' she answered. 'It's so lovely to see you again.'

'You don't look too horrid for having been forced to marry.'

'How do you know about that—Clara—isn't that your name?'

'Everyone knows, of course.' She nodded with a serious expression.

A woman sat down at the table across from them. Madeline recognised her as Clara's mother.

'It is rather talked about when a passenger nearly dies and marries a stranger within a matter of hours,' the woman said. 'I can't say how horrible I feel about all of it. You were so kind to us. You did not deserve that misfortune.'

Misfortune? Or was it a great gift?

Confusion was what it was. Life could not possibly take such a sharp turn and be on the right path.

Unless the sharp turn had been not so sharp. Maybe it had been arranged by a Higher Power from the very beginning. It would be a comfort to think so, make her choice easier.

At the same time, it could be wishful thinking.

And if it was wishful thinking, it meant she wished to remain with her groom.

Their marriage was new enough for him to still be a groom.

Groom. She bit her lips thinking about that because in her mind the word suggested something more intimate than *new husband* did.

Something that went deeper than the kisses they indulged in.

Fascinating possibilities drifted across her mind. She ought not to be entertaining them while in the presence of a child.

'Mrs Dalton.' Tears gathered in the woman's eyes. 'What you did for my family—I have no words to thank you.'

'It's no more than anyone would have done.' At least Madeline liked to think so.

'No, my dear. What you did was uncommon. I feel wretched when I think of what it cost you. Had you not given me your ticket, you would have had a room and not been caught out in the storm. You would not have had to marry the way you did. Why, a pretty young lady like you ought to have your pick of men.'

Was that not what she intended when she went away with Bertrand? Having her pick?

Well, she had picked and picked wrongly. Her poor decision had caused her to be separated from Grandfather and Clementine. By making that choice she had very likely taken it away from her cousin.

Running away from a problem had worse consequences than she would have imagined.

This stranger thought her to be a good person. She was far from it.

For all Madeline knew, Clementine cried herself to

sleep every night while hugging the corner of the bed, putting as much distance between her and the Earl as possible.

Not so Madeline. She who had caused the trouble invited her husband to share a bed—was looking forward to tonight to see if he would.

'Clara, run to the cabin and get the project I have been working on.'

'Yes, Mama.' Clara grinned, winked, then dashed away.

'My name is Martha, by the by. Since you were travelling alone, might I assume you need the guidance of one long married? I'm certain your mother would speak to you of being newly wed were she here with you.'

'My mother's name was also Martha. But she died when I was very small.'

'You poor dear.' Martha reached across the table and squeezed her hand. 'Will you be living in Liverpool? Perhaps we can remain in touch with each other. A new bride should not be without someone to confide in.'

'My husband has a place in Liverpool. But I don't know how long I will be—'

In the instant Clara rushed back into the dining room with something tucked under her arm. She handed it to her mother.

'This is for you.' Martha opened a shawl for her inspection. 'I made it for you as a thank you. It's rather feeble as a thank you goes. I'm only glad I met you again before Liverpool so that I might give it to you.'

Madeline wrapped it about her shoulders.

There was nothing feeble about the shawl. It was beautiful, knit in shades of blue and tan. The fact that Martha had made it with her own hands made it feel more like a hug than yarn.

'I can't even—' Her throat clogged with tears. It was amazing that a stranger would be so kind to her. She found people to be that way—kind for the most part. She had rarely met a person who did not quickly become a friend.

Rees had become that and more swiftly than made sense. The more time she spent with him, the more time she longed to.

'I do thank you for this,' she said, stroking the fine stitches. 'I will always cherish it, Martha.'

She stood, picked up Rees's coat and the food for his dinner. 'Perhaps I will see you again before we make land.'

'And after, my dear. If you need anything at all, our family name is Adlebackmore. Liverpool is a large city, but it's an odd name. I hope we can find each other.'

Madeline hurried along the deck, grateful that she was, at last, able to move swiftly. She would never take good health for granted again.

Things were looking much more hopeful. When she had boarded the ship she had been utterly alone. Only a week later she had a friend.

And a husband.

She had but to accept what he offered.

Oh, but did she dare to? What if she found she had made a mistake the same way she had before? What if she ran away from it?

She would feel the most unworthy of souls.

Rees lingered a few moments at his post even though one of the men he'd hired to help watch stood by waiting to take over the shift.

The fellow was competent, but even so, it was difficult for Rees to hand over the watch.

'I'm ill at ease with the worker at the third furnace down, Mr Hayes.'

'I agree. I've noticed that he's different than the others. He's a shifty one, at best. Won't look anyone in the eye, I've noticed.'

'You'll recall what I said about him smelling of spirits?'

'Aye, yes, I'll keep it in mind. If he is up to no good, I'll know it soon enough, Lord Glenbrook,' he whispered.

'I thank you, Hayes.'

Hayes nodded, cast a severe glance at the suspected derelict. Rees knew he was leaving the watch in good hands.

Tired to the bone and hungry as a fiend, Rees trudged up two flights of stairs, then walked the length of the deck to his cabin.

Every step was an effort. He wanted his bed, not that he would be sleeping overmuch.

The worrisome fact that there might be a problem in the fire room was not all that was going to keep him from his rest.

His lovely legally wed bride, whom he wanted to be his in more than name alone, had invited him to share the bed. She might not intend all that came with it. Chances were Madeline had no idea that the things entertaining his mind even existed.

Damn it! In his mind they would need to remain. He could not indulge in the smallest of them. Not until he was honest with her about everything.

Opening the cabin door, he was greeted with the scent of burned something or other.

'It's your dinner—or it was.' Madeline shook her head, her mouth puckered in a grimace. Funny, how even her frown was endearing. No matter how she tried, the gesture did not appear stern. 'I'll admit, I've never been called upon to prepare a meal.'

'I'm sure it's wonderful.' Or was at one time.

'I scooped off the top of the stew. It's only the bottom of the pot ruined. The bread and cheese are edible.'

He washed, then sat on the bed, it being the only place to sit other than the floor. He'd had quite enough of floors for a lifetime.

Even so, he might lie there again tonight. His options were to tell the truth and maybe share the bed or continue to lie and sleep on the floor.

Or, in the event he confessed, spend the night in the lifeboat. There was no reason to believe she would forgive him just because he finally told the truth.

She set a tray on his lap, then settled beside him.

'I don't suppose it will make you sick.'

'Are you going to eat?'

'I filled up with cheese and bread before you came home.'

Home? What a wonderful sentiment. She called this dreary little space home and with those words it seemed to become one. Not because of the walls, but because she shared them with him.

'I didn't spend all your money.' She nodded towards the table beside the basin. 'I put what remains over there.'

'It's yours. There's a woman selling goods for ladies. Please buy whatever you want to.'

'That's generous of you, Rees. But I know how hard you work. I would feel wicked being frivolous with your money.' She hugged a shawl around her shoulders. 'You should spend it on your children.'

Now would be the time to admit he spent a great deal of money on his children—as Viscount Glenbrook would have the privilege of doing.

It was far past the time he opened up. Fear of her reaction at discovering he had lied kept him from it. She thought him to be an honest man and nothing could be more wrong.

In the beginning he had had good intentions in keeping the truth to himself—fearing she would not keep his secret and all that rot. Now he knew it was nonsense.

She was completely reliable and clearly she valued truth much more than he did.

'I have something to tell you.' He felt the words on his tongue, but they seemed to be glued there.

Even his twin girls, who were barely more than babes, knew there were consequences to lying.

'That's a pretty shawl,' he said in a cowardly sidestep. 'I'm glad you purchased something.'

'It was a gift.' She stroked the blue yarn. 'From the woman I gave my ticket to.'

'It matches your eyes.'

'I was thinking that it matched yours.' She hugged the shawl tighter about her. 'Does that taste all right? Don't feel you have to eat it. There's plenty of bread and the cheese is delicious.'

'I'm hungry enough that anything will taste delicious.'

'Is your mother a good cook?'

Such a simple question, yet he found himself in a tight corner. Mother had never as much as boiled water. With the kind of life he claimed to live, cooking would be a required skill.

'Not very,' he answered vaguely. 'How was your day?'

'I'm feeling much better—stronger and hungrier.'

He memorised the curve of her smile. He'd come to crave seeing it—would, in fact, rather see it than a spectacular sunrise over the Atlantic.

'And curious,' she added.

'Curious about what?'

'About you and your life.' She shrugged. 'We are considering spending a lifetime together, yet I know less about you than you know about me. It's an odd situation, you must admit.'

'For some levels of society, it's common.'

'Yes, and I'm worried that I might have forced my cousin into one of those marriages.'

'If she is anything like you, she will have refused to wed where she did not wish.'

'Oh, but she is nothing like me.' She shook her head. 'Clementine is level-headed and loyal. She would not betray Grandfather the way I did.'

'I'm certain that in spite of everything they love you.' He set the bowl of burned stew on the floor. A lock of golden hair trickled across her face. He stroked it behind her ear, making sure his fingers brushed her cheek. 'Love can forgive anything, don't you think?'

Yes—please let her answer be yes.

'I hope so. I'll need it, don't you think? When it comes time to beg it of Grandfather. Of course, that makes me something of a hypocrite because when it comes to forgiving and forgetting Bertrand, I'm not so sure I can let bygones be bygones, as I ought to.'

'That man is your past. I'm sure in time what he did will not sting so badly.'

'It doesn't sting now. It only shames me that I did not recognise his false character from the beginning. He lied so gracefully. It is a fortunate thing I figured him out before it was too late. Can you imagine being bound to a liar all your life?'

'I—well—no. It would be unpleasant.'

'Unpleasant? It would be far worse than that! One would always need to be on guard to make sure one was not being duped.'

He was doomed—damned if he told the truth and damned if he did not. He feared that if he carried on this conversation any longer he would— Damn it, he did not know what he would do, but it wasn't good.

'Don't worry, my angel. We will find your family and they will welcome you.'

'Do you really think so or are you trying to make me feel better?'

'I'm a strong believer in forgiveness. So, yes, I do.'

'I hope you are right.' Her smile returned.

He'd heard of hearts melting. Until this moment he hadn't believed one could have a warm puddle simmering in one's chest and yet he did.

'Now,' she said. 'Since we have a long evening in this little cabin, I'd like to hear about your family. Is it only your children and your mother?'

At some point she was going to ask him something he could not answer.

Had he not fallen in love with his bride—and he might as well face the truth of it that he had—he would blurt out everything and consequences be damned. If she left him, he would quickly recover.

But he was in love and he would not quickly recover.

'I have a brother. He is only a year younger than I am.'

'Does he also live in Liverpool?'

'No, Derbyshire.' All of this was gospel.

'But your mother lives with you. Is she a widow, then?'

'My father died when I was a small boy.' Too small a boy. It seemed to Rees he had been Glenbrook most of his life.

'We have that in common, then.'

Shyly, she brushed the backs of her fingers against his hand. He needed no more invitation than that to fold them up in his palm.

'I'm glad we have this time to get to know one another,' she said. 'Since we are considering remaining together, we should be well acquainted before we make a hard-and-fast choice. Don't you think so?'

'I do.' Getting to know her better occupied a great deal of his attention. 'For instance, I'd like to become more acquainted with your lips.'

'My lips?'

He nodded, traced the shape of them with his thumb.

'Ah, well, they are ordinary lips. They enjoy smiling,

speaking, laughing and eating. They are much the same as any others.'

'I think they are not, but what I wonder most is if they enjoy kissing.'

'They have not had a great deal of experience in that, but—' She stared at him silently for what seemed a very long time. 'But they do enjoy kissing you. They enjoy it beyond what is wise.'

'Why is it not wise? We are married.'

'In an odd sense we are.'

'We spoke vows like anyone else.'

'I have a feeling the vows you spoke with your late wife were nothing like ours were.'

Madeline was correct. His first wedding had been an elegant society event with hundreds of guests in attendance.

He nodded. 'And yet I knew less of Margaret on our wedding day than I did of you.'

'Oh, well—' she glanced at the ceiling, clearly hiding her embarrassment '—needs were what they were, after all.'

'Madeline.' He turned her face so that she could do nothing but look into his eyes. 'When I promised myself to you, I did know you. I don't mean just the birthmark or anything else I learned about you that night. Before that, on the docks, I knew you put other people's well-being ahead of your own. I knew you were brave, you were bold and adventurous.'

'You saw all that through a spyglass? From across the street? Truly, in only a few moments you came to those conclusions?'

'They were obvious.'

'Really, Rees—did you miss the part where I was running from a man? Surely you did not see a woman who broke her family's heart in the spyglass?'

'It would have made no difference.'

'It ought to have. You married someone who nearly died because she did not know to come out of the cold.'

He shook his head. 'No difference.'

'I was not at all resourceful and—'

Her lips moved, but he no longer paid attention to what they were saying.

He had to kiss them.

She stopped talking.

'Madeline, it doesn't matter.'

'Oh,' she murmured.

'I want you, all of you—I want to be your husband in God's way. Do you know what I am saying? What I am asking of you?'

'Yes, Rees, I know.'

He, a grown man and peer of the realm, felt as though he might weep. For joy and for fear.

Inside him truth and lies were at war. His heart was the battleground, but his wife's would be the casualty.

Now was the time to tell her—now before things went too far between them and she could no longer seek the annulment.

Another kiss, an intimate touch, and it could happen.

He let go of her waist to capture her hand. He kissed her knuckles, took a great breath, then held her gaze.

'Do you remember when I said there was another reason I wanted to marry you?'

'I've been intensely curious over it.'

'It has to do with—' He tried to huff, but choked instead. The words he needed to say became cramped in his throat and would not emerge. 'When I saw you in the spyglass, I thought you were the prettiest woman I'd ever seen.'

'That is very sweet, Rees. And now you may kiss me.'

'I would, and I will. But I've only just recalled I must go out—speak with the Captain.'

What a wretch he was. A compound liar. One who uttered one lie to cover another. But he had to get outside, have a moment alone to confront the state of his soul.

'I forbid it. Whatever it is can wait until the morning. You will lie down on the bed and sleep.'

Clamping his hands about her waist, he lifted her off the floor and set her down behind him.

'My mother will adore you. I'll explain all this when I get back, I promise.'

He opened the door and found himself eye to eye with Mr Hayes.

'Come quickly, sir. There has been a fire.'

Chapter Seven

The inebriated man, the fire-starter, sat on a cot, his back against the wall of the ship's only cell. His head sagged forward; his narrow chin nearly touched his chest. With his gaunt body and slumped shoulders, he reminded Rees of a spindly-legged insect.

Even in the dim lamplight he could see that the man's face was bruised.

'Have you sent for the doctor?'

'I don't know that he deserves it. He might have caused a disaster.'

'Perhaps he does not, Captain Collier. That does not change the fact that he will have medical care.' Rees cast a glance over his shoulder. 'Hayes, fetch the physician.'

'Yes, Lord Glenbrook, right away. But I agree with the Captain. Mr Harrow deserves what he got.'

'Dr Raymond will attend him, nonetheless. And, Captain, light a fire in the stove.'

'I didn't mean no harm to anyone.' The drunk's voice was slurred. Rees wondered if he even understood that the fire he'd accidentally started might have caused an explosion and killed people.

Even now he did not know how much damage had been

done. He would no doubt spend the better part of the night with the ship's mechanic finding it out.

Which meant he would be away from Madeline all night. He had needed a few moments away. But only that, just long enough to gather his courage to become an honest man.

His fear now was that he might not have time to do it.

Once the ship neared land things aboard would become hectic for the crew.

No matter, he would have to make the time. It did not bear thinking that she would discover who he was because it was in front of her face.

Madeline absently brushed her hair while wondering why it was Rees who had been called in the emergency. The timing of it had been wickedly disappointing.

The intimacy sparking between them had been intense. So intense that he apparently needed a moment away to catch his breath.

And truly, she was glad for it. She also needed a moment to consider the step she felt they had been so close to taking. Once she gave herself to him, she would never go back from it. There would be no annulment.

But a moment was all either of them needed, not these endless hours while he saw to what was happening.

A fire? Really, it did sound rather frightening, although it must have been put out since no alarm had been raised.

The night dragged by. Once or twice steps tapped on the deck, but passed on by. Later someone paced back and forth in front of the door, cooing to a fussy infant.

As soon as it was dawn, she was going to have severe words for the Captain. It was hard to believe that on this huge ship there was no one to call on but Rees.

Important decisions regarding the future were so close to being made.

It touched her more than he would ever understand that he had left the decision of what was to become of them to her.

Funny how the fact that he had given her a choice made her want to choose him.

If she walked away from this marriage, she had no idea what would come next.

In the event Grandfather took her back, he would probably marry her off to another peer of his choosing.

The room seemed to close around her.

She snugged the shawl about her shoulders and went outside.

The wee hours were clear and still. She was hit anew by the glorious display of stars blinking from horizon to horizon.

Someone else was on deck. A woman sat in a chair, hugging an infant to her breast. The child was asleep.

'Good morning,' Madeline said softly. At least she thought it was morning, perhaps about two o'clock. 'Is your baby ailing?'

'She's only teething. I hope we didn't bother you. But I can't stay in my cabin or she'll wake her brothers.'

'You didn't disturb me.'

If she had to be sleepless, it was rather nice to have company, misery loving company and all that nonsense.

Of course, she could not count this as misery since her companion seemed a pleasant sort.

'Would you care for tea? I have some water already warm. My cabin is just behind us.'

'It is a bone chiller tonight and the offer is tempting, but I'll need to get back and check on my boys soon.'

'We're lucky the wind isn't blowing, at least.'

Even without the wind, Madeline did not think the baby

would be warm enough under her mother's thin coat. She took off her shawl and tucked it gently about the tiny figure.

She could go back inside and get a blanket for herself, but instead she sat down in the chair beside the woman.

There was something magical about making a new friend in the silent splendour of the wee hours.

'I'm Madeline Macooish—Dalton now.'

'I'm grateful for your company, Madeline. My name is Lena Brown.' She pulled the shawl higher over her baby's head, covering her daughter's blonde curls. 'Aren't you the lady who nearly died in the lifeboat and then married the man who rescued you?'

She nodded. 'I fear my fate must be rather well known.'

'And envied.'

'I can't imagine why anyone would.'

Lena chuckled under her breath. 'Your husband is quite the hero for one thing, coming to your rescue the way he did. And then offering marriage to honour your virtue?'

'He didn't offer marriage. He insisted upon it.'

'So that makes him honourable as well as handsome enough to capture the heart of any woman. I know of five or six young ladies who dream of walking in your slippers.'

The baby whined, but was comforted when Lena rubbed her back.

'Even though I had no choice in the matter?'

'Oh, my friend, we rarely do. Most of the time life does not offer choices.'

'Did you choose your husband?'

'I did. And I'd do it a hundred times over. But I didn't choose to become his widow.'

'Oh, I'm sorry to hear it, truly sorry. I hate to imagine how hard it must be for you.'

'I've learned some things because of it. Grown stronger than I knew I could be.' She dabbed her eyes even though she was smiling. 'One thing I can tell you, if you care for some advice.'

'I think it's what I need most right now, advice.'

'From what I've seen of Rees Dalton, he's a fine man. If you care for him, tell him so. You don't know when you might not be able to.'

Well, she did care for him—cared for him greatly.

'But I've only known him for a week.'

'I knew my George for only a day before I knew he was to be mine. I think that love is rather like yeast. It's the same ingredient no matter if it's newly mixed into the dough or it's had time to rise and grow. Yeast is yeast.'

And love was love. It was just as real new as it was when it was mature.

'And with that sage wisdom, I've got to get back to my twins.'

Lena stood up, handing back the shawl.

'Where are you going to from here?' Madeline asked.

'To my brother in London. He's a bachelor, never been wed, so I imagine we'll be a jolt to his life. But he says he wants us.'

Madeline hugged her quickly, careful not to wake the baby. 'I wish you and your boys the best, Lena.'

'And I hope you will have a long and blissful marriage.'

Madeline watched her new friend walk away and then went to stand at the rail to watch the night pass for a bit before she went back inside.

The universe was amazingly vast. She could not hope to understand it.

But Lena's advice? Yes, she understood that quite clearly.

Yeast was yeast no matter how long it had been set to rise. Love and yeast were the same.

Gazing out at the countless, unending display of stars, she made her decision.

Her life would rise alongside Rees.

The hours passed almost without notice while Rees accompanied the mechanic and the Captain while they checked to make certain the furnaces, valves, tubes and engines had not been damaged.

It had been fascinating how everything worked. Frightening, too, seeing all that might have been damaged, the injuries that could have resulted.

There had to be something illegal about what the drunk had done. He would check with the police when they reached Liverpool in the morning.

But what time was it? His mind had been focused only on the soundness of his ship, so he had lost track of the hour.

Opening the door to his cabin, he wanted to curse in frustration at the hours he had lost with his wife.

The sound died on his tongue when he stepped inside and saw his bride asleep on the floor, her hair tumbled loose over her shoulders and one delicate hand tucked under her cheek.

A meal waited for him on the small table, but it had no doubt grown cold hours ago.

He crouched down beside her, smoothed a strand of hair away from her forehead. He did enjoy touching her hair.

She looked nearly recovered from her weakness. It was no trick of the lamp she had left burning for him that her cheek looked pink where it had been pale. Now that he looked closely, he thought she had already gained back a bit of the weight she'd lost.

He'd know for sure if she were not covered from neck to knee in a nightgown.

How thoughtful she was to take the floor and leave him

the bed. From the first he'd thought her an angel walking the earth.

Even so, she could not imagine he would take the bed while she slept on the floor.

Crouching, he scooped her up in his arms, being careful not to wake her. The selfish side of his nature wanted her to rouse and kiss him, make him feel as though this was all going to come out right.

For a moment he held her close to his chest just to feel her breathe, to catch a whiff of her feminine scent.

Perhaps once they reached the Glenbrook town house she would share his bed, become his wife and forget the blamed annulment.

What devil had made him promise it anyway?

It might be possible for this to happen. First, he would need to confess his lie. She did believe in forgiveness. But then, she adamantly believed in truthfulness, too.

'Perhaps it could be, my angel, unless you hate me.'

'Why would I?' Her voice was soft, dreamy sounding.

'You're awake.'

'Halfway. Rees, I want you to have the bed.'

It was a fine idea—but a better invitation if one looked at it just so.

He laid her on the mattress. She hadn't opened her eyes while she spoke and did not do it now.

When he lay down beside her a smile curved her lips.

The only way for them both to fit on the mattress was to lie on their sides. He folded one arm around her, scooped her to him spoon-like.

Before, when he had lain with her like this he had been as frightened as he'd ever been, thinking that each breath might be her last. Now she snuggled her warm behind against him and sighed.

'No annulment, Rees. I want to stay with you.' Her murmur stirred the hair near her lips.

'Do you, my angel? I'm glad of it.' Stunned, overjoyed more than that. But fearful, quaking, trembling scared. 'We'll speak more of it in the morning.'

He wasn't sure if she heard him. Her lungs rose and fell under his hand in the slow regular rhythm of a dreamer. The strand of hair near her mouth shivered with each warm breath.

Yes, in the morning.

Madeline came awake slowly, feeling the need to stretch.

She was loath to do so because she was warm—nice and toasty, but not only that. Rees's large, rough hand, resting on her shoulder, was tangled up in her hair, and she did not wish to dislodge it.

Blissful, that was how she felt. She had been content in her life, many times, but this was a far different gladness than any she had ever felt.

Beyond a doubt, she could be happy living the simple life with what society considered a commoner. Not that Rees Dalton was in any way common. No, he was exceptional.

Grandfather might not be pleased that she was married to a working man, but she was pleased and she was the one who was married, after all.

What difference did it make how large her home, or how elegant? While she adored pretty gowns with lace and flounces, she could be happy in something more serviceable. As long as she woke with Rees's long limbs wrapped all around her, it did not matter what she was wearing or where she was wearing it.

She thought a humble life would suit very nicely. Having grown up with servants to attend her every need, she was grateful for the chance to learn to do things on her own.

How long could it really take to learn the art of cooking?

And motherhood? If she loved Rees, it only followed

that she would love his children. Until most recently, she had not given children of her own a great deal of thought. Now that she had, she believed it would be the sweetest of sounds to hear two little voices calling her Mama.

Drat it, this bed was far too small for two people. As much as she regretted to do it, she needed to stretch the cramps out of her limbs.

She lifted her arms over her head. Rees's hand slipped from her shoulder to her waist. She turned towards him, kissed his nose.

Good, he was deeply asleep as he ought to be. He worked far too hard, and now that she had something to say about it, he would get some rest.

How long before they made port? Noon, was it not?

That gave her a few hours to find Lena Brown. The young widow had been so kind. Madeline would like to say goodbye to her. Also, she needed to bid farewell to Mrs Adlebackmore and her family.

Of course, visiting new friends was not her only motive for going out. If no one was in the cabin to answer a knock and Rees was still asleep, they would leave him in peace.

Given the fact that he had been out all night in the service of the *Edwina*, he deserved to miss his morning shift.

She dressed quietly. Then, with her hand on the doorknob, she smiled at Rees and blew him a kiss. When he awoke rested, he would thank her for letting him sleep.

This business of being a wife was rather nice. She found she liked having a man to fuss over, a husband whose wellbeing was hers to see to.

Madeline enjoyed a pleasant hour with Clara and her mother. The visit with Lena Brown had been somewhat more hectic. How would one expect it to be otherwise with three small children to keep in order and all their belongings to gather up? Madeline helped for as long as she could, but if Rees awoke, he would wonder where she was.

Rushing past scores of people standing by the rail, she came to the cabin door. It was closed, so she paused by the rail to watch water rush past the hull.

For the first time in ten days she saw land. It was far off, but she could feel the excitement of her fellow travellers when they also spotted it.

Liverpool was still a distance away, but a thrum of anticipation hummed from person to person.

It pulsed within Madeline, as well. Her new life waited on those shores.

Not only did anticipation for her future make her spirits sing, but somewhere on those British Isles were Grandfather and Clementine.

She had missed them more than she could have guessed when she ran away.

Soon, though. If they had gone to London as she suspected they had, she would find them. She did not want to burden Rees with train fare to get there, but perhaps she could do something to earn a bit of money. He had promised to help in the search, but if duty kept him in Liverpool, she was capable of going alone.

Her family was close, so close. She could feel it was so in each salty, fishy breath she took.

A large, firm hand settled on her shoulder. She knew whose it was without having to look, so she reached up and squeezed it.

'I missed you when I woke up. Where did you go?' His voice stirred her hair when he spoke. It tickled, made her smile.

'To bid farewell to friends.' It was a difficult thing to do. At least she would not have to say goodbye to Rees. 'Do you know,' she said, watching the city come ever closer, 'as anxious as I am to find Grandfather, there is a part of me wishing the voyage lasted longer.'

'I'd have thought you would dislike boats intensely.'

'It hasn't to do with the boat. It's to do with you. Once we arrive in Liverpool, life will draw us here and there. As it is now, it has only been the two of us getting to know each other more deeply.'

'I've enjoyed it, too.' He leaned down to brush a kiss across her cheek. 'We haven't much time. Come, let us gather our things.'

Rees led her by the hand, going inside in a hurry.

'Rees, we need to say something to each other. I want to do it before we leave the cabin.'

Indeed, she had told him she would not seek the annulment, but not why.

He closed the door, but kept her hand curled firmly in his. He brought it to his lips, gave it a lingering kiss.

Oddly, his gaze was sombre. Perhaps one of his fellows had been injured in the fire.

'Are you well, Rees? Has something happened?'

He shook his head, smiled, but it was not with his usual playfulness.

'I did say we would speak about something this morning. I just don't know how to begin.'

'If you are uncomfortable about saying it, I will speak first.'

He looked confused. How odd. The state of her heart was perfectly clear to her. She had thought the same was true of Rees, but maybe he found it difficult to express profound words.

'What did you want to tell me, my angel?'

'It has to do with bread.'

'You're hungry?'

She shook her head, cupping his whiskered face in her fingertips. 'With leaven more than bread.'

'So you want to bake?'

Yes, bake in his arms, simmer under his kiss.

'I'm using it to illustrate love. How quickly it can happen. Yeast is the same ingredient no matter if it has only begun to ferment or has risen fully.'

'Are you saying you are fermenting for me?'

She shook his chin in the negative. His mouth ticked up on one side. Whatever had caused his good humour to fade was now gone.

'I love you, Rees Dalton. It does not matter how short a time it has been. Love is love and I love you.'

He lowered his mouth to hers. She slid her fingers from his cheeks to his neck, tangling her hand in the red bandana he wore.

She felt his breath feather across her lips, so warm and moist. 'I love you, too, my wife. Did you know you are my angel?' He hugged her tight. She felt the solid thud of his heart. 'I need to tell you why.'

A whistle blew, the sound so deep it reverberated throughout the ship.

'I think we have arrived!' She pushed out of his—grip? Odd that what had begun as a sweet embrace now felt as though he was trying to prevent her from stepping away from him. 'Life is going to be grand, Rees. Let's get to it!'

Freeing herself, she snatched up the bag of clothing and other belongings she had packed. She stepped towards the door, but he caught her elbow.

'Madeline, wait!' He took the satchel from her and slung it over his shoulder. 'There are things about me that you do not know.'

'Well, naturally, the same as there are things you do not know about me.'

'They are not the same.' He caught her arm, gently drew her away from the door. Why did he look so distraught?

Whatever his expression was, and she could not quite read it, it broke her heart.

'Life is going to be grand.' She slipped free of him and walked out the door. When he did not follow, she peeked her head around the doorframe. 'Let's get to it! We will learn every little thing there is to know about one another once we get home.'

Chapter Eight

Rees rushed out of the cabin after Madeline. She kept several paces ahead of him as she hurried across the deck.

With one word—*home*—she had sliced his heart wide open.

She had to imagine they were going to a sweet little cottage where flowers and children grew. Unless he could catch up with her and finish his confession, there was a very good chance they would never share a home, be it cottage or manor.

He lunged forward to close the distance, but a woman leading a small child stepped in front, blocking his advance.

At the flight of stairs, he nearly caught her, but once again someone stepped between.

It was all he could do not to curse. This felt like some bizarre nightmare where he was prevented from reaching his goal by waist-deep mud.

The air began to feel damp. A swathe of clouds crept over the harbour. He smelled rain coming even over the scents of smoke and fish.

There! He spotted her with her blue shawl drawn over her hair. She waited for him at the gangplank, waving and smiling.

He did curse then, cursed time, cursed himself.

'It's not so different here than in New York,' Madeline said when he reached her. 'Is your home far away? Will we walk or summon a hackney?'

Not forty feet from where the gangplank touched the shore his coach waited, the family crest seeming to pulse on the door in rhythm to his heartbeat.

Spinning her away from the carriage, he dropped the bundle and clamped his hands on her shoulders, trying without success to keep his fingers from trembling. 'Madeline, I—'

He heard the click of the carriage door opening, the creak of springs when someone stepped out.

His valet would descend upon them before he had a chance to explain.

'Whatever happens right now, I love you and that's heaven's own truth.'

She reached up, frowning while she touched his fingers, stroked them comfortingly. 'Yes, and I love—'

'Lord Glenbrook?'

Bethany's voice hit him like a blow. What the blazes was she doing here?

He looked over Madeline's shoulder, felt it when her hands fell away from him. He spotted his valet, Hendrick, following close behind Miss Mosemore's swaying skirt.

'Oh, good gracious!' Hendrick exclaimed, casting a critical eye over his appearance. 'What has become of you, Lord Glenbrook? I never should have allowed you to travel without me.'

Trapped, he returned his gaze to Madeline, fastening it on her face to try to read what she was thinking.

It sliced to the bone when her blue eyes widened in dismay, when she bit down on her lower lip.

Quite desperately, he wanted to go back to being a fireman aboard the *Edwina*.

Bethany caught his elbow in her gloved hand. 'I hope you do not mind that I've come to greet you, Lord Glenbrook, but there is something…' Her voice trailed off when her gaze settled upon Madeline, who stood so close to him that his ankle was wrapped in the hem of her skirt.

'Rees…' Madeline said, her voice sounding uncertain. 'Who are these people?'

'And who are you to speak to the Viscount with such familiarity?' Bethany arched a fine, upper-class brow at Madeline.

He heard his wife's sudden gasp. Slowly, she slid her gaze from Bethany to him. 'Viscount?'

A response would be appropriate, but if he opened his mouth he did not know what would come out—gibberish, he imagined.

'He doesn't look it at the moment, but, yes, he is. And I am Miss Mosemore, the Viscount's fiancée.' Bethany tipped her rather sharp nose in the air, as if it did not look haughty enough without the gesture. 'And who are you?'

Madeline's expression speared him.

'Viscount? Are these people telling the truth, Rees?'

'Good gracious! Even for an American you are brash. No one addresses Lord Glenbrook like that.'

'Madeline does.'

Bethany did not appear to hear what he said, so incensed was she by the perceived disrespect to his title.

Rees noticed his valet cover his mouth and look down, no doubt hiding a grin. Hendrick had never been pleased with his engagement to Miss Mosemore.

The cobbles began to smell damp with drizzle.

Madeline turned her gaze back to Bethany. Instantly, her expression softened. With her kind heart, she no doubt felt pity for the woman who was about to discover she had been jilted.

'If it's true that this man is who you say he is, then I suppose I must be Viscountess Glenbrook.'

She backed away when he reached for her, shaking her head to warn him off. He had an ugly feeling that Bertrand Fenster might look appealing by comparison to him.

'You needn't worry, Miss Mosemore. It's only for a short time. You may proceed with your wedding plans and no one will be the wiser.' Madeline dashed the back of her hand across her eye. 'I don't understand any of this, Lord Glenbrook.'

All he'd ever meant to do was protect his family. But now, looking at two women with dampness sparking in their eyes, he believed the word *cad* did not do him justice.

Silence fell upon them, broken only by the steady tap of drizzle on the dock.

Madeline broke it when she said, 'A man of your position ought to be easy to locate. I will advise you where to find me when our time is up.'

She spun about and ran, disappearing into the crowd while Bethany clutched his sleeve, demanding an explanation.

'Madeline!' he shouted, shaking free and running after her. 'Wait!'

But she didn't wait and the crowd closed around her.

He zigged this way and zagged that, calling, shouting and looking quite mad, no doubt.

Heavy rain came down suddenly, so hard and cold it felt as though it was being poured from a bucket.

His clothing soaked through in an instant. If his was, Madeline's would be, as well.

Last time, she had nearly died from such exposure. Now, like then, she had no place to go, no roof to shelter her.

He stood still, turning in a circle while people dashed about trying to get out of the storm.

Perhaps he ought to go back and tend to his jilted fiancée. Explain that while she would face shame for a time, in the end she would have a lifetime to love his brother.

Honour demanded he do so, yet it also demanded he find his wife.

'Madeline!' he called, ignoring the sound of Bethany Mosemore's voice calling stridently after him.

There would be time for her later, but now he would find his bride and plead his case.

If pleading did not work, he would pick her up, toss her over his shoulder and carry her home.

Three months had been his promise. He would honour it. But, damn it, she was going to spend those months with him!

Another curse stung his tongue. He let it loose.

What chance did an innocent like her have on the mean streets of Liverpool? With no one to turn to, this town would break her.

'Madeline!' His shout made heads turn, but he did not see the face he sought.

'Madeline!'

'Lady Glenbrook,' Madeline grumbled, winding her way quickly through the throng of people at the docks. 'Viscountess!'

Oh, she heard Rees calling her name clearly enough. Not that she was going to respond to it.

No, rather she would use it as a guide to tell her where he was and judge which way to best avoid him. She was no novice at eluding men, after all.

Quickening her pace, she made a sudden turn down a charming cobbled street. Rees might be a trickster, same as Bertrand, but her husband was no fool. It might take more skill to outwit Lord Glenbrook.

Just the name made her temper flare. Anger was a rare emotion for her and she did not care one whit for it.

If only she was not wet, shivering to the bone.

Memories of nearly dying of the cold made her shake all the harder. At least this time she was on land, a circumstance which she was immensely grateful for.

She glanced about at the brick buildings on both sides of her, thinking that it was awfully dark for midday. No doubt it had to do with the storm and with the way the lanes were so narrow as to keep the light out.

For all that the street she dashed down was quaint, with hat shops and bakeries flanking pretty little homes, she longed for the wide, open spaces of Los Angeles. For sunshine and—and Grandfather. In the moment she longed for him most desperately.

What a great fool she had been to leave him. No matter what, she was going to find him. It might take longer without Rees to help her, but she would do it.

For now, what she needed was shelter—a few moments to dry by a warm fire.

She ducked under the porch of a dress shop. Even though rain no longer fell upon her head, cold leached out of the bricks.

Through the shop window she spotted a stove. A warm orange glow surrounded a woman standing on a dais while having a hem fitted.

There had been a time when she was the pampered one, warm, dry and standing on the dais being fawned over by the dressmaker. If she walked inside the shop now, she would be turned out straight away. No one wanted a dripping waif ruining their polished floors.

She thought she saw an auburn-haired man rush past the lane she'd turned on to. Pressing back against the stones, she wanted to weep.

Could it only have been an hour ago that she had been

looking forward to living with Rees in a sweet little house like the one across the lane from her?

A woman stood at the window, rocking a baby on her hip. She peered out through the glass, looking worried.

It just went to show that trouble was all around. Being warm and dry did not keep it at bay.

However, it would make problems easier to confront if one was not shivering.

Certainly, she was far from the only one caught out in the miserable weather. Just there, turning on to the lane, was an older gentleman leaning on his cane and making slow progress to wherever he was going.

Perhaps he would want to share her shelter and wait for the rain to end before travelling on. His gait looked unsteady on the slippery stones.

She lifted her arm to invite him over, but he slipped.

'Oh!' she cried, making a dash towards him. Kneeling on the cobbles, she patted him on the back, looking him over for injury.

'Are you hurt?'

'Dead, maybe.' He studied her face. 'Are you an angel or just a pretty lady?'

'Flesh and bone, same as you.'

'Reckon I only hurt my bum, then.' He tried to stand, but could not quite manage.

'Let me help.' She braced her shoulder under his arm and tried to lift him, but he was heftier than he seemed.

'You sound like an American, but you look like an angel. You're certain we're on this side of the coil? Old man like me can take a fall and that's the end of him.'

'I can't say for sure, but I think it is not as cold and wet in heaven.'

'Grandfather!' a woman screeched.

Madeline peered through the dim, watery light to see a woman racing towards them. As she came closer, Madeline recognised her as the one who had been watching out her window.

No wonder she'd looked worried.

Between the two of them they managed to lift the old man.

'Haven't I told you that you can't go out all on a whim?'

'Have you? I don't recall, but look, I've met a heavenly being.'

'I'm Madeline Dalton from Los Angeles, California.' She surprised herself in using the name Dalton. For as angry as she was at her husband, she might have used Macooish instead.

There was no time to puzzle the reason for that now, because it took both women to make sure the elderly man made it down the lane and up the stairs without slipping again.

Thankfully, they made it into the house without mishap.

The woman did not complain about water soaking her floor, so Madeline judged her to be easy natured. Her only concern seemed to be getting her grandfather dry.

'I don't know how to thank you, miss,' she said while rubbing the old fellow briskly with a towel. 'He wanders lately, and with everything, I can't keep up—oh, there is a dry gown in the back room.' She indicated the direction by inclining her head. 'I'd not want to see you catch your death from cold and I believe we are of a size.'

Those words rang closer to the recent truth than the woman knew. Madeline hurried to the back room and put on the gown with great gratitude. It was not as fine as the one Rees had given her, but it was dry and she was thankful beyond words.

By now she was indebted to so many kind people that she hardly knew how to keep count. But she did intend to show her gratitude once she found Grandfather.

The search might be a long one without Rees to help, but she would manage. Somehow, she always managed.

When she came back into the front room the woman was preparing tea. The baby she had seen earlier through the window was in the cradle and clearly not content to be. It flailed plump little arms and legs while making fussy sounds.

'If you'll pick him up, we'll have tea sooner, Miss Dalton.'

'That sounds like a bit of heaven, thank you, and I'm Mrs Dalton.' Lady Glenbrook, to be exact, but she felt no need to be quite that forthcoming.

Madeline picked up the baby. It stopped fretting and smiled at her. She was not sure she had ever seen anyone quite so enchanting.

Surprisingly, it hurt to know how close she had come to being a mother. Given that she hadn't paid a thought to motherhood before last week, she ought not to be this sad for losing the chance. Yet there it was, a great empty space in her heart.

'Ach! Has something befallen your husband, then, for you to be wandering about in the storm? I'm Mrs Fitzmore, Mary. Not a widow, but you'd never know it by the way my husband is always away from home on business.'

'I've run away from my husband,' Madeline admitted because it was best to tell the truth when one could. Had Viscount Glenbrook been so inclined, she might not be sitting here now.

'Was he a brute, then? Some men are.'

A brute? Not at all, but assertive as would be expected of a man of his station. She ought to have recognised him as a peer from the first.

'Not a brute, Mary. Only dishonest.'

'I've a discreet ear if you wish to speak of it. But don't

feel you need to. You are welcome to stay with me for as long as you need to.'

'Our very own angel to live with us?' The old fellow grinned.

'She's Madeline Dalton, from America. But, yes, she is welcome to our couch for as long as she needs.'

'I'm more than grateful to you. I'll make sure you are repaid for your kindness.'

'Another pair of eyes to make sure my grandfather doesn't wander is all the repayment I need. Besides, I think my baby, Stewart, is taken with you. But then, I suppose any man you've met is.'

It was true and more a curse than a blessing.

'Tell me about America.' Mary set down her teacup, leaned forward on her chair. 'Are cowboys as gallant as they are in Buffalo Bill's *Wild West* show? My husband took me to see it in London when we were first wed.'

'They work harder than the show might portray.'

And so the talk went for hours about life on both sides of the pond, as Mary called it.

In Madeline's opinion, the Atlantic was a very large and perilous pond. One she did not wish to give much thought to.

Giving thought to anything at the moment was painful. She could hardly avoid it, though, when she lay down on the couch to sleep. Those hours she had spent at sea with Rees were among her happiest.

Which made her all the sadder while she lay here listening to the quiet creaks of the house and the tapping of rain on the cobbles beyond the window.

Of course, she wasn't really listening to rain as much as footsteps in the rain. For Rees's footsteps, coming for her.

She tried not to want it—but there it was, causing a rather large lump to swell in her throat.

No doubt he had given up his pursuit by now.

Rees had a fiancée, a life to live with Miss Mosemore. Now, with Madeline gone, he was free to go on as he had planned before he lifted her from the lifeboat and carried her to his cabin.

Before—before everything.

Pelting rain felt like needles nicking Rees's head. His coat had become soaked through so long ago it no longer provided protection against the elements.

He had searched, asked person after person if they had seen a woman who resembled a lost angel. No one had.

At last, only hours before dawn and with very few people about to ask, he met a lamplighter on his rounds.

The fellow did remember a woman from earlier in the day. She had rushed past him appearing distressed, so he'd followed her.

He told Rees the name of the lane she had turned down. The lamplighter remembered seeing her go into a house about halfway down, along with another woman and an old man.

It had taken a further half an hour to find the lane. Thirty minutes in which he wondered if he could go on.

Any second he expected to keel over face first on to the cobbles. He had stopped feeling his feet hours ago. When was it that his hands had grown numb?

He could only imagine what the temperature might be—just shy of snow, he figured.

This had to be the right lane, if not— Ah! Halfway down, a window glowed as if someone had left a lamp burning low.

Coming closer, he saw a woman passing back and forth in front of the glass while carrying a baby in her arms.

She wouldn't appreciate a knock on her door by someone who looked a half-frozen fiend. No matter, he had to know if his wife was inside or if she had gone on her way.

Lifting his hand, he noticed his fingertips were blue. An odd sight, that. He felt detached from it, as if he were looking at someone else's hand.

He pounded on the door with the side of his fist. He could see the woman glaring at him, but she did not move from her spot at the window.

Once again, he hammered, this time with both fists. When he could pound no more, he leaned his weight against the door for support. The frigid temperature robbed him of the last of his strength.

All at once, the door flew open. He grasped the frame, looking into the eyes of the irate lady.

'Have you no sense, man!' Her glare at him accused him of all sorts of idiocy. 'Pummelling the door when a woman is trying to get her child to sleep?'

She seemed to be swaying, but more likely he was the one listing.

'I'm looking for my wife.'

'And you imagine I have her stashed away on my couch, perhaps. Ah, my wee lad is wide awake now.'

'Please, if you have seen her…'

If she had, it might have been some time ago. Just because Madeline had sought shelter here did not mean she remained.

'Can you not stand, man? You seem near to death.'

'My wife ran away and—'

The woman tipped her head to one side, frowning severely at him with a brow arched.

'Did you heartlessly lie to her?'

Somehow, he managed to straighten up.

'You have seen her, then—my Madeline?'

Madeline did not believe she could have fallen asleep, but she was clearly dreaming. How else would she be hearing Rees say her name?

Reality tried to intrude, so she dug deeper into sleep. But the harder she dug, the more wakeful she became.

'Perhaps I have. I'll need to make sure.'

She was not dreaming Mary's voice. Within seconds she was bending over the couch, the baby hugged tight to her chest.

'I believe your husband has found you. Shall I send him away?'

'Yes, do.'

'You ought to know, he looks rather poorly. Even the walk back down the lane might do him in.'

Do him in! Her great strong husband?

Madeline bounded from the couch.

Good heavens!

Rees stood in the doorway, swaying on his feet.

Holding tight to the doorframe, he smiled weakly at her and said, 'Thank the good Lord.'

His voice sounded like sand.

She slipped under his arm, but he straightened and made it to the couch on wobbling legs.

He closed his eyes, let out a great sigh. 'You're safe.'

With that, he fell asleep. But then again, because of how pale he was, how cold his hand felt, he might be unconscious.

Madeline knelt beside the couch. Mary peered over her shoulder.

'He must be a very big liar for you to run away from him, my friend. A man who looks like that? If I were not completely devoted to my husband, well... I'll just say there's many who would want to be in your shoes.'

'I've been told it before.' She had also seen the not-quite-subtle glances of dreamy-eyed women.

A circumstance which did not change the fact that he had grievously lied to her.

But about everything?

Were the feelings he had declared for her true in spite of the way things appeared? Madeline could hardly ignore the fact that he must care for his fiancée.

Ah, but he did look done for. The question in her mind was, had he been searching for her out of guilt or out of the love he claimed to have for her?

'Since I'll not put myself into a situation to lust after a man who I'm not wed to, I'll leave it to you to change him out of his wet clothes.'

With a wink, Mary picked up her fussing child from his crib and walked towards her bedchamber.

'I'll set some of Long's clothing outside my door, although I expect they will fit a bit snug.'

'Rees…' She shook his shoulder. '…can you hear me?'

He grunted, but his mouth ticked in a weary half-smile.

Good, not oblivious, then, only exhausted.

'I need to get these wet clothes off of you, but you'll need to help me.' Was that a nod? If so, it was very weak.

He tried to lift his arm, but it flopped back on the couch. She picked up his hand. It was far too frigid for her peace of mind.

'How did you injure your knuckles?' She didn't dare touch them, as swollen and bruised as they were.

'Doors.'

Knocking on them, looking for her, he must mean. She felt wretched.

Very clearly she had a character flaw: she was a weak-spined runaway. First she had fled from her grandfather, then from Bertrand and now from her husband.

Taking to one's heels was no way to solve a problem, but rather to create one.

'You've got to help me, Rees. I cannot do this on my own. You are far too—' *muscular, strapping, brawny and well built* '—heavy.'

He sat halfway up, groaned. Eventually, with a great

deal of tugging and yanking, she managed to remove his coat and shirt.

And then to blatantly stare.

She had seen him bare chested before, but apparently it was not a sight one got used to. No, it was a sight one brazenly indulged in with great longing.

She blushed, felt heat creep up her chest to her neck. She pressed her cheeks with her fingertips. As she suspected, they were sizzling. Her red face was not due completely to her reaction to seeing him this way, but because—well—he knew she had that birthmark on her hip and possibly a good deal more than that.

If his feelings in the moment had been anything akin to what hers were now, it was no wonder he insisted they would marry.

All of her was ablaze. He had touched her, to warm her only, but after that he had kissed her quite ardently.

Yes, he'd done that in the full knowledge that he had a fiancée waiting for his return.

'Let's get you out of those trousers.' Her voice sounded like a frog croaking. 'Then I'll make some good hot tea. That should set you to rights.'

In spite of how much she wanted to, she was not going to warm him with her touch. There was much to be settled between them and just now she was not certain it was even possible.

The man was hers in a legal sense, but she had to wonder if his heart was hers. He had claimed so, but he also claimed to be a working man making a living shovelling coal.

He lifted his hips. She closed her eyes and yanked the sodden fabric down his legs, tugging it over his feet.

With her eyes squeezed tight, she fumbled about for her shawl. It had fallen off her shoulders when she had bounded up from the couch and now he sat on it. She only hoped, prayed even, that her fingers would not close about anything that was not yarn.

Drat it! That springy substance her palms brushed across was not wool, but hair. She did not allow herself to imagine where it grew.

She nearly sighed in relief when her fingers found the shawl and it slid free from under him without her having to—never mind that. She had the shawl and that was all that mattered, that and getting hot tea into him.

She spread the shawl over him, then opened her eyes. It covered what it could, but he was a large man.

Spinning about, she raced for the kitchen.

He needed warming and she needed cooling.

Chapter Nine

Something burned his lips, but at the same time, gentle fingers pressed the back of his neck, lifting his head.

'Drink it up.'

He did, one sip only, then said, 'Lie beside me.'

'It's a narrow couch.'

He opened his eyes to see her frowning at him. She could be hurling profanities at him and he wouldn't mind. Finding her safe was the best thing to have happened to him in a very long time—maybe ever.

'Not much narrower than our cot in the ship's cabin.'

Relief slowly restored his strength, even more than being dry did.

Madeline did not answer, but withdrew the cup from his lips.

'What do you think your fiancée would think about that? I hate to imagine.'

What she would do was run for Gretna Green with Wilson.

He sat up. Her wool shawl puddled in a heap on his lap.

'Sit beside me.' He reached for the tea. While he no longer feared freezing to death, he was still just this side of shivering. 'We need to speak of what happened.'

'I'll spread your clothes in front of the fire so they will be dry when you leave.'

'When we leave, you mean.'

'That is not at all what I mean.' She turned away, crossed to the hearth, then spread his garments on it.

'I wonder how long the lady of the house will allow us to remain here. I have no intention of leaving her house without you.'

'I suppose as a grand lord you believe you may dictate to me.' She plopped down beside him, her arms folded defiantly across her chest. 'But I am an American. I do not recognise your noble precedence.'

'A viscount. That is all. Only a baron is ranked lower.'

'I despair to imagine how arrogant you would be as a duke.' She popped back up from the couch, paced a moment, then spun around to face him, her hands balled firmly on her hips. 'We agreed to a temporary marriage. You will leave here without me.'

'We also changed our minds.'

'I would not have if I'd known you were promised to another.'

'Madeline, sit down.' He patted the cushion. 'Had I met you first, I would not have proposed to Miss Mosemore.'

'How very noble of you.'

While she spoke, her gaze slipped from his eyes to his chest. Her blush hit him square in the heart. He wouldn't, under any circumstance, leave here without her.

'You did not meet me first and you are promised to another.'

'That promise became null when I recited vows to you. I never loved her, Madeline. When I said I loved you, my heart was not bound to another.' He patted the couch again.

The bedchamber door creaked open. Something hit the floor with a thump before it clicked closed again.

'Oh, good.' She crossed the room, then picked up a

bundle of clothes. 'Mary has given these to you to wear until yours dry out.'

She dropped the garments on his lap, then went to the window and stared out.

'Will you not help me dress, as I did you?'

She spun about. 'You are a rogue, Rees Dalton. You know I will not. Why, Miss Mosemore would be broken-hearted.'

'Miss Mosemore is in love with my brother.'

Madeline went utterly still, her skirt swaying about her ankles. She pressed the fingers of one hand to her mouth, slowly shaking her head while tapping her lips.

'And so you decided to have her for yourself? That is rather twisted, even for a man as despotic as you are. I fear I do not know you at all. The man I professed to love would not betray his family. And you, a father—an example to your little girls!'

'But you do know me.' He stood up. Clutching the shawl to his middle, he crossed to the window.

'Have you no shame? You are standing bare as a jay in front of the glass!'

He lifted her chin with his free hand, peering deeply into her eyes. 'I do not. But I will agree to go back to the couch if you promise to sit beside me. I have much to say.'

'All right, I will. But for Mary's sake. She would be hard put to explain a naked man standing in her window!' She spun away from his touch, hurried to the couch and sat down. 'But you must agree to put on those clothes.'

'Agreed.'

He dressed while she stared at her lap, neatly spacing the gathers of the skirt she wore. His borrowed garments were too small, so he had to leave several buttons unfastened and the sleeves of the shirt rolled up at the cuff.

'You may explain now,' she stated curtly. 'Although I do not know how it is possible.'

'From the beginning I told you there was a reason our marriage benefited me.'

'I can hardly forget. You ought to have told me what it was before the vows.'

'I should have.'

A quiver of poisoned arrows would not have stung more than her pointed glare did.

'When I made the marriage agreement with Miss Mosemore's uncle, I had no idea of my brother's attachment to her, nor hers to him. The time was right for me to remarry and my daughters needed a mother. So when Milton Langerby, Bethany's uncle, pressed most insistently for the union, I accepted his offer.'

'But you must have been in love with her, otherwise why would you?'

'I was not.'

'Very fond of her at least?'

'I barely knew her. If I had, I might have been aware of the attachment between Miss Mosemore and Wilson. To me she seemed as respectable as any other woman I might wed. I honestly had no feelings for her one way or another.'

All at once Madeline shook her head and nodded, making it seem like one wide-eyed gesture. 'I ran away with Bertrand, in part, to avoid being that sort of bride. I wanted to be loved.'

'And so you are.'

'I am not ready to hear that from you. Even though you are at last explaining to me what happened, I do not know you. The man I loved was a fireman aboard the *Edwina*.'

'I'll get to that, but can you not see now why our marriage was a great boon to me?'

'Make me understand it, Rees.'

He'd rather stumble into a patch of nettles, but— 'I saw straight off what a mistake I'd made when, after the betrothal was announced, I came upon the pair of them in the garden. They didn't know I was hidden behind a bush, so they spoke freely of their devotion to each other. Wilson wanted to elope to Gretna Green on the spot, but Bethany was not willing to stand against her uncle. I'll tell you, Madeline, he is a severe fellow, so I don't blame her for not acting against him.'

'Well, poor thing, her future determined by the whim of a man. It seems she was stuck in a mess she had no control over. I hate to think of the great scandal the poor girl will be subject to if our marriage becomes known.'

'She hasn't a bit of your spirit.' Or compassion. Madeline might have been bitter towards a woman who turned out to be her husband's fiancée, but, no, she seemed more concerned for Bethany's fate than anything else. 'But don't you see I was also in a mess I had no control over? I needed a miracle. I could not betray my brother and take the woman he loved as my wife. It was unthinkable. But at the same time, agreements, promises had been made between me and Milton Langerby. I sailed before I had time to even think of what to do about it.'

'All right, I'll admit you were in a difficult place.'

'An impossible one, until I came across you. You were my miracle.'

'It hardly felt like a miracle to me.' She sighed deeply, leaning her head back on the couch to expose the fair column of her neck. She was his wonder, his heart and every bit a miracle, no matter how she might see it in the moment.

'Were you running from the situation—?' Suddenly she looked away from him, biting her bottom lip and frowning. 'Perhaps avoiding facing your problem by taking a job aboard the *Edwina*?'

'Ah, no.' The weight of his lies felt crushing. The only way was to press on. 'I own the *Edwina*.'

She swung her gaze back at him. Her eyes narrowed

upon him, but given the fact that her face looked angelic, her expression could look nothing but sweet, no matter how she might be striving to make it otherwise.

'It makes sense now. I always wondered why the Captain jumped to do your bidding. But it does not make sense that you lived in steerage and worked such a difficult job.'

'The first owner of the *Edwina* did a careless job of running it. He was more concerned with making a fast Atlantic crossing than seeing to the comfort of his passengers. I worked as a crewman in order to discover which employees had become lax under his employ.'

'Most men of your station would have hired someone else to do it.'

'My mother will tell you that if something important needs doing I don't trust anyone else with it. But in this case, with so much to see to, I did hire a couple of men to help watch.'

'You are assuming I will meet your mother in order for her to tell me that.'

'As I've said. I will not leave here without you.'

'Have you considered that we would not be in this situation had you been truthful from the beginning? And why lie about who you were? Did you not think I would keep your secret?'

He gripped her shoulders, but gently in spite of the tension within him. He turned her so that she had nowhere to look but at his face. If she would not listen to his apology, perhaps she would see it in his eyes. 'The truth of it is, I married a stranger. I could not know whether you would or not. Everything happened so quickly between us. One moment we were strangers and the next we were married and the one after that, in love.'

'And later, after you did know me? You could have told me then.'

She tried to arch her brows at him, but the gesture failed.

'I meant to. But the plain bald truth is, I was scared. I thought when you knew you would not give me the three months.'

'I was a convenient way for you to be rid of the commitment to Miss Mosemore? Yes, I see it now.'

'No, you do not, not completely. In the beginning I offered the three months because I was afraid you would not marry me. But then, Madeline, I did not want three months with you. I wanted for ever. If I had told you everything, I feared you would leave me.'

'And so I have. But just so you know, it is not because of the title, but because of the lies.'

'I wanted to tell you—I tried to. I thought I had more time, but things happened to get in the way. In the end, though, I was simply a coward.'

'Yes, there was the fire. You were in charge of the passengers' safety. With all of it, I imagine I was not uppermost in your mind.'

'You imagine wrong.' He looked into her eyes, holding her gaze and praying she would see what was inside him. 'You were always first in my mind.'

Her shoulders rose and fell under his hands when she exhaled a great sigh.

She stood up, breaking his hold on her, then paced in front of him. The swish of her skirt swirled a cool draught around his bare ankles.

She stopped suddenly, frowned down at him, her fingers beating a rhythm on the satin sash at her waist.

'All right. I will meet your mother.'

'And after that?'

'I agreed to three months and I will honour it, unless I find my grandfather first. If I do—'

Leaping to his feet, he wrapped her up, kissing her until she returned it.

'We have gone beyond needing three months. I take them back.'

'You can't just—'

He kissed her again, taking possession of her in a way words could not.

'I can—I have.'

'Do you always get your way?'

'Mostly, yes,' he stated with more confidence than he felt. Having been a viscount from a very young age, he expected to get what he wanted.

Until he'd met Madeline Macooish Dalton. Now nothing was as expected.

'How do you know you will this time?'

He smiled, lowered his lips close to hers, felt the brush of skin on skin when he murmured, 'There's this between us.'

'Oh.' Her breath was warm, sweet as the memory of summer peaches on his face. 'Not three months, then. I'll stay until I find my grandfather. Then, after that, we'll see. For the sake of this, we will see.'

'We will find him. You and I together.'

'Together, then. We will find him and my cousin together.'

'You forgive me?'

'I understand.'

'It's not the same thing.'

'I forgive you.'

'My angel.' He buried his face in her hair, rocking her tightly in his arms. 'It won't be long, I promise. We will find them. I vow it.'

It might be an easy thing if his thoughts about them being in Derbyshire were correct.

He tried to ignore the selfish voice suggesting that he take his time finding out.

The time he had with Madeline was no longer a set three months, less than that now, but it was to be determined by locating her family.

His fate rested on an event. An event he might have the power to hasten.

He only needed to convince her of his devotion before it occurred.

After waving goodbye to Mary from the carriage window, Madeline pressed back against the seat cushions, looking at the finely appointed cab.

While she would not have minded travelling in a rented hackney, this was quite a bit more comfortable.

Rees sat across from her, but close enough that their knees brushed when the wagon bounced over uneven cobbles.

'I'm sorry I made you look for me all night in the rain.' Even now he did not seem recovered from the ordeal. He huddled in a blanket, his eyes halfway closed.

'It was worth it.'

'Not if you take sick.'

'I won't, not as long as I get a bit of rest before we reach home.' He yawned, then closed his eyes completely. 'I'll need my wits to explain all this to Mother.'

'Will she be angry?'

'Not angry as much as in a tizzy with all the wedding arrangements to be cancelled and explanations to be invented. She'll want what's best for both her sons, though.'

'What will she think of you bringing home an American wife?'

He opened one eye. Even in the dim light of the carriage his blue gaze gave indication that he didn't care. 'Funny, but most marriages of the sort are gone into for financial gain, or for position. I don't need your money and you don't want my title.'

'The title might help, though, when it comes to begging Grandfather's forgiveness. I will have fulfilled his goal for me, however accidentally it came to be.'

The other eye opened. 'I suppose that what he really will want is for you to be happy. It's what I want, as well.'

He closed his eyes again. She ought to let him rest.

She watched out the window. Liverpool was a busy place with people strolling the pavements and wagons rushing here and there. It was noisier than she cared for. Birdsong and leaves rustling in the breeze were more to her liking.

If she decided to stay with Rees after he found her grandfather, she would need to get used to the bustle.

She would get used to it because, in spite of the fact that she clung to the appearance of having a choice in remaining married to him, she desperately wanted to.

One did not lightly skip away from the man one loved.

Watching her husband sleep, wanting to reach across the way and touch the dark-red hair that slipped over one eye, she thought of Oliver Cavill, the Earl of Fencroft.

Grandfather had thought them to be an ideal match since the Earl was fond of gay times and laughter, the same as she was.

Clementine, however, was not. If she was married to the Earl, she would be miserable.

Madeline was not sure how she would live with the guilt of being blissfully wed to a viscount when she had forced her cousin into a union with someone unsuitable for her.

Tears welled in her eyes, so she closed them tight, hoping to trap them. With the battle lost, she dashed the moisture away with the back of her hand.

She opened her eyes to find Rees looking at her.

'Are you so unhappy, Madeline?'

'I need to know my cousin is all right.'

Rees opened the blanket, motioning for her to join him under it.

She snuggled against his side and he hugged her close with his strong, comforting arm.

'Don't think the worst. If she did marry, I'm sure she knew her groom better than you knew me when we said our vows. If she didn't like him, she could have refused.'

She shook her head. 'Clementine would not disappoint Grandfather.'

Her cousin would never run away from her obligation and leave others to deal with the consequence.

Madeline did not say so aloud, because the vow she was about to make was between her and the good Lord.

Inhaling deeply, she recited it in her mind. *I will not run away from a problem again. No matter what happens, I will stand and face what comes.*

There was a rap on the hood of the cab.

'We're here—are you ready to meet Mother?'

'I am eager to.'

'I wish I was.'

The door to the coach opened before the driver even stepped down.

A small woman with springy silver strands poking from her coif climbed into the cab. She plopped down on the bench across looking distressed and clutching a sheet of paper in her fist.

'Hello.' Madeline felt the need to say something because the woman stared at her, her face gone from pale to bleached bone.

'A note.'

Rees's mother shoved the damp parchment at him, her attention shifting between him and Madeline.

He'd best set the facts straight before she thought he'd brought home the governess she'd been asking for and was behaving inappropriately with her under the blanket.

Shaking her head, his mother turned her agitated gaze fully on him.

'It says—oh, I hardly know how to speak the words.' Her gaze flashed once more to Madeline, who had slid away from him and was hugging as close to the wall as she could get.

'Mother?'

'I'll just say it quickly—rip the bandage off, so to speak. It's from your brother—from Wilson. Oh, but he's run for Gretna Green with your fiancée.'

'Ah, good, then.'

'I know you are heartbroken over it—but have you lost your mind?' She grabbed his hands and squeezed them between her own. 'No doubt the shock has left you senseless, my poor boy, but you need to be prepared. The scandal will be unmatched by any we've seen. Worse than when your father—' She pressed her lips together, clearly reluctant to discuss Father's mistake with an outsider. 'Well, much worse than that.'

'Better a scandal than a disaster.' He extended his hand towards Madeline. With a nod he urged her to take it.

With a small smile she placed her fingers in his, slid back towards him.

'Mother, I'd like you to meet my wife, Madeline.'

Normally a strong woman, the news of the morning was apparently too much. She fainted where she sat.

Rees carried her up the steps and into the house. It took three minutes with the smelling salts to bring her around.

That was all it took for half the household staff to gather. Less time than that for Victoria Rose and Emily

Lark to come paddling into the room, porcelain dolls tucked under their arms.

Victoria Rose stood beside the couch, nose to nose with her faint grandmother. Emily Lark clambered up, sat on top of her and peeled up her eyelids.

'Granny napping,' Victoria Rose said, reprimanding her twin.

Even at such a young age Rees knew that Victoria Rose was bossy and Emily Lark mischievous.

'Don't worry.' He caught his sweet imp to him, saving his mother from further indignity. 'She'll wake soon.'

Mrs Warren, the housekeeper, clapped her hands. 'Back to work, all of you. It's as the master says—Lady Dalton will be right as rain in a moment. She will not wish to see you hovering.'

Murmuring, they did as Mrs Warren ordered.

Victoria Rose stroked fat little fingers over her grandmother's cheek while Emily Lark smeared wet kisses all over his.

'Faddie scratchy.' She puckered her lips and scrambled out of his hold.

Apparently finished welcoming him home, she dashed over to Madeline and stared up at her. After a moment of consideration, she lifted her arms to be picked up.

Without visible hesitation, Madeline knelt and scooped her up.

'Whose you?'

'I'm Madeline.'

Victoria Rose's attention snapped away from her grandmother.

She scurried over to Madeline and tugged on her skirt. 'You's pretty.'

Madeline bent over, then set Emily Lark on the floor beside her sister. She cupped Victoria Rose's chin in her fingers. 'So are you—both of you are as sweet as newly hatched chicks.'

Something inside Rees shattered in that moment. Seeing the unreserved affection Madeline offered his daughters, again he knew she was his miracle and nothing less.

During his engagement to Miss Mosemore, he had never seen her give more than a passing word to the girls.

He heard a gasp and fabric rustling on the couch when his mother sat up.

'Ach! You're back with us, my lady.'

Luckily Mrs Warren bustled about his mother, because Rees's attention was caught up with the other ladies in his life.

For all that Madeline had claimed to have no experience with young children, she took right to them. And they to her.

What she did have experience in was kindness. Practice had not taught it. A loving, generous spirit came as naturally to her as breathing.

During the carriage ride from the docks to the town house, she had instructed him to send unstinted financial gratitude to no less than four, or perhaps five, people who had been kind to her on her journey, one of them a ticket master in New York.

Kind, generous, gracious and beautiful—what more could he ask for in his Viscountess?

'Do you feel like standing, my lady?' he heard the housekeeper ask.

It was time to return his attention to the trouble that would soon come tapping on the door. Or not tapping as much as pounding and rattling until it came off the hinges.

'I suppose I must, after all, if I wish to be informed of what is befalling my family.'

Rees thought it best to speak first. 'Mrs Warren, please meet my wife, Madeline, Lady Glenbrook.'

Mrs Warren did not faint. To her credit she looked taken aback for only a moment before she smiled.

'Welcome, my lady. It will be a great pleasure to serve you.'

'Faddie?'

Victoria Rose tugged on his trouser leg. Her still-babyish voice wrapped him up, squeezing his heart. He hoped she never learned to pronounce the word *father* correctly.

'She is our mama?'

He wanted to tell her it was true, but did not. He could hardly compel his wife to commit to caring for them all their days. She had not even given him that commitment.

He waited, breath held to hear how, or if, she would answer.

In spite of the fact that she loved him, she was not ready to give him her future.

Who could blame her? Their short marriage had been founded upon deceit.

Patience was what he needed now, along with honesty. While he waited for Madeline to understand her heart, he must be above board in all his doings.

What he also needed was time to convince her of the rightness of their marriage. The problem was, he might not have much of it.

With Fencroft Manor so close to Green Knoll, he did not feel at ease. If the Cavills were in residence, he would need to discover if Madeline's family was among them sooner rather than later.

He needed later.

The longer the family remained in Liverpool the more time he would have to woo his wife, to prove they were meant to be together.

Whenever the reunion for Madeline and her family

came, it would be a wonderful surprise. He could think of no better wedding gift.

He could tell her what he suspected about the neighbours being more than simply neighbours, but he would not cause her heartache if it turned out not to be true.

No, he would investigate and then surprise her.

Surely when he arranged the surprise reunion she would be more inclined to remain his wife. Such a thing would prove, in a way words could not, how much he loved her.

Rees watched Madeline's face while she looked down at his baby girls. Her smile was hesitant at first, but grew warmer by the second. He could not recall ever seeing her so lovely.

There was admitted love between them. All he needed was a little more time to let it grow deep roots.

Yes, the longer the family remained in Liverpool the better. He was going to insist they remain for a while.

'You our mama!' Victoria Rose hugged Madeline's skirt, her small arms getting lost in yards of fabric. It was a gut punch to his heart, seeing the longing in his child's round brown eyes. 'Pweese!'

Rees held his breath. He ought to step in, prevent them from hearing what she might say. It was one thing for him to be broken-hearted if Madeline went away, but quite another for his small girls. He could not allow their desperate need for a mother to harm them.

But what if she consented? By promising herself to them, she promised herself to him.

As he saw it, there would be no waiting for her to decide for or against him.

His heart thudded against his ribs so hard he thought everyone must hear it.

'We will leave for the country immediately,' Mother declared, coming to her feet and clapping her hands. 'Mrs Warren, please inform the staff to be ready to travel.'

* * *

Madeline felt useless, a stranger with nothing to do but watch while the servants bustled about and the Dowager urged them to greater speed.

If her mother-in-law meant to outrun the scandal, Madeline thought it unlikely.

Disgrace was the crown perched upon the heads of the Dalton family. As Lady Glenbrook, Madeline's crown would gleam as infamously as anyone else's would. It was on her account that poor Miss Mosemore had been jilted, after all.

As far as public sentiment went, it mattered not that what had happened worked for the good of those involved.

Even Rees's mother had quickly seen the wisdom in her eldest son's hasty marriage. When the facts were explained, Abigail Dalton had simply pressed her hand to her bosom, shook her head, then declared she was grateful that Wilson would not pine his life away and Rees not spend his guilt ridden.

After that she wrapped Madeline in a great hug, thanked her for saving them all from ruin and welcomed her to the family.

There was still ruin to be faced, of course, but of the social kind that would be overshadowed when another outrage to polite society was unearthed.

In Madeline's opinion, if titled members of society had productive work to do they would not fall to pieces over every social faux pas.

And yet here she was, an accidental peer standing in the parlour and uselessly observing others rush about.

Well, not completely useless. Victoria Rose and Emily Lark trailed her skirts like a pair of giggling bubbles, which kept them out from underfoot of people who were actually working.

A movement at the doorway caught her eye.

'Faddie!' Emily Lark rushed for her father and he scooped her up.

He nodded at Madeline with a smile, then carried his daughter to the far side of the room where his mother wrapped a silver candlestick in cloth.

'Mother.' He kissed her cheek. 'Do you not think it a bit hasty to leave Liverpool so quickly?'

'I do not. Really, Rees, the sooner we leave the less chance we have of a visit from Lord Langerby. I would just as soon avoid that.'

Emily Lark clamped her chubby arms about her father's neck, pressing her smooth cheek to his unshaved one. 'Ouchy!'

'I'm afraid that is unavoidable,' he answered.

'Perhaps so, but we will avoid it for as long as possible. Besides, I'm certain Wilson and his bride will not come back here and I would like to greet them in Derbyshire.'

'No doubt—' Emily Lark tickled her father's ear, probably trying to get him to laugh at her, but to no avail '—you do, but they—Emily Lark, I'm trying to speak with Granny—want to be alone for a time. It's better we remain here and not make it look as if we are running away.'

'Running away! Saying it that way sounds cowardly. But we are not running, my son. We are simply stepping out of the way of an oncoming train, which is a wise thing to do. It will appear that we are simply going home for Christmas.'

At last Madeline found something useful to do. She picked up Victoria Rose, then relieved Rees of Emily Lark.

'Come, sweet chicks,' she said, with a bright smile which she hoped would defuse the tension of the discussion between Rees and his mother. 'Let's go play in the garden.'

'Play with Mama!' Victoria Rose announced, which made her twin clap her round little hands and dance about,

What a pickle I am in, she thought while going out a pair of wide doors leading to the garden. The girls had laid claim to her as their mother. She was their father's wife, after all, and they had every right to expect it to be so.

Madeline wanted it to be true! Still, for now she could promise them nothing. At the same time, she could not deny them the affection they craved.

Poor little motherless babies. Her heart longed to wrap them up as much as it recoiled from doing so.

She had vowed she would never run away again. But what if she weakened and did it? And after giving herself to them as their mother? She would be the worst human on the planet.

For now she had only offered to play in the garden. All that was required in the moment was to enjoy it—to laugh and indulge in childish games.

A cool breeze tumbled the last of autumn's leaves over stone paths, but the clouds had blown away and the sun shone down to give the impression that it should be warm.

The thought occurred to Madeline that the weather mirrored her feelings. Her storm had cleared, but doubts crossed her path like the scuttling leaves. Love shone in her heart and gave the impression that she would live a happy life with Rees, but did she not need time to know if he could be completely trusted? Or that she could?

'Find us!' both young voices cried at once.

A good game of hide-and-seek ought to set her spirits to rights. She closed her eyes and counted to ten slowly, then set off to search under benches and behind statuary.

Emily Lark's pink ruffle peeked from behind a tree trunk, but she chose to ignore it for a moment. It was no fun to be caught out right away. Better for the suspense to build while she called their names and pretended to be at a loss as to where they had gone.

Suddenly a man's voice came from the street beyond

the garden wall, cursing viciously. The peace of the tranquil spot was ruined.

The stone wall was tall, so she could not see him, and he hadn't spoken so loudly that it disturbed the girls' play, but still she urged them to a deeper part of the garden.

Such vitriol was not meant for innocent ears.

Madeline walked back to the wall. Her ears were not unsullied and she did want to know what the angry fellow was about.

'Uncle Milton, perhaps you ought to return when your temper has settled?' urged another man's voice.

Milton Langerby? It could only be him.

'Perhaps you ought to shut your mouth. I demand satisfaction over this outrage!'

'Duelling has been outlawed for years. No one does it any more.'

'Satisfaction can be had in many ways.'

'I say we come back when you have thought things through.'

'There is nothing to be thought through. Lord Glenbrook has broken our contract!'

Madeline sorely wanted to stand on a bench, pop into view over the wall and point out that all parties had been in agreement over it—or, if not in agreement exactly, done what was necessary.

She could not, of course, for in that moment Victoria Rose's curly-haired head popped out from behind a statue of Cupid. 'Here I is!'

While appearing to continue the game, Madeline tried to hear what the men said, but got only disjointed words: *betrayed, ruined, humiliated, revenge.* Hopefully she had heard that last one wrong.

But what she did know was that the man was not going away before he confronted Rees.

No wonder Lady Glenbrook was rushing to get them all to the country so quickly.

Rees's encounter with the man on the other side of the wall would not be a cordial one.

Dealing with unkind gossip was one thing. Facing the anger of a man whose niece had wed a second son rather than a viscount would be quite another.

She would have run to warn Rees, but already the man and his angry words had ploughed a path towards the front door.

Knowing her husband, he was well capable of handling the situation on his own. She would best serve him by staying here and keeping his children away from the ugly situation.

'One! Two! Three!' she counted loudly, in order to ensure the girls did not hear anything they ought not to.

The carriage ride from Liverpool to Green Knoll had been a long and mostly silent one.

Silent when his daughters were sleeping, that was. Little girls, Rees was quickly learning, loved nothing more than to talk. Even if what they had to say made little sense, they jabbered on.

The encounter with Langerby had been hard on everyone, even the staff. The man's boisterous threats of legal reprisal had rung from one end of the town house to the other.

Rees had remained mostly silent throughout the tirade. The fellow was not the most pleasant of men even when he attempted to be. When he had explained in the calmest voice he could that Wilson and Bethany were in love, it only incited Langerby to further anger.

Apparently the man did not believe in love.

He wanted his niece to be Viscountess Glenbrook and Miss Mosemore's heart played no part in the matter.

Milton Langerby was unreasonably bitter at what he considered his niece's disloyalty, dangerously so in Rees's opinion.

He was wrong about Bethany's loyalty. Had Rees not married Madeline, the girl would have gone through with their marriage bargain.

Doing so would have dashed her life and Wilson's, but she would have been obedient to her uncle.

He could not fault her for it. It was what well-bred British ladies did—married for the benefit of family position or to bolster sagging fortunes.

Until Langerby was able to see matters in a sensible light, Rees thought it best to warn Wilson to keep his bride away from Liverpool, perhaps even London.

Glancing across the dim interior of the carriage, he could just make out the profile of Madeline's face. She appeared to be asleep with Emily Lark tucked under her chin. Without a doubt his daughter was smiling contentedly and having sweet dreams.

Let Milton Langerby carry on until his lungs gave out. Rees would do everything again, much in the same way.

The carriage rocked gently over the road. In time he drifted off to sleep like the rest of the people in the carriage.

It seemed only a moment before the driver rapped softly on the hood.

They were home. Away from the acid tongues of society and safe from the threats of Bethany Mosemore's uncle.

Safe for a time. Rees did expect his solicitor to be paid a call by Langerby's solicitor.

In the end, the matter would be sorted out. For now his attention would be better spent on the future of his marriage.

The carriage door squeaked when it opened. Mother and Madeline awoke.

Rees helped them down the steps, taking Emily Lark from Madeline and Victoria Rose from his mother.

He'd missed his little girls while he'd been away and cherished the weight of their small sleeping bodies in his arms.

Too soon the manor staff rushed out the front door to take them from him.

His mother trailed wearily after them, but Madeline remained behind with him.

Coming home, he always paused for a moment before going inside. He'd travelled many places, but coming back to Green Knoll Manor always gave him a sense of belonging.

It always felt right to stand a moment and let a sense of peace, of thankfulness, wash through him.

'It all looks magical by moonlight,' Madeline murmured. 'I can only imagine how beautiful it is in daylight.'

She was right—everything appeared washed in enchantment. With the fat moon so low in the sky, it seemed to be sitting atop the chimney. Beyond the house, peaks of rolling hills were glazed in pearly light.

She slipped her hand into the crook of his elbow while they made their way slowly towards the stairs. He did not imagine she leaned into him going up.

'I hope you will be happy here.' *For ever.* Of course, he kept that last to himself.

It would have been good to hear her say she believed she would, but she did not. She didn't speak again until they reached the top step.

From here the dim illumination of lamps in the hall invited them inside.

All at once, he scooped her up, carrying her over the threshold of his home.

She squeaked in surprise. Perhaps she did not consider

herself to be a proper bride, but he was going to treat her as if she were.

'Where will I sleep?' she asked, no doubt concerned that he might carry her off to his chambers. Oh, he did want to do that. The image of it pulsed vividly in his mind's eye.

'The staff will only now be discovering we are wed. They will not have had time to prepare for you.'

He did not put her down, but strode across the grand hall.

'Is there a cot in the children's quarters? I'll be content there.'

'I will not be content to have you there.'

'But don't you think it is best we sleep apart? There is an annulment to be thought of.'

If she wanted to be separated from him so badly, he assumed she would be attempting to get out of his arms, not snuggling closer to his chest.

'Ah, my angel, there is. I'm going to do my best to convince you not to seek one.'

'But you did promise and until then we—'

'I only promised because I was afraid you would not marry me unless I did.'

'Oh, Rees, you know how I care for you. But I'm afraid at the same time.' She sighed, sadly, he thought. 'I need time, that's all. Enough to know you meant what you said—that I can trust you to keep your word.'

'I will let you go if it is what you want. But here's another vow.' He'd like to seal it with a kiss, but knew he should not. 'I vow to do my best to make you stay.'

'You can't do that!' she exclaimed, still making no attempt to free herself. 'I do not accept your new vow. The choice is mine to make, one way or another.'

So it was. 'What can I do to convince you to choose me?'

'Simply be honest with me—in everything.'

Suspicion about the neighbours was not knowledge—exactly. Remaining mum about a suspicion was not dishonesty. Especially not when it concerned the greatest wedding gift he could present her with.

'You will take my chambers. I'll find someplace else to sleep.'

'Thank you.' She snuggled her cheek against his neck. What a contradiction she was, trusting him and not trusting him all at the same time.

But no doubt he was a contradiction to her as well, given the way he had loved and yet deceived her.

To have believed him to be an honest, hard-working man and then to find he was a dishonest viscount? It was no wonder he was leaving his wife off at his chamber door, then going to sleep on a couch in the library.

He did not deserve a goodnight kiss. Which did not mean he would not try for one.

'Here we are, my angel.' He set her down, pulled her closer.

Damn it! It was her fingertip touching his lips, not her mouth.

'I think it best if you do not kiss me. Certainly do not call me yours.'

'You are wrong, Madeline. It is not best, but I will honour it.' Quickly, before she could react, he did kiss her cheek. He would have that at least. 'I'll see you at breakfast.'

When he was a step away she caught his hand, squeezed it, then let go. 'I miss our cabin aboard the *Edwina*.'

'As do I. Sleep well, my angel.'

Before she could contest the endearment, he hurried along the hallway, down a flight of stairs, across the hall, then down another long hallway to the library.

The room was cold and dark. Since no one would have

anticipated him sleeping here, there was no fire in the hearth.

Dash it, but he did not want to be here. All his life he'd been an honest man, fair in all his dealings.

Now he needed to prove that he was once more that man. He needed to prove it to Madeline and he needed to prove it to himself.

At least she could trust him to keep his word that she would have his chamber to herself.

Once he found her grandfather and gave her a wedding gift beyond all others, she might take him back to her heart.

If she did not, he would stand by his promise and grant her the annulment. Dash it, even the word made him feel sick.

So did thinking about how voiding his marriage, treating it as if it had never been, would hurt his children.

Already his babies were calling Madeline 'Mama'. He could not let that continue without knowing she would be willing to be that for them.

It hit him that the time he had longed for, depended upon, was more his enemy than his friend. Yes, he needed it to properly court Madeline and win her trust. But hour by hour his daughters were becoming attached to her, putting her in the place of the mother they never knew.

All they had ever known was a father. A father who could not possibly place his well-being above theirs.

There was but one thing to be done.

Go to Fencroft Manor and discover what he might. It would be foolish to put it off. He had learned that lesson aboard ship. He had nearly lost Madeline over it.

Hopefully he would not again.

What he most fervently prayed was that her love for him was as great as her love for them—that she would choose to remain Lady Glenbrook.

* * *

'A Christmas ball!' Rees heard his mother exclaim when he walked into the dining room the next morning. 'Or if not that, then New Year. We must get you introduced to society as soon as possible.'

'Oh, yes! There is nothing quite as wonderful as a winter ball.' Madeline looked as pleased with the notion as his mother did.

'Not everyone will make it, naturally. It is short notice and many of the neighbours are still in London. It will be a smallish gathering, but lovely all the same.'

It was hard not to smile seeing the pair of them becoming close so quickly. Of course, it was nearly impossible to be anything to Madeline other than a friend. She gathered them like a botanist gathered flowers.

'Good morning, Rees.' His mother stood up, kissed his cheek, then pointed to the buffet. 'We saved you a slice of ham.'

'One?'

'If you'd not slept the morning away and been here at a proper hour, we would not have indulged as we did. I put it solely on your shoulders if our waistlines thicken.'

Slept? He nearly laughed out loud. He'd scarcely sat down before he'd left the library to walk the grounds and visit the stable. He'd come inside at dawn. Then he had bathed, shaved, dressed and spent time in the office going over ledgers.

It was essential to become reacquainted with the estate after an absence.

That was what he told himself, but the truth was, it might have been done later. The true reason he had lost sleep was because he missed sleeping close to Madeline and was tempted to sneak into her chamber to sleep on the floor near her bed.

'Good morning, Rees.'

Daybreak and his wife's smile seemed one and the same to his way of thinking—both were sunshine to his soul.

Madeline Dalton was so beautiful, smiling and making plans with his mother.

'Where are the twins?' he asked.

Madeline lifted the hem of her skirt to reveal Victoria Rose, lying on her belly on the floor and peeking out while she hugged her doll.

His mother did the same and he spotted Emily Lark in an identical position.

'You finded us!' Victoria Rose laughed while scrambling out from under Madeline's skirt.

'It's time and past you hired a governess, Rees. Surely you do not expect your new Viscountess to tend them all day long? It would be improper.'

'We wants Mama!' Emily Lark declared, then crawled from her grandmother's skirt to Madeline's, wrapping herself in the grey woollen skirt.

'See if you can get Mrs Warren to watch them for the day, Rees. My daughter-in-law and I must visit the seamstress.'

He would rather she did not go to the village. Gossip surrounding his sudden marriage would have reached here by now.

If he could prevent it, he would not have people casting judgemental glances at Madeline as if she was the reason for Bethany Mosemore's disgrace.

It would be better if she remained at home.

Soon enough curious neighbours would come calling. He would give her a bit of time to prepare for it.

'I'm sure Mrs Warren is busy. I'll call for the seamstress to attend you here.'

'Would you not rather see the village, my dear?' His mother poured a cup of tea and passed it to Madeline.

'Perhaps it would be better to wait until Rees finds a governess. I imagine he is correct and Mrs Warren is busy.'

'Sit with us, my son.' His mother patted the table. 'Once plans for our ball begin in earnest, we won't have much time for you, or you for us.'

And yet time with Madeline was what he needed.

Rees took his slice of ham, buttered a piece of toast, then slathered it with strawberry jam. He sat down beside Madeline.

'Are you sure you would enjoy a ball?' he asked. 'Wouldn't you rather take time to settle in?'

Hopefully his mother would listen to what Madeline wanted.

'I would adore a ball. It seems like for ever since I've attended one—yes, it was all the way last April.'

'And this one will be in your honour!' His mother clapped her hands gleefully. 'And Bethany's, too, of course. What a boon to gain two daughters within such a short time. It will be quite the event.'

'We ought to wait until the scandal subsides.' He was right in this.

'Nonsense.' His mother liked to say he was authoritative, but he'd clearly got that trait from her.

Who else would dare to contradict a viscount?

'Your mother is right. A ball will put the wagging tongues to rest.'

Evidently his American wife would dare to. He was certain Wilson's bride would do no such thing.

Why was he grinning when he ought to be frowning?

He was grateful to be wed to a woman who convinced him she was correct with a pretty smile and a happy blue-eyed wink—that was why.

It did occur to him that her agreement to a ball meant that she was willing for people to know her as Lady Glenbrook. He dared to hope this meant she was considering keeping her title—and him.

'A ball there will be, then. Just keep in mind that people still talk about Father galloping into the ballroom on his favourite horse.'

'You should be aware of the scandal, Madeline.' Mother shrugged, shook her head. 'Although over the years it has grown more humorous than offensive. But you see, Lord Glenbrook took it into his mind that such a thing would be funny. The noise those big hooves made on my beautiful polished wood was deafening, but not more deafening than the screams of the ladies fleeing the dance floor or the curses of the gentlemen. Hmm, as I recall, a few of them screamed, too. Oh, but my husband thought himself grand, swinging his grandfather's sword over his head. He even managed to lift a glass of whisky and shout "God save the Queen". It might not have been so bad had he not started singing afterwards and if the horse had not made a mess for Lady Fenwick to slip in. It was an exceedingly expensive gown.'

'I'm told my father enjoyed his fun, but I scarcely remember.'

'Ah…' His mother sighed, gave a soft smile. 'It was not always appropriate but, yes, he did.'

He'd always thought Mother must have loved Father very much. Numerous times over the years she had been offered marriage and each time refused her suitor. Either no one measured up or she feared someone would.

'I worry Emily Lark takes after him,' he admitted.

'But Victoria Rose is more like you, Rees.' His mother picked her granddaughter up, nuzzled her soft brown curls.

'Me like Mama,' Emily Lark declared, then climbed up Madeline's skirt and took possession of her lap.

His sweet Emily Lark was nothing like the timid woman who had given birth to her.

But like Madeline? He had to admit his stomach lurched. He suspected his child would do whatever she needed to in order to have her life be the way she thought it should be.

Even run away from home.

He saw himself one day standing in James Macooish's shoes. He saw it with a painful squeeze of his heart.

Where was Macooish? If he was only miles distant, there was only one thing to be done. Go to the man and inform him that his granddaughter was safely wed and living close by.

If that were the case, the reunion between Madeline and her family must happen more quickly than he wanted it to.

'Come, Madeline, let's take the children to play in the garden.' He caught his mother's frown. The invitation did sound more like a command. 'If you would not mind. It looks like snow before too long and I'd like them to take the fresh air while they can.'

Chapter Ten

'Snow! Truly?' Madeline covered her mouth with her hand, suppressing the urge to jump up and down. *Snow? Here?* 'I've only ever seen it from a distance on mountaintops. Oh, but even that is a rare thing.'

She set Emily Lark on the floor, then stood up.

'I'll have your coats brought.' The Dowager Lady Glenbrook set Victoria Rose down, then stood, brushing the wrinkles from her skirt. 'I've a million things to do. I hope Wilson and his wife come home straight away. It won't do for them to miss the party.'

With everyone bundled up they left the dining room, going out through the glass doors leading to the garden.

Clouds hung low and grey in the sky, but nothing white fell from them.

'All of the Christmas cards show images of snow, but where I come from, December the twenty-fifth is almost always an idyllic sunny day. Once in a while it rains, but even that is rare.'

Walking after the girls, keeping an eye on them as they ran down garden paths, she imagined what the place would look like cloaked in snow.

Right now the garden was washed in shades of brown

and gold, which was lovely, but to see everything white and glittering would be like stepping into fairyland.

'I hope you like it as well once you've lived in it for a while.'

For a while? Those words so casually spoken meant much more. He cast the thought out like bait on a hook. As though he was planting a seed in her mind, hoping it would take root.

Lord Glenbrook was a sneaky fellow. She could do nothing but carry on as if she had not noticed.

'Oh, it is cold, but it is not as penetrating as it was out on the ocean. And now we both have warm coats, not just the one to share between us.'

'I didn't mind that.'

No, she hadn't minded it either. Especially when they had been wrapped together while watching the stars, sharing a kiss.

'I'll have the seamstress make you a few of your own so that you need not borrow Mother's. You'll need gowns and everything, I imagine.'

The children found a bush and dashed in circles about it, trying to catch one another.

She and Rees sat on a bench, smiling at them.

Madeline could not recall a specific instance, but she was certain she and Clementine used to play the same game many years ago. She missed her cousin—her best friend—dreadfully.

She had faith that Rees would help her locate her family as he promised to do. As anxious as she was to begin the search, she understood he needed some time to get things caught up at the estate. More than that, he needed time with his daughters.

For her the wait was hard, but after everything she could wait a bit longer. Until then she would enjoy where she was and the people she was with.

Very quickly, she was becoming fond of these new people in her life. For so long it had been only Clementine and Grandfather.

'I did come to you rather lacking. But don't worry—I'll have Grandfather repay you for what you spend.'

Rees's expression changed, subtly as if he were trying to hide it.

His gaze shifted from watching his daughters play to looking deeply at her, seeing inside her in that way he had of doing.

'Do you like Green Knoll Manor? I know you've not been here long enough to know for certain, but do you think you could be happy here?'

Oh, she did like it. It was lovely, yes, but would she be happy here? She honestly had no answer. Which was a surprise because only a short time ago she believed there was only one place she would be happy. With Grandfather and Clementine.

Had he asked if she loved him it would be easier. Of course she did, no matter how swiftly it had happened. She remembered the analogy of yeast and believed it to be true. What troubled her was what to do with love when it was conflicted.

All she could do was answer what he asked, not what he meant.

'It's a wonderful home. I haven't seen it all, but I'm sure the rest is no less welcoming than the first. Your mother is wonderful. I cannot recall my own.' Was she going to cry? Her tightening throat gave every indication that she might. She swallowed hard. 'But your mother—right off, at breakfast this morning, she asked me to call her "Mother" and—oh, Rees, it touches me deeply.'

If, when the day came, she went away with Grandfather, she would not only be saying goodbye to her husband, but his family.

That was a cost she must count when making her choice.

'What about them?' He nodded towards the children. 'Would caring for them be a burden?'

'No, Rees.'

It ought to frighten her how quickly she was coming to care for his children. It was a lifetime bond she was considering making with them. Oh, but were they not sweet playing like a pair of lively pups? Her affection for them was growing faster than she'd expected it to.

Then again, perhaps she should've expected it to, given how quickly she had come to care for their father.

Yeast. Love and yeast, not so romantic a notion, but accurate for all that.

Ah, but these precious ones, parting the shrubbery to peer after a bunny, were not bread, but endearing little girls. And their father—well, she had no words to describe how handsome, strong, virile and manly he was.

Apparently she did have words because *potent* and *kissable* came to mind, as well.

She adored him; she adored his children.

She mistrusted herself.

In spite of her vow, she feared she would run if Rees kept the truth from her again.

Victoria Rose fell, hit her elbow on a stone and began to cry.

In an instant Madeline was on her knees, gathering the child and rocking her against her bosom.

'Mama,' she sobbed. 'Hurt!'

She had never encouraged them to call her 'Mama'. Right there on the cold ground something inside Madeline went soft.

The name sounded right; it felt right. Perhaps it was because she had been them once, longing for a lost mother.

It did not have to be so for those sweet babies. She could offer them what she and Clemmie had never had. Not only could she, but she wanted to.

'It's all right, sweetling. I imagine it feels better already, doesn't it?'

Victoria Rose nodded, then dashed off to resume her game.

Now it was Madeline whose throat tightened. In her mind's eye she saw the twins growing, becoming happy girls and then young ladies with bright futures. She saw herself being a part of it.

Still kneeling, she glanced up at Rees. 'They are wonderful. No one would think it a burden to raise them.'

'Bethany would have, I believe, but you would not?' He reached a hand down to help her up.

She sat beside him, closer than she had a moment ago.

'Oh, no, it would be a joy. A complete and utter privilege.' She closed her eyes, tipped her face towards the clouds. 'But I must be honest with you. I don't know how to act when they call me "Mama". I like it, of course. It touches me in a way I can't quite explain, but how can I allow it, not knowing our future? But at the same time, how can I tell them no? I understand what it is to want a mother.'

'Let us be your future, Madeline.'

If only it were as easy as murmuring the word *yes*.

She could not utter it. At the same time, she could not outright refuse. All she could do was look into his eyes and get lost in the love she saw in them.

She touched his cheek and wanted to cry. If only love was all that mattered.

In the end, maybe it was.

'Do you want me to speak to them about it? Ask them to stop?'

Make her decision right now? That was what she would be doing, whatever her answer to him was. Still, she could not.

'I think I should go back inside and help your mother.'

'There is no need. She'll have the servants dashing about. She is hardly a novice at putting together a gathering on short notice. She delights in it.'

'In any case, it's getting colder. We ought to take the girls inside.'

'Sit with me, my angel, just a while longer. We can talk about the weather in Los Angeles or the latest fashions ladies are wearing—whatever you like. Just be here.'

'I can't think in a straight line when you call me that. Please do not.'

He did not say he wouldn't. In fact, he shot her the half-smile that was always her utter undoing.

Oh, and he was aware of it! Used it against her as the most seductive of weapons.

'If I see one little shiver from them we are going inside,' she uttered sternly because she was feeling softer than she ought to. 'Now, tell me what it was like growing up here. Who were you as a child?'

'Mother claims my brother and I were hooligans.' He put his arm about her shoulder, hugged her close to his side. Wisdom would advise her not to allow it. But wisdom had never been her strongest trait, so she snuggled into his warmth. 'She smiles when she says it, though.'

'My grandfather says the same about me and Clementine! Not hooligans, though. Pixies up to no good was the way he described us.'

'And all you wanted was a bit of fun. Same as we did. We never thought staining our clothes while rolling down hills was the wicked thing Mother and the laundress did.'

'Just so! It was simply good fun rolling in the surf and getting our bloomers full of sand and our hair caked with salt water. But our nanny always complained to Grandfather about it. We told him she was simply envious because she was too old to join in the fun. Of course, he knew us better than to believe it.'

'What mischief will those two get into, do you think?'

Whatever it was, she doubted he would ever do anything but smile indulgently at them.

'They've already begun, Rees. Look, Emily Lark has torn her dress.'

He nodded, a restrained smile ticking the corners of his mouth. 'Look at those leaves stuck in Victoria Rose's hair.'

'Pixies and hooligans,' she pointed out.

His strong, solid shoulder shook when he laughed under his breath. 'I'm a blessed man, am I not?'

Greatly blessed, she knew, looking at his face and loving the way his blue eyes shone for his children.

She could be blessed along with him. He'd offered this to her.

The choice only needed to be made.

The couch in the library was too short for his frame. Rees shifted position. Too narrow, as well.

He turned on to his back with his legs dangling over the arm, recounting the day as he tended to do before falling asleep.

There had been no success in his most urgent order of business, which was finding out if Madeline's family was in residence at Fencroft Manor. He'd advised his wife and his mother that he had business in the village and would be gone several hours.

He did stop there for a few moments to have coffee and a biscuit. As much as food and drink, he wanted to know how deeply gossip about his family had spread.

Naturally, no one spoke openly of his rejection of Bethany, nor did they bring up his hasty marriage. He did get curious, sidelong glances which let him know there had been talk.

In the end, the excursion had been a waste of time. The family was not present and the staff had had no word as to when they would return.

His day would have been better spent courting his bride. As it was, he'd barely shared more than a few private words with her.

Coming home, he'd found her where he'd hoped to, in his chambers. What he had not expected was that the dressmaker would have responded to his summons so quickly.

Fabrics of every hue and texture were tossed about the room. Three women clucked around his wife as she stood on a wood box in the centre of the room.

Mother gazed on, giving advice while holding Victoria Rose in her arms.

'Gween,' his child stated. Apparently even ladies of a tender age had opinions when it came to fashion.

'Where's my Emily Lark?' he asked, seeing a mound of brocade shift on the bed.

'Here, Faddie!' She popped out from among the folds, then scurried off the bed, coming for him with lifted arms.

At that point his mother handed Victoria Rose to him and told him to keep the girls entertained until business here was finished.

He'd been going out the door when Madeline asked, 'Is it snowing yet?'

'Not yet, but it's getting colder.'

As the day went on, he had tried to get his wife alone for some private conversation, but the coming social gathering captured all of his mother's attention, which meant it captured Madeline's, as well. No one could involve a person in her cause more thoroughly than Mother could.

The hour was now late. The children asleep, his mother and wife retired for the night. Only a few servants going about the last duties of the day remained awake.

If he could only get comfortable, he— The door burst open.

'Is it true? You've married an insolent American?'

Rees sat up slowly, plopping his bare feet on the floor.

'Yes and no. Good to have you home, Wilson.'

His brother leapt over the back of the couch, then landed with a thump beside him.

'You and Bethany are married, I understand.'

'Didn't think you would mind since you married someone else.' His brother stretched, yawning as if weary from a long, hard journey. 'And I know there is an interesting story there.'

Rees got up, stirred the coals of the fire, then turned back to look down at his brother.

'You might have mentioned you were in love with Miss Mosemore. Had I not heard you crying all over each other in the garden, I would have gone through with the marriage contract.'

'It was a poignant moment. We believed we were star crossed. But you? What happened? Bethie can only conclude you were trapped.'

'Your wife was taken aback when she met Madeline. From the shock of it, I imagine. I can understand her confusion, but if anyone got trapped in this mess, it was my wife.'

'But she managed very well for herself. Who would not want to become Viscountess?'

'Madeline would not. I had to offer her an annulment in order to get her to agree to marry me. If she had not accepted, I have no doubt you would have thrown yourself in front of a hackney cab by now.'

'Neither of us knew what her uncle had planned for her until your engagement was announced. Did you know he threatened to give her to old Baron Manderly if she did not accept you?'

'Manderly is so old he can't even button his own trousers!' As threats went, this was an effective one. 'It's a good thing you married Bethany as quickly as you did. Langerby paid a call. He is furious, as you might expect.'

'So, as I understand it, you convinced the American woman to marry you so that I could marry Bethie?'

'I saw no other way around it. Any reason besides me already having a wife might be got around.'

'I'm grateful, Brother, truly. If there is anything I can do to convince her to grant you the annulment, I will. No doubt she went title hunting no matter that you think otherwise.'

'I'm going to overlook what you are suggesting about Lady Glenbrook since I suspect it has been coloured by your wife's words.' He sat down on the couch, speaking quietly. 'Madeline is completely innocent in all of this. I never told her who I was.'

'She married you thinking you were a sweaty fireman?'

He nodded. 'Indeed. She liked me better when I was. When we got off the ship, she had no more idea that I was Lord Glenbrook than Bethany had that I was married.'

'I wish I'd been there.'

'You always did like to see me squirm. But as I just said, I'll excuse your insinuations about my wife's character, but only this once since you have not met her. And so you know, the last thing in the world I want is for her to leave us.'

'Well, then, that's the last thing I want, too.'

'Might not be.' He probably shouldn't be grinning, but

how could he stop? 'Mother's planning a ball to introduce our wives to local society.'

'Our mother knows no fear.' Wilson stood up, scratching his hair, which was the same rich brown shade as Victoria Rose's. 'Anyone else would hide away from scandal, not invite it in.'

'Well, there was Father. She did develop a rather strong backbone.'

'Are you sleeping down here?'

He nodded, grunted, 'Annulment.'

Wilson grimaced. 'Ah, well, I'm going to bed my wife. I do appreciate your sacrifice on my behalf.'

Watching his brother walk towards the door, he would have pitched something at him had anything been at hand besides an antique vase.

Instead, he lay back down on the couch, bent his legs over the arm.

Dash it!

He leapt up and sprinted out of the library.

Madeline's bed jostled; the mattress sagged. All of a sudden, the coverlet was no longer covering her. With the room so dim and cold, the bare skin of her arms and throat pebbled with chill.

'What are you doing here?' she asked of the figure hovering over her.

'This is my chamber. This is my bed. You are my wife.'

'Nevertheless, I—'

'I miss you and I've come to kiss you goodnight.'

She eased up on her elbows, wishing she could read his expression in the dim light.

'It is a common practice.' Had she actually said that? She must have gone daft—or—she missed him, too.

It would be untrue to say she had not been thinking

of—all right, longing for—the nights they had shared in the ship's intimate little cabin.

His big hand closed over her upper arm, stroking away the gooseflesh.

Was it not interesting how one could go from icy to sizzling in a blink? When his long fingers circled her throat, when his thumb stroked her collarbone, it left her breathless, that was what it did.

'You said—'

And speechless, as well.

'I said I was going to kiss you.' He shifted his weight and somehow it ended up with her lying flat on the bed and him on top of her, his great strong body braced on his elbows to allow inches of air between them. 'And so I am.'

He tangled his fingers in her hair, dipped his mouth so that the heat of his breath grazed her lips.

Giving herself over to his kiss, Madeline was fairly certain she would never be cold again.

'You are my angel. I will not stop saying so,' he whispered, then pushed off her. 'Choose me.'

Getting off the bed, he covered her with the blanket. Tucked it with great tenderness about her.

'You should not tell me things like that, Rees.'

And yet those were words any woman longed to hear. Had she not dreamed her whole life of such a declaration? 'It's cheating.'

He was standing in the doorway when he answered softly, 'Not cheating as much as tweaking things in my favour.'

He remained there for a long time, looking at her, saying with his eyes what she had asked him not to.

I love you, she heard with her heart.

'We can have this and more. All you need do is say so.'

And then he was gone.

Yes, her heart whispered after him, wept after him.

If only love was all there was to it.

* * *

The next morning at breakfast Madeline stood alone in the dining room, staring out the glass doors.

The servants said it was too cold to snow. Was there such a thing? She desperately hoped not.

Wait! Just there! Was that not a snowflake drifting past a tree limb? She stared at the way it lazily fell to the stones, as if it were a feather.

Drat it! It *was* a feather.

'Good morning,' came a voice she recognised, but did not particularly want to respond to.

While Madeline excelled in making friends, she feared she would never win over Bethany Dalton. The circumstances of their first meeting had been a blow and left them both dumbfounded.

Still, she reached within her heart for a smile, then turned around. 'Good morning, sister. May I call you that, Mrs Dalton?'

'I'm rather surprised you would wish to, given how condescending my attitude towards you was when we first met. I thought you—' She bit her bottom lip, shook her head. 'I did not understand everything until last night when Wilson explained it all.'

'Given that I'd married your fiancée, no one would have faulted you had you tossed me off the dock.' She reached for Bethany's hand and gave it a quick squeeze. 'I did not know about you until the second we met. By rights we both ought to have tossed Lord Glenbrook off the dock.'

'Perhaps we will think of something yet.'

Madeline breathed in a secret, but relieved, sigh. It was a great relief to know that she would get along well with Wilson's wife. It would be horrible to have bitter feelings towards a member of one's own family.

She went utterly still inside, realising that without a second thought she had counted Rees's family as her own.

What could that mean since she had not yet made her decision?

Had she?

Certainly not!

All at once, Emily Lark and Victoria Rose burst into the dining room, trailed by their grandmother.

'They have already eaten,' Lady Glenbrook announced.

Emily Lark smiled at her through a smear of red jam while her sister licked something that could be butter from her fingertips.

If Madeline had ever seen anything as sweet, she could not recall the event.

'Look at the two of you,' Lady Glenbrook declared with a great smile. 'I can scarce believe I have daughters after all these years. Let's eat our breakfast and you can tell me your ideas for your party.'

Madeline glanced at Victoria Rose. The child seemed to have ideas and not good ones. Greasy fingers reaching, she dashed towards a ruffle on Bethany's fashionable blue skirt.

Bethany gasped, backing up and swiping her skirt to the side.

Intercepting her, Madeline scooped her up and settled her on her hip. A memory stirred in her heart of mauling someone's skirt when she was small, but she could not quite bring it forth. Whatever it was made her miss her mother dreadfully.

Victoria Rose touched Madeline's cheeks with buttery fingers. 'My mama.'

Bethany's face looked flushed as she pressed one hand to her heart. 'I'm sorry I reacted so badly, truly I am, but I'm not good with little children. It's worked out for the best that you are their mother. I fear I would have failed them miserably.'

'I'm sure you will be a top-rate auntie,' Lady Glenbrook declared. 'And when the time is right you will be an admirable mother.'

Madeline buried her nose in Victoria Rose's soft brown hair. Was the time right for her to be a mother? She could not say for certain. But she did know that a smear of butter on her skirt would not have bothered her.

'Lady Glenbrook,' the butler announced, standing in the doorway and looking distressed. Rees's mother and Madeline turned in response. 'Lord Langerby has come to call on the Viscount, but he's gone to visit his tenants. Shall I send him away?'

'No.' The Dowager sighed. 'Ring for tea and I'll see what is to be done about him.'

'It's for me to do.' Bethany squared her back, lifting her chin. 'He's my uncle and he'd not be here if I'd stood up to him in the beginning.'

'We'll all go,' the Dowager insisted and sailed out of the dining room as if blown along by a stiff wind.

They rushed after her, Emily Lark lagging behind.

Hearing the child's whimper, Madeline paused for her to catch up.

'Come, sweetling.' She bent and Emily Lark rushed to be picked up.

They all hurried after the Dowager, down two corridors and into the formal parlour.

Milton Langerby stood in the centre of the room, hands behind his back.

He rocked on his heels, smiling as they came in one by one.

Odd, she had not expected him to appear congenial. The angry voice she had heard on the other side of the garden fence in Liverpool did not fit with the man giving effusive greetings to his niece.

Odder still, his voice was louder and deeper than was seemly for his diminutive body.

Lord Langerby looked like a skinny bird, his movements quick and fidgety. Madeline had the distinct feeling that at any moment his show of affability would burst and he would turn into a small, fighting cock.

It was not hard to imagine talons flying at Bethany's throat.

Luckily the footman wheeled in the tea tray before her imagination took her further down a nightmare path.

Lord Langerby sipped his tea and complimented the little tarts. He was lavish in praise of his niece's marriage, even complimented her blushing appearance, then chuckled at how wedded bliss agreed with her.

Yet Madeline had the distinct impression his words did not match his heart. This was a man to be wary of.

If Lady Glenbrook felt the same, she gave no indication of it. She smiled and chatted politely until Lord Langerby stood up, signalling that the visit was at an end.

And not a second too soon. While Madeline had held the twins, one on each knee, she was privy to their quiet conversation. They thought the visitor had a long, pointy nose. It could only be seconds before they shared the opinion with everyone else.

'Come, my dear niece,' Langerby said. 'I've something for you, a gift, but I would like to give it to you in private.'

The fine hairs on the back of Madeline's neck stood to attention.

Bethany did not answer, but trailed slowly after her uncle as the butler led the way to the front door.

'Follow them,' Lady Glenbrook whispered, taking the twins from her arms. 'But be careful. Stay hidden.'

Staying hidden was one of her greatest talents. She could not recall a time when it was more useful than now.

Dashing to the hall, she peered through a lace rose in the curtain.

Rather than going directly to the waiting carriage, Lord

Langerby took Bethany by the elbow and led her down a path that ran parallel to the drive.

Madeline was in luck. Tall shrubs grew on both sides of the walkway. As soon as her quarry vanished behind the greenery, she lifted her skirts and dashed after them.

Full of arrogance, the man must not expect to be trailed because he stamped along the path, making a noisy business of it.

Really, this could not have worked better to her advantage. She might have been an elephant tramping through the brush and he'd not have noticed.

'Aren't you the clever one?'

For half a second Madeline could not determine whether she'd heard spoken words or a hiss. Either way the sound gave her a chill.

'It was not my doing that the Viscount married someone else, Uncle.'

'No? You ought to have done something to ensure it was you the Viscount married.'

What sort of something? The image popping into Madeline's mind made her feel rather angry—possessive, to put a finer point on the emotion.

Rees was her husband! Even the suggestion of another woman in her place made her want to steam.

Yet what did she think would happen if she annulled the marriage? Some woman would snatch Rees up in a heartbeat—that lady would become a mother to Emily Lark and Victoria Rose.

The woman was only imaginary, yet Madeline wanted to—

'I have not spent a fortune raising you all these years to get no profit from it.'

'I have always been dutiful to you. Obedient in everything.'

'You failed me in the one thing that counted most.

Doors that would have been open to me because of your title will not be. Business ventures I would have made from your contacts, lost.'

'Do you not see I had no control over any of it?'

'You married a second son rather hastily.'

'I love him, Uncle.'

'A complication only. Let me think upon it for a time. There might be a way to turn this problem to our advantage.'

'But I—'

'Will be obedient in whatever I decide. Your loyalty belongs to me.'

'No—'

'I will return to inform you of what I will have you do,' he said, cutting off Bethany's protest. 'In the meantime you will be attentive to Lord Glenbrook—you do understand my meaning?'

Why, the great diminutive devil!

A truly odious laugh whispered through the leaves.

Madeline was thankful for the thorny thicket that separated her from Lord Langerby. She wanted desperately to burst through the thorn bush and stamp on him! Squash him flat like a bug.

Making friends of foes was all well and good, but sometimes one encountered people who made it impossible.

Indeed! Bertrand Fenster on his worst day was a better human than Milton Langerby on his best and she had left him behind without a parting smile.

Skirts and petticoats made a whooshing noise. Footsteps tapped rapidly up the path to the house.

'Stupid chit.'

Langerby kicked something. A thorny branch slid under the shrub, came to a rest inches from her hand.

Oh, my, she should not. But, oh, it would only take a little shove and— She heard him take a step.

What she was about to do might be wrong…but it would be gratifying.

She shoved the branch back through the shrub, held it inches off the ground. She felt the tug when his trouser leg caught on a thorn, heard the rip and his gasp when he lost his balance.

Hitting the ground, he flailed about, grunting and snorting.

Oh, yes, it was gratifying. She scurried back towards the house. If only somehow Clementine could have magically watched it happen. She knew her cousin would applaud.

'And so I tripped him,' Madeline declared, sitting upon the bed in the master suite and grinning proudly with her bare feet tucked under her sleeping gown.

Having come to kiss his wife goodnight, Rees felt as if he was the one to have fallen face first on the path.

'That was risky—far too dangerous. You will not do such a thing again.' He stood on the rug at the foot of the bed, arms crossed, legs spread and knees locked in a stance of authority.

'How do you know I will not?' What kind of smile was that? Not a promise of future obedience.

Dash it, the reason should be obvious. He had just decreed she would not.

And she had challenged him on it.

'Let's not veer from the point of the conversation,' she said.

Given the importance of what she had just told him, it ought to be easy to focus.

Sadly, his attention wandered more to the pretty ivory nightgown she was wearing than to what she was saying. It was held at the neckline by a pink ribbon tied loosely in a bow.

Why was it loose? Perhaps she anticipated another goodnight kiss and wanted more.

Or perhaps he ought to stop staring at the pink ribbon and concentrate on the matter before him.

At this late hour everyone was in bed and the house quiet. The only noise besides their softly spoken conversation was the gusty wind rattling the shutters, that and the crackle of fire in the hearth.

Focus, he reminded himself again, then again. It was no use—he was obsessed with the fragile, slippery ribbon. All right, it was not the ribbon as much as what it hid from his sight.

Really, one tug would—

'Rees Dalton…' She snapped her fingers in front of his nose. 'Our sister-in-law is being coerced. Do you not care what her uncle's wicked scheme will be?'

He did, of course, but apparently not as much as he cared about making Madeline his wife in deed as well as name. He stood up, then walked to the window, staring down at vague, dark shapes in the dark garden. In the end, it did not help all that much to put a bit of distance between him and temptation.

'At least now I understand why Langerby pushed so hard for the marriage. The man was relentless in his pursuit of me.'

'He has a corrupted soul. Even knowing that his niece loves Wilson, he wants her to—"be attentive to you" were his words.'

'The only woman's attentiveness I will ever respond to is yours.'

He heard the bedclothes shift when she got up from the bed. The cloth of her nightgown whispered around her when she walked.

He turned to look. Fabric undulated about her body like mist.

He'd given a vow to wait for her decision on their future—he was a man of honour—he was stronger than he knew, wasn't he?

Never, though, had he vowed not to influence her decision. On the contrary, he had promised to do so.

'I believe you, Rees. If I stay, I will want the attentiveness of no other man,' she said, blinking up at him with those lovely blue eyes.

And if she did not stay? She would be with another. The thought made him sick to his stomach. Made him need to pound the glass and shatter it. A bleeding wound would feel better than the pain of thinking of her wed to someone else.

'Oh, I wish I had done more than trip him! He is hatching up some foul plan for the family. I wonder what he means to do to us.'

Us? She had included herself among the Daltons. He prayed it was intended and not merely a slip of tongue.

He was rather glad now that he had not smashed the glass. Now he was free to touch her hair. It was incredibly beautiful, catching the shimmer of lamplight as it did. Slowly, deliberately, he reached for a strand, caressed it between his finger and thumb.

She frowned at him and slid her hair from his hold. She did not hurry doing it either, but reclaimed it slowly, the same as he'd taken it.

'I can't think of what has got into you, Rees Dalton.'

'You can,' he whispered in a voice that resembled a low growl even to his own ears.

Ah, there! The blush suffusing her face told him she was not insensible to his attempt to woo her. She was as aware as he was that they were alone in the master's chamber and that while he was fully clothed, she was not.

'Are you trying to distract me from what we have discovered on purpose?' she said and at the same time glided a half a step closer to him. He wondered if she noticed.

'What is it we are trying to discover, Madeline?' He traced the backs of his fingers over her cheek. 'Something of more importance than Langerby, is it not?'

'Oh…' She took another small step towards him, blinked and set his heart thumping.

'Which,' he whispered, his hand on the back of her neck to press her ever closer, 'is why I am going to kiss you.'

'Goodnight?'

'All night, if you so choose.'

'We won't find an answer to our problem that way.'

'But we will, my angel.' He lowered his mouth. 'Trust me.'

'I say, next time Langerby comes to visit, I spy on him again.'

'What?' Startled, he let his hand fall away.

'Bethany will not tell us anything. She is too frightened of her uncle. If we intend to discover what he had in mind, we will have to do it ourselves.'

Clever lady, but she was not going to distract him so easily. She knew good and well what their conversation had been about.

'And you believe I will allow you to do this?'

'I do, because you know it is an excellent idea and you also know that you cannot keep me from—'

Perhaps he could not. What he could do was keep her from talking about it by kissing her.

Which he did, for a very long and indulgent time.

'We will do it together,' he murmured, letting go of the kiss.

'All right, good.' She gazed up at him, heavy lidded and nodding.

It was time to go back to the couch in his library because there was a point when enticement became coercion.

For as much as he wanted her, he would not cross that line. Until he presented her with his wedding gift of the reunion with her family, it would not be right.

It was early when Madeline heard laughter coming from below in the garden. It could only be a little after sunrise.

She opened her eyes, stretched, then got out of bed and padded sleepily to the window.

The chambermaid had already come to light the fire and draw open the shutters. The heat was wonderful. She would never take being warm for granted again.

The girl deserved an extra-monetary thank you for her quiet service and her thoughtfulness. First thing when she saw Rees she would tell him to do it.

With a yawn she drew back the curtain and looked outside. Wilson and Bethany were out for a morning walk in the sunshine.

As desperately as Madeline had wished for snow, it seemed it was not to be.

A circumstance which seemed to suit the couple rather nicely. Even from up here she sensed their happiness. It was sweet how they could not walk twenty steps without stopping to kiss.

But they were newlyweds, after all, and it was to be expected, rejoiced over.

Madeline dropped the curtain, sat down in the chair in front of the fireplace feeling rather—cross?

Yes, cross and sad.

She was also a newlywed, but she was not free to openly kiss her husband when the whim took her.

A condition which she had created. She thought she had been right to do so. It made sense if she meant to come to any sort of logical decision regarding her future.

Oh, but remembering the way Rees kissed her last night—it seemed right in every way.

In spite of that she had fought against the intimacy.

Fought and failed. For all that she tried to avoid it, there was a bond between them whether she willed it to be or not.

Dodging it by trying to redirect the course of a conversation did no good because as soon as she looked at him she knew what he wanted of her. His eyes shone with wanting her. Not only did she know, but she responded to it.

She felt like a bee hovering over a flower laden with the most beautiful golden pollen. She wanted it. She had passed by other flowers not nearly as nice. Clearly this was the one blossom she had been seeking—and yet?

And yet she was not a bee. If she were, she would take what she wanted and move blissfully to the next promising flower.

Just there was where the trouble really lay. Her decision as to whether she would 'move on' or remain married to Rees did not have to do with her trusting him because, when all was said and done, she just did.

While he might not have always been forthcoming in revealing his circumstances, she understood, she forgave.

Forgiveness was rather a forever thing. It could not be taken back at a later time or it meant nothing to begin with.

Rees was who he was. A dependable man; a trustworthy one.

If only that was all to be considered, life would be flowers and smiles. If that and the state of her heart were all to be considered, she would run to him this moment. She would hug him about the neck and through a hail of kisses announce there would be no annulment.

Oh, yes, she would drag him back to that bed right over there, the one too big to be slept in alone. She would become his wife for ever.

Yes, if only.

What held her back from acting on the impulse had nothing to do with him, but rather with herself.

She was a runaway, not to be trusted. The worst thing she could do was agree to stay, to promise herself to Rees and his children and then, when the first sign of trouble arose, leave them.

If she could betray Grandfather the way she had, a man she owed her whole life to, who knew what she might do?

She owed her life to Rees, as well. Yet even that had not prevented her from dashing away from him at the dock.

Clearly, it was not Rees she needed to learn to trust; it was herself. But given her past decisions, she did not believe in her own good sense.

With the right provocation she might take to her heels again.

Two things were needed, in her opinion, to correct wrong behaviour. Repentance and transformation.

Repentance, she had in abundance.

Transformation was trickier. Facing her flaw was a start, but only the first step.

Perhaps when she found Grandfather, sought his forgiveness, somehow there would be healing in it.

How, though, did she even begin to go about finding him? The British Isles were huge, so many people called the place home.

Her best chance at finding Grandfather was to wait for Rees to help her. He knew places; he was acquainted with people who could help.

It might need to be after the ball since it was all hands on deck for that.

She half-wished she had not agreed to Lady Glenbrook's ball. The sooner she threw herself upon Grandfather's mercy and Clementine's—most desperately upon her cousin's—the sooner she would be free of the guilt that she suspected kept her from making a decision to remain with Rees.

He was wonderful and she was flawed. A runaway and a breaker of hearts was who she was.

This very day she was going to admit with all sincerity to Rees how sorry she was to have made him search all night for her in the rain and cold.

She had apologised, just not with all her heart.

At that time she had not understood what he had been going through. Now that she did, everything was changed. Especially her.

Nothing he could do would make her run from him again. Problems would come, it was the way life was, but whatever those might turn out to be, she would not run.

Sitting up straight in the chair, she took a deep breath and smiled. What a relief it was to no longer feel cross. It was not in her nature to be so.

Life was much better now that she knew what to do.

Glancing at the bed, she decided that it was not as big and lonely as she had first thought.

No, rather it held a great deal of—well, of something wonderful.

Chapter Eleven

'I'm grateful that you are a level-headed bride, Madeline,' Lady Glenbrook declared later that afternoon while removing a Christmas ornament from a box. 'Bethany is quite overcome with…let us call it wedded bliss…to be of any help.'

Madeline wanted to be overcome, as well! Hopefully by tonight she would be. Sadly, every time she tried to get Rees alone so that she could tell him what she had decided, his mother assigned him an urgent task that needed doing.

This morning, before she could have a private word with him, he had been sent off to cut down a Christmas tree.

He had seemed to be reluctant to go, but Emily Lark and Victoria Rose screeched with such joy that he could do nothing but bundle them up and go get them a Christmas tree.

Madeline had been reaching for her coat, intending to go along with them, but Lady Glenbrook assigned her a task involving the ball. She could not refuse, given that the ball was in her honour.

No sooner had Rees returned with the tree than he'd been sent out again to gather garlands because, as his mother explained, the ball was three days after Christmas, which was only five days in total from today, which was already halfway spent.

Drat it. Now that she had made up her mind to be his wife in deed as well as name, every delay seemed achingly long.

'No one knows how much work goes into a celebration this time of year—even a smallish one like this will require all hands on deck, in ship's talk, but we have one, so it is appropriate.' Lady Glenbrook placed the ornament on the tree and then smiled at it. 'I can't say how I appreciate you, my dear. So many years without a daughter, and now, here you are beside me. Oh, look! Here is an ornament that Rees carved when he was ten years old. It's a boat. And look there. That small dark spot is from when he cut himself.'

She placed it in Madeline's hand for her to arrange on a branch.

'Has he always liked ships?' She placed the ornament in just the right spot to be admired.

'I think *boat* was his first word—for all that I'd hoped it would be *Mama*.'

A thrill skittered over Madeline's nerves. Mama was a title she'd been given, but had not yet accepted. Hopefully she would do it very soon.

But first she needed time alone with her husband in order to tell him.

'I hope Rees gets back with those branches soon.' Lady Glenbrook swiped a greying strand of springy hair away from her face with the back of her hand. 'There is still so much to be done. Just because there is a party does not mean we can neglect Christmas.'

'I wonder if there will be snow.'

'It's hard to predict, but for your sake I hope so.'

The front door opened and six men led by Rees entered the parlour, their arms laden in fresh greenery.

All of a sudden, it smelled like Christmas.

She had never spent the holiday away from Grandfather and Clemmie. If only—but, no—it was too much to hope Rees would find them before Christmas.

'What is the weather like outside, Rees? Your wife is hoping for snow.'

He dropped his boughs on the hearth.

'It's about to.' He made a dash, caught her hand and hurried her outside before his mother could object.

Which she would not have. In glancing back, Madeline spotted a smile on her mother-in-law's face. At least it seemed like a smile, but it could also be seen as melancholy. Madeline felt her heart twist, thinking Lady Glenbrook might be recalling days spent with her husband and missing them.

Following quickly behind, Madeline wanted to dance about in joy. She could scarcely believe she was about to see snow!

Out on the front steps, she stopped. Yanked her hand out of the strong one wrapped around hers.

'Rees Dalton! The sun is shining!'

He captured her again, pulling her along to—she did not know to where, but scarcely cared.

'It will snow eventually.'

'What will your mother think?'

He shrugged, laughing softly.

'She'll think we are trying to get out of helping,' she pointed out.

'Come this way. I know someplace where we can be alone.' It was not as though she could do otherwise since he would not let go of her.

He led her to the stable, through the great open doors and past several empty stalls.

'Where are the animals?'

'This is their time to run in the pasture. Here…'

Coming to a door at the far end of the stone structure, he opened it and drew her inside. There might not be snow, but it was cold enough for there to be.

The room was small but cosy-looking, having a couch, a desk, and a bookcase crammed with volumes looking well read. The room smelled comfortably of leather, polish and old books.

Over in the corner was a small black stove.

She looked longingly at it, wishing it had a fire blazing. Leaving the house as quickly as they had, neither of them had taken the time to put on a coat.

Ever since the lifeboat, she hated being cold, feared it, really.

Although snow was cold, she was eager to see and touch it, perhaps catch a flake on her tongue and taste the ice.

'Would you like a blanket?' Before she could answer, he opened a cupboard, took one out and placed it over her shoulders.

Kneeling in front of the stove, Rees opened the squeaky iron door, then stacked small logs inside. He poked them about to get the flames going.

'What is this place?' Being so small, it brought to mind their cabin aboard the *Edwina*. The cosy intimacy was the same.

'My second study. The one in the house can get busy with people wanting my attention.' He glanced over his shoulder, shot her a smile that made her insides tickle in the oddest way. 'I come here when I want to be alone.'

Standing, he crossed the room and locked the door.

All of a sudden, she felt hot. That was odd since the stove hadn't had time to heat the room.

Nerves had to be the cause. She was about to say something that would change her life. Certainly something like that would account for the dampness slicking her skin.

A spring creaked when Rees sat down beside her. He laid his arm over the back of the couch, but did not touch her as she would have liked. Oh, but the way he looked at her made it seem as though he was touching her and in a way that went deeper than mere flesh.

Apparently a woman did not need a glowing stove to warm her. The intensity of that blue-eyed gaze was enough to singe a lady's undergarments.

'This reminds me of our cabin aboard the *Edwina*.' Of the times when she wore no undergarment, but his shirt only.

Now that her heart and her mind were in agreement over what she wanted, well, she was glad that the door was locked and the curtain over the window drawn.

He plucked a pin from her hair, then another and another. When it was loose he drew it out of the fashionable coil, wove the freed strands between his fingers.

'You've told me you love me, Madeline.' He stared intently at the hair wrapped up in his fingers. 'Do you still? Now that we are here, settling in at Green Knoll, with my children and all the rest of the household—would you be happier living with your own family?'

His gaze shifted from her hair to her eyes. Worry lines creased the corners of his mouth.

The sight fairly crushed her since she was sure that she had caused them.

'I still love you.' She cupped the side of his face in her palm, watched his eyes close, his lids press together and then slowly open again. 'There is no place—there is no one—I want to be with more than with you.'

'But I can't imagine why you would trust me.' He stood

up suddenly, walked back and forth, looking down at her. 'After everything, you would still?'

'Yes, completely.'

'Why? What if I fail you again?'

'You are afraid I will run. I'm sorry, Rees. I've given you no reason to believe I would not.'

'I'm not a perfect man, you know that. What if—?'

'There is no what if—I promised myself and now I promise you. I know, it took too long for me to figure this out, but—' She rose from the couch, standing in front him to stop his pacing. 'Love does not run. I will not run.'

'But I—' His voice sounded ragged and it broke her heart.

'Let me just tell you—' She silenced him by placing her fingertips over his mouth.

Tears moistened her eyes, but there was nothing to be done about them.

How could she not wonder if, upon reflection, he feared trusting her with his heart, even more with the twins' hearts?

It did not seem so, he had never given indication it was true, but she could be very wrong.

Clearly he had something to say and she'd stopped him.

First she would say what she needed to, and then, if he still wished to say it, she would remove her fingers from his lips.

If after he'd heard it, if he changed his mind about wanting her, so be it. She would leave, but she would not flee.

'I do not want an annulment. I want to be your wife.'

There, it was done. One by one she withdrew her fingers from his lips.

Rees stared, gravely silent, at the weave of the curtain with his hands shoved deeply into the pockets of his trousers.

Why would he not even look at her?

Her chest felt heavy, like cold lead encased her heart. She walked towards the door, feeling so numb that that she was not aware of the wood floor under her shoes. There was no one to blame this on but herself.

Rees caught her elbow, swung his gaze up. Even had he not been gripping her, she would have been unable to walk away from what she saw in his eyes.

How wrong she was to believe, even for a moment, that he did not want her. It was not rejection, but utter relief she read in his expression.

He yanked her to his chest, pressing her close to his heart. His breathing came hard and fast.

'But what if I—?' Whatever he had been about to say seemed caught.

'And what if I do? Rees, we are married. I am yours and you are mine.'

'You are certain?' At last the smile she loved spread across his face, slowly like dawn rising on a new day.

'Vows spoken, my husband, commitments agreed upon. I will continue to be your wife, come what may.'

'I promise to do my best to make sure whatever comes brings you joy.'

He led her towards the couch, drew her down with him.

'I've been carrying this around just hoping. I'm surprised it's not worn out by now, but —' He dug about in his pocket, drew something out. It was the cigar band he had given her when they recited vows.

'You kept it?' For some reason, the fact that he had made her want to weep, more than she already did.

'It meant something to me, even then.' He slipped it on her finger. 'I think I loved you from the first, Madeline.'

'And I will love you to the last.'

Then, all of a sudden, words died between them.

* * *

His wife wanted him—not the annulment.

The master of Glenbrook, always in charge and in control, could not control his shaking fingers when he reached for the buttons on the front of her dress.

In this moment, perhaps control was better forgotten.

They had pledged their futures to each other, standing before the Captain of the *Edwina* as strangers. Seconds ago, they had done it again, this time in full knowledge of each other, of their virtues and their weakness.

Love would stand against anything.

Not so the frilly gown she wore. It melted away under his fingers as if of a mind to desert its wearer with all haste.

He hadn't noticed when his clothes deserted him. One moment they were a hindrance and the next they lay pooled on the floor.

The thought flitted across his mind that he must surprise her with a reunion with her family as soon as possible.

Flitted, then vanished because her skin smelled like heaven when he slid her down beneath him on the couch.

Ah, but the feel of her smooth, soft body under his fingers, that was earthy, carnal and consecrated.

Madeline woke up in her bed, stretched and felt delightfully sore all over. Judging by the way light filtered through the curtains, they had missed breakfast.

Certainly no one would wonder why. They had missed dinner, as well.

Madeline doubted that they were the first newlyweds to miss a meal or two.

As much as she hated to, they must rise and go downstairs. Surely the twins wanted to see their father—and mother. She could hardly wait to see the girls for the first time, knowing they were hers for all time.

'Wake up, Rees.' She pinched his bare behind. 'We can't leave your mother to do everything.'

With a grunt he shifted to his side, gave her a big blue-eyed wink along with a smile that made her wish she had not mentioned getting out of bed.

'There's the servants. She's not alone.'

'The children—they will wonder where we are.'

With that, he grabbed her by the hips and pulled her to him, belly to belly.

'Won't take long,' he murmured against her neck.

No doubt. Passion tended to spark between them like flint to tinder.

All right, what harm could it do to go down after lunch than before?

In the middle of a deep kiss, a noise from outside caught her attention. She jerked her mouth free.

'Did you hear that?'

'No.'

'Listen!'

'Hmm…' he drawled, seeking her lips again. 'We have a visitor, apparently.'

'Not just any visitor, Rees.'

All of a sudden, he sat upright. 'Langerby!'

That disagreeable voice could belong to no one else.

He scrambled from under the covers, pinched her behind on the way. Good for the goose and all that, she figured.

'Quick, let's spy on our sister-in-law,' he said.

'How?'

'We'll figure it out on the way down.'

Even though Madeline was not one to curse, she might take it up. To think of how Bethany must feel as he made such evil suggestions to her, which he had now evidently woven into a plan.

How conflicted she must be over it—it just broke Madeline's heart.

* * *

Hurrying out of the house, they stood at the top of the steps, listening.

For all that Milton Langerby had spoken loudly before, he was silent now.

Rees went down the steps, squatted and stared at the dirt.

'There.' He pointed to the path leading to the garden. 'His footprints go that way. Step quietly.'

Really? Did her husband not think she knew how to sneak about?

What she would not give to be able to arch her brows the way Grandfather and Clementine did. If the day came when she was reunited with Clemmie, she would ask her how to do it. Now that she was a married woman, she would need the skill.

She grabbed his sleeve, motioned that she ought to be the one leading the way.

He shook his head, auburn hair flying wild about his face. Since he had longer legs and quicker strides, she had no choice but to fall in line behind him.

When he would have gone crashing down the path, she indicated with a tip of her head that they should tiptoe discreetly down a tunnel-like space between the shrubs. They were tall and dense, so it would be easy to spy. If they were not to be heard, Rees would need to tread more quietly on the fallen leaves.

From where Madeline stooped, she could make out three shapes. There was Bethany. Her eyes looked dark, worried. The second was Langerby. She saw his profile well enough to make out his malicious expression.

The third was a small dog, held firm in Langerby's grasp. The scruffy brown creature wriggled in an attempt to get free of the bony fingers clamping its chest.

'Why have you come, Uncle? Why have you brought Spiffy with you?'

'I told you I would come. Surely you recall. I've come up with a plan for you to regain the title. The dog is here to make sure you agree to it.'

Langerby lifted the pup in the air when Bethany tried to grab it. 'Oh, careful now. He's a fragile little thing. Think of the harm a fall might cause him.'

The pup whimpered.

'I never had the title to regain it.'

Beside her she felt Rees turn rigid, his muscles grow hard and tense.

'Only because you did not ensure Glenbrook could not back out of it. Now listen closely. I will not repeat this.'

'I have no wish to hear anything you have to say.'

'Oh, surely you do—it is to your benefit, to say nothing of Spiffy's.'

The dog yelped, scrambled to be free.

'Please, put him down!'

Glancing aside at Rees, Madeline saw the anger building inside him, felt it radiating from his body.

'After you have heard me out and agreed to what I tell you to do.'

In the instant she thought Rees was going to make a rush for the man, she heard laughter.

Victoria Rose and Emily Lark came skipping around a corner, dolls tucked under their small arms.

All at once, they stopped, stared wide eyed.

'Doggy!' Victoria Rose shouted.

The girls dashed forward. Victoria Rose yanked on Milton Langerby's trouser leg while Emily Lark took the moment to go up on her toes and neatly pluck the pup from her captor.

'We has a puppy!' Emily Lark declared joyfully as both the girls dashed back towards the house.

Lord Langerby appeared perfectly stunned. So did Rees. Madeline wanted to applaud her sweet, clever daughters. She would have had she not wanted to know the next thing Langerby was going to say even more.

Halfway back to the house, the dog scrambled out of the eager arms gripping her middle. She ran headlong towards Lady Glenbrook, who neatly swooped her up.

'There you are, my little scamps! What is this you have found?'

'A puppy, Grandmama!' Victoria Rose hopped up and down, clapping her hands.

'Poor thing looks thin. Come, let's give it a bite to eat.'

Shooting a fast glare at her red-faced uncle, Bethany spun about and strode after them, but he grabbed her elbow.

'You will seduce the Viscount, keep at it until you are with child. He will divorce the American and marry you. We will think of what to do about your husband if he refuses to let you go.'

'You have gone mad! I will not do this.'

Red-faced, Langerby yanked her down so that he was nose to nose with her. It appeared he was within an inch of having an apoplexy.

Beside her, Madeline felt movement.

Rees stood up, then walked through the thorn bush as if it was of no consequence.

'Release my sister-in-law.' Rees's voice sounded like a blade.

Langerby jumped away from her as if, indeed, he had been sliced.

Madeline rushed for Bethany, drawing her further from the men since she was not sure what was about to happen.

'You will leave my property and never return. If the misfortune occurs when we meet in public, you will not address anyone who belongs to me.'

'I'm sure, Lord Glenbrook, you misunderstood the conversation with my niece. Perhaps she had poisoned your heart against me for some reason I do not understand.'

'Understand this. Under no circumstance will I betray Lady Glenbrook. Nor will I betray my brother or his wife.'

'I did not mean—'

'He did mean it!' Bethany shouted. 'You have always meant to use me to your gain.'

'No, you misunderstood my affection for you, my girl.'

Rees was fuming now. It was only a wonder he did not pound Lord Langerby into the dust.

Madeline would do it if she were able.

Rees gripped the wicked little man by the collar of his coat, lifting him off the stones.

Oh, Rees Dalton was magnificent. She had never seen anyone more valiant.

'There is no gain to be made here. You may leave here under your own power or I will escort you out, just this way.' Rees gave the villain a quick shake.

Langerby resembled a toy that small Spiffy might shake about.

Had the situation not been so serious, she would have laughed aloud.

'I'll go.' Rees set the man down quite a bit more gently than he had snatched him up.

Bethany spun about and rushed for the house. It was a shame she had fled so quickly, otherwise she might have seen her uncle trip in his hurry to get away. Very likely she would have appreciated the way he scrambled for footing and landed on his rump.

Madeline covered her mouth, but the giggle escaped.

Rees came to her, a frown narrowing his eyes.

'This is a serious matter. You should not—' His mouth ticked up on one side for all that the matter was severe.

'Well, it's not as if his scheme would have succeeded.

It would mean that I would have to be out of your bed in order for someone else to be in it.'

Just there, he burst into a marvellous grin.

'You, my angel, have taken my plain life and made it brilliant. I love you more than you can imagine.'

Chapter Twelve

Later that afternoon Rees left the stable office, where he had gone with Bethany to help explain all that had taken place. His sister-in-law had not seen a bit of humour in anything and was quite shaken. Of course, she had not seen her tormentor hit the dirt. It might have made a difference.

He curled his coat collar up around his neck. Dark clouds massed on the horizon, so low they appeared to be sitting on the distant hilltops.

Biting wind whipped under his coat while he ran towards the house. Smoke curling from several chimneys promised warmth and welcome.

Coming inside, he crossed the grand hall and entered the parlour.

It was as warm and welcoming inside as he imagined it would be, but the heat did not emanate from the fireplace. Madeline stood in front of the Christmas tree, gazing up at the angel on top and cradling a cup of steaming tea in her palms. The room could have been stone cold and all he'd feel was a gut-deep simmer.

She appeared to be lost within her thoughts and did not hear him come in.

'Merry Christmas,' he said. 'A day early.'

She took a sip, turning to him with a smile.

'You're back.' She set the cup on a side table, then crossed the room, wrapping her arms around his ribs in a hug. 'I missed you.'

'What were you thinking about just now? You seemed lost in whatever it was.'

'Christmas. Since tomorrow is Christmas I wanted to spend time with the tree. I love everything about them, don't you? The way they are so lovely and green. And the scent? It makes one feel happy inside. Excited and peaceful all at once.'

'Yet you looked rather sad.'

'Not sad. Wistful is all.' She lifted to her toes and kissed him. 'I've so much to be grateful for—you, the children and the rest of the family. I feel so at home here. But the thing is, even though I feel as though this is where I belong, I miss—' She bit her bottom lip and glanced away.

'Your grandfather and your cousin?'

She nodded.

Rees had been to Fencroft Manor only a short time ago and found no sign of Madeline's kin.

He would go again, this afternoon. If the family was in residence, and the Macooishes among them, he would make this a Christmas gift rather than a wedding gift. He would take Madeline with him. There was no need to make her wait longer than necessary.

Madeline's heartache was his own.

'Are you going to make me wait for ever?'

'What?' he asked, a bit startled. She was clever, but was she a mind reader, as well? Had she caught him out?

'Are you going to tell me how Wilson took the news?'

'He's got mayhem on his mind, as you can imagine. Where is everyone? The house seems quiet for this time of day.'

'I'm sure someone will make an appearance soon.'

He took her hand and led her to the couch. The pressure of her sweet body snuggling against him felt the most natural thing in the world. It was as if she had been here for ever. God willing, she would remain so.

'Your hair smells good.'

'I've been in the kitchen with Cook, making mince pies. It must be cinnamon you smell. Did you find anything out?'

He kissed her nose because it was so close and exceedingly cute.

'There is something that would mean the world to me.'

'What is it, my angel?'

'A real wedding. Not a lot of guests—only a vicar and our loved ones. Once we find my family, I would like to marry you again, but properly with flowers, and a beautiful gown having yards of satin and lace. Even pearls and rhinestones would not be amiss.'

'And you shall have it.' He kissed her bright smile. 'Put on a warm coat, my angel. We are going for a carriage ride. It's time you met the neighbours.'

Madeline climbed into the carriage, keeping a close eye on the sky while she did. It was cold and, with the clouds so heavy and grey—well, one never knew.

Perhaps on the way to meet her new neighbours she would encounter the great wonder of falling snow. If she did, she was going to stick her head out the window and catch a flake on her tongue, or capture enough snow in her hands to make a snowball and toss it at Rees.

The carriage shifted when he stepped in behind her. He lifted his hand to tap on the roof, the signal he used to let the driver know they were ready to depart.

A flash of movement from the porch caught her eye. The housekeeper ran down the steps, waving her arms.

Frowning, Rees got out of the carriage.

'What is it, Mrs Warren?'

'Your mother says to go for the doctor. The wee lassies have taken ill.'

Madeline hurried down the carriage steps after him.

'With a fever, my lord. She says to go at once.'

'Go, Rees. I'll see to the twins,' Madeline urged.

'Ask the groom to saddle Darvey,' he called up to the driver.

Madeline ran close behind Mrs Warren, up the steps and into the mansion. She heard Rees's footsteps pounding on the marble floor behind them.

He passed them on the stairs and entered the nursery first.

By the time Madeline and the housekeeper rushed into the room, he was holding Emily Lark in his arms, rocking her and crooning soft loving words against her red curls.

Lady Glenbrook cradled Victoria Rose.

For all that Rees sounded composed and in control, he looked pale and stricken with fear.

Mrs Warren must have thought the same, for she gently took Emily Lark from him. 'Go for the doctor, my lord. No one will be quicker at it than you are.'

He nodded. Madeline followed him to the door, touched his sleeve as he was going out. He glanced down at her, fear marking his features.

'Children are strong.' She patted his arm. 'They recover from fevers all the time.'

'Emily Lark feels so hot and her skin—it is too dry. It's—' He glanced over his shoulder, back at the room. 'It's the way their mother looked when—and I could not help her.'

'But you can help the twins.' She urged him towards the staircase. 'Go get the physician.'

When he was halfway down the steps she went back into the nursery.

'I'm here now, Mrs Warren.' She eased Emily Lark out of her arms and into her own. 'Will you make us some tea while we wait for the doctor to come? It would be most welcome.'

Or, if not welcome, at least a distraction.

'Certainly, my lady,' she answered, then hustled out of the room.

It was difficult holding a fevered child. Madeline had not done it before. It seemed an endless ordeal, feeling hot cheeks and foreheads, imagining they were cooling them, fearing they were growing hotter. Oh, but the waiting, waiting, waiting was the worst.

It seemed forever, but Rees returned with the doctor in under two hours.

Madeline stood back with him, gripping his hand tight while the doctor bent over the girls and examined them, first Victoria Rose and then Emily Lark.

It seemed a dreadful eternity before he straightened up, turned to look at them.

'Influenza,' he stated. 'Many children in the village are coming down with it. Most of them will recover if due diligence is given to their recovery. And these two little girls are strong. I have reason to believe they will, as well. But they must not be left alone. They will need lots of water, clean water, boiled, or willow bark tea if they can manage. It helps with the fever.'

'They are not in danger?' Rees asked.

Please, oh, please let the doctor say they were not.

'No one can tell how this will go. Some influenza outbreaks are worse than others. But your children are strong, Lord Glenbrook, and that will go in their favour. And so far I have not lost one of the village children, no adults either. Take heart and do not wear yourself down. If the twins are not improving within a few days, summon me. I will return straight away.'

With a nod and a reassuring smile the doctor went on his way.

'You see, Rees?' she said. 'All will be well. We just need to do the things he told us and take care of ourselves at the same time.'

She told him this, but would have been more confident in what she said had she not known influenza outbreaks which resulted in tragic ends.

On Christmas morning, Victoria Rose was well enough to come downstairs and open her gifts. While the fever had broken, she was still weak, and Rees carried her up to bed as soon as the ribbon and paper settled.

'Want to play, Faddie.' She touched his cheek, turning his face so that he had no place to look but at her pleading expression.

'You may play in your bed and tomorrow you may come downstairs.'

Entering the nursery, he kissed the top of her head, set her on her bed, then went to Emily Lark.

His sweet baby lay listless in Madeline's arms. Her fever had grown no better. Sometimes it was worse.

'I'll take her. You get some rest.' Rees glanced at the pallet of blankets on the floor that they took turns using as a bed.

'Being a parent is not an easy thing.' She stood up and handed off Emily Lark. She had not weighed much to start with, but now she felt like a feather in his arms. 'I did not expect to feel like a mother so quickly, but here I am worried to death. I don't know how I will sleep.'

'You fall in love very quickly. I suppose that must be why you take to motherhood so easily.'

She lay down on her side and tucked her hand under

her cheek. 'You must be right. I fell in love with you in a heartbeat, after all.'

And she deserved the best Christmas gift he could give. He'd hoped to have her reunited with her family by now, but it was not to be.

The moment the children were well enough, he would take Madeline to Fencroft and hope that the family was home and Macooish among them. At the very least they might know something.

Even though she claimed she would not sleep, Madeline's eyes closed.

A moment later his mother tiptoed in. She stopped to ruffle Victoria Rose's hair before coming to where he sat beside the window.

'How is she doing?' she whispered.

He shook his head.

'Perhaps I will postpone the ball.' She crouched down beside him and trailed her fingers across Emily Lark's forehead. 'We can dance when she is well.'

'No, Mother. Carry on as planned.' She would be better by then. He would not act as though she would not. 'She will come around by tomorrow.'

With a sigh, his mother stood again, ruffled his hair the way she had Victoria Rose's. 'I'll send a note to the doctor, ask if we ought to do anything differently.'

Passing by Madeline asleep on the floor, she paused to gaze down at her. A softly affectionate smile curved her lips. 'You picked well, my son, although you did not have a choice in it.'

'I was lucky,' he said.

Although the word *lucky* was not quite right. *Blessed* seemed a better assessment.

'Faddie…?' Emily Lark looked up at him, her eyes red and unfocused.

He wished he could make the day move faster. This time of watching and waiting was slow agony.

But it was as he told his mother—tomorrow would see her health restored.

Madeline sat up from the pallet on the floor with a start. She had slept far too deeply and for much too long. Rees ought to have awoken her by now.

She glanced at his chair. He was not in it. Neither was Emily Lark.

And where was Victoria Rose? Not in her bed.

She had no idea what time it was, but the house was still, the night beyond the window deep black.

What had happened? Rising, she hurried out of the room, then rushed down the stairs and across the hall.

Coming to the parlour door, she stopped, simply staring while her heart rolled over on itself.

Rees stood on a stool, lighting the candles on the Christmas tree.

Emily Lark and Victoria Rose sat on the rug, staring up, their faces reflecting wonder.

A pile of unwrapped gifts surrounded Emily Lark.

Madeline came into the room slowly, quietly, loath to spoil the magic of the moment.

'I is all better now, Mama.' The pallor of Emily Lark's face said she was not completely well, but she did not appear to be flushed with fever.

Victoria Rose hopped up, dashed to Madeline and wrapped her thin arms about her skirt. 'Father Christmas bringed presents.'

'We were waiting for you. We could not open them without you.' Rees blew out the large candle he had used to light the smaller ones, then stepped down from the stool.

He crossed the room, took her by the hand, then kissed

her cheek. 'Emily Lark is on the mend, praise the good Lord.'

'You ought to have woken me.'

'You were already stirring. I figured you would be down by the time I finished lighting the tree.'

Rees sat down on the rug beside the children. She settled hip to hip beside him.

Victoria Rose scrambled on to her lap while Emily Lark grinned at the treasure of packages with pretty bows set before her.

As frail as the child was, she managed to open them all within ten minutes.

She clutched her new doll to her chest. Her smile held no indication of how ill she had been only hours ago.

Even though it was the small hours of the morning on the day after Christmas, the magic of the day lingered.

'Where's your present, Mama?' Victoria Rose asked, curling her arms about Madeline's neck and squeezing.

The thought of exchanging gifts had not entered her mind over the past several days. She doubted it had crossed Rees's either. Judging by the dolls, books, new dresses and games under the tree, it had occurred to someone. Their grandmother, no doubt.

'Why, you are my gift, Victoria Rose.' She kissed her cheek. Then she leaned across to kiss Emily Lark's. 'And so are you. I could not have a better present than the two of you. I love you both so very much.'

'We loves you, too, Mama,' Victoria Rose said.

Emily Lark, one arm still clutching her new doll, climbed on her lap. Victoria Rose moved over to make room.

How, Madeline thought in complete wonder, could one go from not knowing anything about motherhood to embracing it so thoroughly? All of a sudden, she had two precious little girls whom she had come to love—and in a shockingly short time.

She looked over at her husband, watching moisture well in his eyes at seeing his babies with the mother they had so wanted, and it was all so very clear.

Once again she knew that love was yeast. It started small and now it consumed her.

Completely and unalterably, it made her their mother.

Later the sun shone brightly. Madeline thought it would be a good time to let the girls come outside for the first time since their illness.

Mother Abigail and the rest of the household were rushing about like a hive of busy bees getting ready for the ball. It would do everyone a great deal of good to take the children on an outing, even if it was only for a short stroll in front of the house.

Madeline listened to the girls sweetly chattering while she pulled them down the drive in the wagon.

Life was quite lovely. So much had happened to her in a short period of time. She had run away from all she loved, then run away from a fortune-hunting cad, felt desperately guilty over all of it and then, of all things, to find love and a home again.

It was a miracle, clear and plain.

'Horsey!' Emily Lark laughed. Victoria Rose tried to climb out of the wagon.

'No, sweetie, it is not safe to stand.' That sounded very motherly. She thought she might be a success at this business in time.

In the distance she spotted a horse galloping towards the house.

The rider was too far off to recognise, but there was something in the way he sat in the saddle, the way his slim form leaned forward over the horse's neck ever so slightly, that seemed familiar.

Naturally there was no way he could be familiar since she knew so few people in Derbyshire.

Whoever it was seemed to be in a great hurry. She turned about to roll the wagon to the side of the drive where the children would not breathe in the dust that the horse kicked up.

'Madeline!' She heard her name shouted over the thud of hooves hitting dirt.

Funny how her heart heard Grandfather's voice. She had heard it many times since she ran away, but it was never real.

She could only be listening with her heart.

Even hearing her name called again, she did not turn about because this was only one more instance where she imagined what she wanted to hear.

The hoofbeats stopped.

She turned to greet the rider and— *Grandfather!* Her mouth formed the word, but no sound emerged.

Surely she was dreaming, yet the sound his boots made crunching the dirt while he ran towards her was no dream.

'Grandfather!' she screeched while lifting her skirts and running towards him.

He caught her up in a great hug, rocking her, nearly crushing her in his embrace.

'Madeline, oh, my girl.' Then he held her away at arm's length, looking her over closely. 'Are you well? Nothing wicked has befallen you? If it has, I will carry you away this minute. You've only to say so.'

'You are here—really here? I don't understand.'

'Do you not know I have been searching desperately for you all these months? I've hired countless Pinkerton fellows. It was as though you had vanished.'

'I'm sorry—so very sorry for what I did to you,' she

cried into his coat, and not with pretty little sniffles, but with great racking sobs that surely garbled her words. 'It was wicked and I beg you to forgive me.'

'Ah, my darlin', it's not you who should beg—'tis me. I should have known better than to try to force my dream upon you. For all that it was a good dream, mind you, but I ought to have let you choose your own.'

'Oh, Grandfather.' She hugged him about the middle because any second she might blink and find this a dream, gone in a mist like so many others had done. 'But I ought to have refused you face to face and not in such a heartless way. That man I left with, oh, he was not who I thought he was.'

Grandfather cupped her face, peering solemnly into her eyes.

'No matter what may have happened to you, you are still my sweet girl. Even if the worst has befallen you, I stand by you.'

'The worst?' The worst might have befallen her had Rees not been there.

'There is talk in the village that you married rather suddenly. It is believed that—well—I only pray you were not forced to wed where you did not wish. You will recall what I've told you about your great-grandmother.'

'I do recall it and you will be pleased to know that my husband is an honourable man and I did wish it.'

Grandfather's face brightened. 'And a viscount?'

'Indeed he is. After everything, I ended up where you wished me to be. I can only imagine how satisfied you must be.'

'You are aglow, my girl. That is what I wished for. Seeing how it all worked for the good, I'm satisfied. But I only regret I tried to take away your choice in it. Can you forgive me?'

'You well know I do. But, Grandfather—did you take it from Clemmie? Did you make her marry in my place?'

'I simply guided her in the right direction. The choice was hers alone.'

'Clementine chose to marry Oliver Cavill? I cannot imagine it. From what you told me of him, they would not suit.'

'Not Oliver, no—sadly, the poor lad passed to his maker. It was his brother, Heath Cavill, that she chose. And a better match there could not be.' He arched his brows, giving her a hopeful smile. 'I think you have also been blessed by your choice.'

'You'll be happy to know that I have. And not just with the man, but you see those little girls in the wagon behind me?'

'I could hardly fail to notice them. They are enchanting.'

'And they are mine. I'm a mother, if you can imagine it.'

He tapped his chest with his hand. 'I'm overcome, my Madeline. You girls are giving me more surprises than I can keep count of.' He hugged her tight, let go, then stepped around her to squat down beside the wagon. He grinned at the twins and withdrew a pair of peppermint sticks from his coat pocket. 'May they have them?'

'Yes, but since when have you begun travelling about with peppermint on your person?'

'Only recently.'

Hearing wagon wheels on the drive and the hurried clop of hooves, Madeline turned to look. From behind she heard Lady Glenbrook come out of the house and exclaim her surprise.

'Ah, your cousin is here at last. We were in the village when we heard rumours that the Viscount had wed an American. We came as quickly as we could to see if she might be you.'

'Who are the people with her? Children?'

Grandfather pivoted on the balls of his feet, grinned up at her. 'Your cousin is a mother, too.'

The driver of the open-air coach had barely drawn it to a halt before Clementine scrambled down.

While Madeline tried to count the number of small faces peering over the edge of the carriage, her cousin dashed across the courtyard, holding her skirt up from the dirt and scattering a gathering of quail pecking at the ground.

'It is you!' she cried with a great smile. In spite of her being clearly joyful and relieved, her cousin stopped just beyond reach, placed her hands on her hips and shook her red curls. 'All this time I've been wondering if I would scold you when I saw you, or hug you and cry. On the way over I thought to give you a proper upbraiding…but now—'

Madeline opened her arms and Clementine rushed into them. They rocked and hugged for a very long time.

'I missed you so much, Madeline. Grandfather and I worried terribly, but I told him you would land on your feet.' All at once, Clementine broke the embrace, held her at arm's length and examined her head to boot tip, much as Grandfather had. 'You have landed on your feet? Oh, please tell me you have.'

'The rumours are true, Clemmie. I've married Viscount Glenbrook. But I regret what I did to you. Even though Grandfather says it worked out well, still…you wanted to teach and I robbed you of it. I beg your pardon.'

'Yes, what you did was wrong, but somehow everything worked out right. And I do forgive you, Cousin, a thousand times over!'

Taking her by the shoulders, her cousin turned her about. 'Come, Madeline, meet my children.'

'You have been busy, Clemmie. How many are there?'

From a short distance away she heard Grandfather's voice. He was speaking with Lady Glenbrook and sounding even more charming than he normally did.

'I've only the seven with me at the moment. The youngest ones are home with their nanny.'

'How many youngest ones?'

'Another seven.'

'Oh, my. Let's turn the children loose in the garden while the sun is still shining and we'll have tea. There is so much to find out about each other.'

She slipped her arm through her cousin's and led her towards the house.

Lady Glenbrook and Grandfather must have come to the same idea, for together they were in the process of gathering all nine children and herding them up the stairs.

'Is that Lady Glenbrook?' Clementine asked.

'My mother-in-law. Yes, she is. One would be hard put to find a finer lady.'

'I'm relieved to hear it since Grandfather is smiling at her in a very strange way, don't you think?'

It was true. Madeline watched the way he moved, the twinkle in his blue eyes and the flirtatious turn of his smile. Beyond a doubt, Grandfather was smitten.

In that moment, Rees strode out of the house. She did not have to summon a smile for him. It sprang from her heart to her lips without thought.

'Visitors!' Rees's mother had announced a moment ago while peering out the library window. 'There is no time for them, not with the ball in two days, but I suppose we must put on a gracious face.'

He hadn't time for them either, having fallen behind on the ledgers while he was at sea. He wanted to finish quickly so that he could take Madeline to 'meet the neighbours'. It had been put off far too long as it was.

However, his mother was correct. A visitor must be acknowledged.

Jotting down the last thing required in the moment, he'd set the pen aside, risen and followed her…directly into the path of ruin.

The scene before him left him gut punched. It nearly cut him at the knees.

Madeline's family had found her. It was clear that in the short time they had been here she had got the forgiveness she craved.

And he had missed it.

'Rees!' His lovely, sweet and smiling wife released the arm of a woman who could only be her cousin and dashed up the stairs to him.

She caught his hand, led him towards her grinning grandfather.

He felt like fleeing, but here he was, trapped as neatly as an insect underfoot.

'Rees,' she announced, her voice so full of happiness it made him ache. 'Please meet my grandfather, James Macooish.'

'It is good to see you again, Mr Macooish.' And there it was, the words to damn him spoken from his own mouth.

Madeline gave a quiet gasp, dropped his hand and took a step away. He could not look at her, but it didn't matter. Her gaze was upon him, hurt and shocked. What else was she to believe other than that he had once again deceived her? Withheld what was most important to gain his own ends?

Macooish filled the space that Madeline had left empty, pumped his hand up and down, then drew him into an embrace and pounded his back.

'In the village just now Clementine and I heard people talking about how you had married an American while at sea. For all that it seemed too much to hope for, we left the seamstress with the needle in her hand and came at once to see.'

'Indeed.' The red-haired woman who was presumably Madeline's cousin lifted her skirt to reveal the raw edge. 'A hem can wait.'

'Grandfather, are you already acquainted with Lord Glenbrook?' Madeline's voice was frighteningly steady.

He could not look at her, could not watch the trust she had gained in him fade from her eyes. To do so would be unbearable.

'Yes, indeed. And it is my pleasure to say so.' Madeline took a few more steps away from him. Her cousin filled the gap as if she sensed what was about to happen and was attempting to protect Madeline from the heartache she sensed coming. Macooish appeared not to notice, for he continued on quite heartily. 'We met briefly when I attended some business in Scotland. I approve of your choice, my girl. Madeline, are you taking ill all of a sudden?'

'Grandfather...' Clementine led Madeline towards the house even while she was speaking '...watch the children while I take her inside.'

His mother rushed to help Macooish gather the little ones and lead them to the path that led towards the garden gate.

And here he was, left standing alone to stare at the front door closing upon Madeline and wondering if the last he would see of her was her straight back and the lock of blonde hair that had come undone from her coif and now dangled between her shoulder blades.

He ought to charge after her and explain.

How could such good intentions have gone so horribly wrong?

Chapter Thirteen

Madeline felt numb all over, or perhaps not that. Numb would mean she felt nothing. What she felt was—it was everything and all at once.

Betrayed, of course, and angry. Sad and confused, not loved and loved, which made no sense at all.

And through it all she felt Clementine's arm about her shoulder, just as it had always been in times of joy and sorrow.

To think that Rees knowingly kept her from her cousin was a bit more than she could bear.

Shoulder to shoulder, they gazed from her chamber window, watching the children play in the garden below.

She let the emotions run through her, have their way for a time because one could not flee from what one felt.

Grief sat at the heart of it all. She felt that most intensely. Watching the twins playing below, she did not know how she would manage being separated from them.

She was good and furious at Rees for forcing her to be the one to break their hearts.

'Has he done something so awful?' Clementine asked, giving her a reassuring squeeze.

'He has.' She sniffed even though she was not crying as she had every right and reason to be doing. 'He has lied to me about very important things.'

'Has he? I know a bit about that. Heath lied to me, as well.'

'Big lie or little?'

'Rather huge, actually.' She felt Clementine take a deep breath, then let it out slowly, apparently building courage to share what it was. 'He was doing something that on the surface looked very wicked and he did not confide in me about it. He was a wanted man and I arranged for him to be arrested. Oh, you can imagine the shock when I discovered it. Of course, it was his fault. Had he shared the secret with me, I would not have set him up for arrest. For a time I thought he was a man the newspapers called the Abductor. Maybe you heard of him?'

'No. If it was recent, I was aboard ship where I nearly froze to death and, after that, nearly expired from seasickness.'

'Oh, my poor Madeline. It must have been horrible.'

'Oh, it was! But—' At least she was a truthful person even if the man she married was not. 'Well, it was also wonderful.'

'Because you married a man you thought you could respect?'

'I had no reason to think otherwise. This is for your ears only. I was forced to wed Rees because he compromised me.'

'Grandfather will call him out for it, I'm afraid.'

'It's not as wicked as it sounds.' Standing in the window, watching the children dash about, she told her cousin everything—how Rees had warmed her and that they had shared a cabin—his insistence that they do the honourable thing and wed, about the promised annulment. She went on to tell how he tended her through the misery of seasickness and how quickly they fell in love and then to find he was not who he claimed to be.

'I forgave him for all of it. But I don't know about this. I believe he wilfully kept me from you and Grandfather.'

'I understand it—the wretchedness of being lied to, but can you not forgive him?'

'I don't know—perhaps—but, no, maybe not.'

'We've all done things. Every one of us needs forgiveness at one time or another. I imagine your husband is no different.'

It was true. Had she not just been granted forgiveness from Clementine and from Grandfather? Both of them had reason to resent her, and yet here Clementine was, listening to her sorrowful story, giving comfort and advice.

What right did she have to withhold the same from Rees? A part of her thought she had every right, but another part, a better part, knew she ought to give him what she had been given.

What she needed was time to understand why he thought it was acceptable to deceive her, once again.

Down below she watched Grandfather begin to court her mother-in-law, for it was quite clear that was what he was about. He sat beside her on a bench rather too close for having met so soon. For casual friends even. 'What do you think of that?'

Clementine bent slightly forward, squinting her eyes in concentration. 'I don't know. We've never seen him in love before and he has only just met Lady Glenbrook.'

'Hmm.' She tapped her lips in thought. It felt very good to think of someone other than herself. 'But now that we are settled, maybe he will see to his own happiness.'

'Are we settled? Are you going to stay with your husband? It seems to me he looked quite miserable when it all came to pieces.'

'He ought to feel miserable! And, right now, I just don't know what I will do.'

'Do not take too long to decide. It will only make matters worse.'

'Worse? Oh, Clemmie, they are worse than you know.'

'How much worse?'

'Gravely worse. I've discovered I am a runner. I ran from my obligation to you and Grandfather. I ran from that man I went away with, although it was the wise thing to do. But I also ran from Rees when he misrepresented who he was. As soon as I discovered this flaw in my character, I vowed I would not do it again. So if I go home with you, I will betray that vow. But if I remain with my husband, I fear I will turn into a miserable shrew because I will resent him for making me resent myself.'

For some reason, her cousin must have found the revelation funny because she laughed aloud.

'If there is one thing you could never be, Cousin, it is a shrew.'

'No? I feel quite shrewish at the moment. But you are correct. I must decide sooner rather than later. There is to be a ball to present me and my sister-in-law, Bethany, to local society. I will either attend and remain with Rees or will pack a bag and come home with you. Since we are neighbours, I assume you were invited?'

'Oh, well, yes, I imagine so. There was an invitation waiting when we returned from London. Before I read it, one of the children ran off with it and I don't know where it ended up.'

'I won't wait overlong to decide. Two days is all. When you arrive at the ball I will either be dressed for the party or have my suitcase in hand.'

'Give it careful thought, but it's your heart you need to heed. Oh—did you see that?'

'Did Grandfather kiss her already?'

'Not yet, but one of my girls just scrambled up a tree! Am I supposed to forbid it?'

'You could, but it would not have prevented us from doing it.'

'I'd better go stand under the branch just in case she falls.' Clementine kissed her cheek. 'I'll see you in two days.'

From the window she watched Clementine burst out of the house, rush to the tree and stand under it with her arms spread.

Madeline felt as though she was on a limb. If only there was someone to catch her if she fell. She closed her eyes, imagining it happening. She was tumbling, frightened—who would be there in the end?

Rees Dalton. His was the only face she saw.

The question was, once he'd caught her, did she trust him not to drop her again?

Of more concern, did she trust herself? Would she run rather than make a hard choice?

Rees walked in the garden at midnight. He had not seen his wife since she had discovered his perceived betrayal, nor had he heard her voice. It felt very much like the light had gone out of his life.

Yesterday he had been given a lecture about honesty from his mother. It sounded very much like the one he and Wilson had cut their teeth on.

He ought to have paid closer attention, been more diligent in learning what she had to teach him.

Ought to have had, yes. But he hadn't, and so here he was, trying to walk off a guilty conscience. He was quickly finding that it could not be done.

Why had he been so intent on a surprise? He should have told her when he had first suspected her family was nearby.

He did recall not wanting her to be disappointed. Damn

it, she had gone far beyond disappointed. Not gone as much as had been shoved—by him.

A frigid breeze whooshed over the ground, shivering the bare limbs of the trees. He ought to go inside, but he did not want anyone to be bothered by a sudden burst of cursing. The emotion he voiced would be directed at himself and not anyone he happened upon, but since they would not know it, he remained outside.

Besides, from here he could see Madeline's chamber window. Every once in a while he saw her silhouette behind the lace curtain. She was pacing the same as he was.

He imagined her coming down to the garden, unaware of his presence. In his mind he saw himself stepping out from the shadows. He would replace the wedding ring he kept in his pocket for the cigar band, then take her in his arms and convince her of his devotion.

It was not likely that she would believe him. Not the man who had betrayed her trust, put it in a coffin and nailed it shut.

What a morbid thought. He shook it off, then breathed in a lungful of icy air. Somehow he needed to rid himself of this despairing mood.

He did have children to bring up. Emily Lark and Victoria Rose deserved a cheerful father.

Sitting down on a bench, he withdrew the letter that Lady Fencroft had someone deliver to him earlier this afternoon. He had read it over dozens of times, seeking whatever hope it might give him.

As far as hope went, it did not offer much. She conveyed her regret that things had happened as they had. Also that she knew a bit about the events causing the rift and that her cousin intended to make her decision by the beginning of the ball tomorrow. She said a few other things probably meant to encourage him.

It was difficult to feel encouraged. If Madeline meant

to forgive him, she would come to him. Yet if she had decided against him, she would not still be pacing in front of the window. She would have fled to Fencroft Manor.

While he stared up, she stopped, covered her face with her hands. Her shoulders shook as if she were weeping.

This was his fault, curse him. He would do something about it. He ran for the house, dashed up the stairs, then stood breathing hard in front of her door.

He lifted his hand to knock. Behind the door he heard her muffled weeping. He clenched his fist tight.

For all that he needed to rush in and convince her to stay, he did not.

He had taken the choice from her once before. This time it had to be her decision. He would not bend her will to his this time.

Before, when he'd forced her to marry him, his reason had been selfish—in part, anyway. His reason for not telling her he was acquainted with her grandfather had not been, but in the end, the result was the same.

He withdrew the ring from his pocket, took note of how it glimmered and sparkled in the hall lamplight. He knelt, then pushed it under the door, where a thin line of light shone on to the floor.

What would Madeline do with it? This was not how he'd imagined giving it to her. No, very far from it.

Rising, he spun about and plodded down the hall, then down the stairs towards the office. It had become far too cold to pace outside.

Snow was coming; he was nearly certain of it.

Because of him, Madeline would probably not enjoy it. The thought made him sick at heart.

Which in turn might lead to actual illness. He had seen that happen. He owed it to his children to remain healthy. Somehow he would learn to smile for them, to keep the

heated words he used to scold himself behind a cheerful facade.

He folded his arms across his chest while staring at the
fire cheerfully snapping in the office hearth.

He did not deserve Madeline's forgiveness.

Then, of course, forgiveness was not something one
deserved, nor could one earn it. It was a gift, freely given.
A gift he was going to kneel here in front of the flames
and pray for.

Madeline stared at the bed, listening to the faint, off-
key sounds of the orchestra warming up.

Three things lay upon it.

On the end of the bed closest to the pillow was a small
valise. At the foot of the bed lay her blue ball gown. If her
maid had wondered about the valise when she spread the
gown over the comforter as Madeline had asked her to do,
she did not raise a brow about it.

The pillow was where her eye returned time after time.
Square in the centre lay the wedding band that Rees had
pushed under the door last night. The pretty stones sparkled, the gold glimmered temptingly, but she had yet to
put it on her finger.

It was unlikely there was a member of the household
unaware of the trouble between the Viscount and the Viscountess. The fact that she had not emerged from her quarters in a day and a half would be suspicious to anyone.

Someone other than herself had to have noticed Rees
pacing the garden last night.

The ball was ready to begin. In spite of the threatening
weather, she thought she heard a few carriages crunching the drive.

She had promised a decision by now.

For a time last night, she thought she had made it.

When she heard Rees's steps in the hallway, heard him

pause outside her door, she had thought he intended to try to influence her choice.

Staring at the door, she willed him to go away, pleaded in her mind for him to pass by without trying to force her choice.

She pressed her palm on the door, listening to the strike of his boots on the hallway floor as he walked back towards the stairs.

It might have been the sweetest sound she had ever heard.

The unspoken message was clear. She was free to make her own decision in regards to him. No more lies to influence her to remain here.

For good or for ill, only the truth lay between them now.

In that moment when he walked away, she forgave him. She wanted to stay and spend the rest of her life with her new family.

The choice had been made, but then over the hours another doubt had crept in and it had nothing to do with Rees.

It was to do with her character flaw. It was perhaps worse than Rees being less than factual.

Would she run whenever something came up that she did not want to face? Would she do it now?

At least her husband had never run. He had not, except to run after her.

What if loving Rees and the twins was not enough to keep her from fleeing? She greatly feared the weakness inside her.

Loving Grandfather and Clementine had not prevented her from leaving them.

She touched the worn black leather of the valise. It was smooth, but cold and hard.

Next she drew her hand over the gown. So soft—the blue shimmer made her heart stir. Happiness fluttered in her fingertips.

She could not continue to stand here. After reading the letter she had asked Clementine to write, Rees would be waiting for her answer.

She needed to make a choice.

Looking back and forth between the items on the bed, something became suddenly clear.

Choice was a decision. One was not doomed to a certain behaviour. One could decide to indulge in it, or to choose another way…a better way.

She reached for the gown.

Rees stood alone at the foot of the staircase in the hall. The guests had already arrived and gone into the ballroom.

Madeline's grandfather had come in and shaken his hand, but also shot him a frown. Her cousin had greeted him with an encouraging smile which had made him feel better, but only for a time.

While the moments passed with no indication that Madeline was coming down, his spirit sank.

Whatever was going to happen, if she was going to walk away from him or to him, it was likely to happen on these stairs. They were the ones leading to the front door and to the ballroom.

Staring at the wide, elegant stairway was becoming agony. His eyes ached; his fingers hurt from being clenched tight.

He walked to the windows on each side of the parlour doors, staring out.

It was snowing! He wanted nothing more than to rush upstairs and tell Madeline about it. To carry her outside, swing her about and kiss icy flakes off her lips.

He nearly smiled at the thought—nearly wept at it, too.

All of a sudden, he heard the rustle of fabric at the top of the stairs.

He went utterly still, afraid to turn and see that it was

a servant and not his wife. But in his frozen state he did think the shifting fabric was silk and not cotton.

'Rees.' The whisper came softly, as if carried on an angel's wing.

Spinning about, he dashed to the foot of the stairs.

Madeline's ball gown shimmered around her, seeming a blue haze to his moist eyes.

He stopped at the foot of the stairs, gazing up. Tears dampened her eyes, too.

What did they mean?

He knew what his meant. A full heart—full of fear, grief, joy and hope all in one overwhelming instant.

The fact that she stood at the top of the stairs indicated, but did not guarantee, she forgave him.

She lifted her hand, revealing the glint of his ring on her finger.

He lifted his arms.

She lifted her skirts.

The light of the gas lamp winked off her silver slippers when she dashed down the stairs and landed in his arms.

She hugged his neck, sniffling. He pressed his face into her hair, probably doing a good bit more than sniffling.

'I choose not to run away again. If you believe that, I'm here to stay. No matter what mistakes we both make, I will not run from them.'

'Madeline,' he whispered into her hair because he had no idea how to respond. It seemed she was blaming herself and not him when he deserved every bit of it. 'I hardly know—'

'What's that?' She let go of him, staring intently over his shoulder.

'Snow.'

She gave a squeak, that was all he could call the happy sound, then pushed out of his embrace. She ran across the hall.

Fairly dancing on her toes, she drew open the doors and rushed outside.

Luckily he was right behind her and caught her in the instant her feet slipped out from under her.

'Oh!' she gasped.

'Ice.'

'I didn't realise.'

With an arm about her waist he led her down the stairs to the drive, where the gravel made for safer traction.

She lifted her arms and her face towards the flakes.

'It looks magical drifting past the lamps.'

It appeared as if she intended to spin in circles, but he caught her hand, drew her to him.

Her smile nearly brought him to his knees.

'Madeline, you need to know something. Until I saw your grandfather on the steps, I did not know for sure he was the same man I met in Scotland. I had no intention of deceiving you. I simply meant to surprise you.'

'It was a rather large one.' Thankfully she said so while pressing ever closer to him. 'I was greatly surprised.'

'But reuniting you with your family was supposed to be a gift, not a shock.'

'As gifts go, it would have been rather grand.'

'It was meant to be grand, to show you how much I love you.'

'And this—' she waved the ring in front of his nose '—is to show you how your love has changed me. I will not run again, Rees, no matter what comes.'

What could he say when there were no words? Go with his heart. He told her what was in it with a kiss.

'Please believe me when I say I will never deceive you.'

'If you accidentally do, I will remain right here in order to scold you.'

'Indeed.' He cupped her face, kissed her deeply. 'I love you, my angel.'

'I know you do. I love you, too, Rees.' Snowflakes gathered on her lashes and her hair. 'And isn't it interesting that all of our mistakes led us here?'

'More a miracle, I think.'

'Quite so.' She caught a snowflake on her fingertips and laughed over it. 'But love is the greatest miracle.'

Aboard the SS Edwina
First day of spring, 1890

Love might be a miracle, but in that moment Madeline felt rather sick because of it.

Standing at the bow of the ship, she glanced across at her cousin. Both of them gripped bouquets of pink-and-white roses.

Interestingly enough, her cousin looked the very shade of green as Madeline felt.

'I wish Grandfather had chosen to be married in one of our gardens in Derbyshire,' Madeline said to Clementine while waiting for the bride and groom to come on deck.

'Oh, if only this was a garden wedding.' Clemmie drew in a short breath and huffed it out. 'My sister-in-law, Olivia, had the right of it when she decided to remain in London.'

'Grandfather wants to show his new bride our home in Los Angeles. To be honest, I want to visit for a while.'

'The children will be glad to see it. They can speak of little else. You know, if each of them say only one thing it is constant chatter.'

'Yes, my mother-in-law has spoken of nothing else in weeks either.'

Madeline's stomach turned in a sickening flip, but she put on a good face. There was about to be a wedding. Joy abounded.

How many steps away was that rail?

Further than it had been when she and Rees shared a cabin. While she remembered that small space with fondness, life was easier in a first-class cabin. Especially with two busy children.

She had great admiration for women who managed to make the crossing with little ones in the steerage area. She would give great thought as to what might be done to make it easier for them. She did have influence with the owner of this vessel, after all.

'She is double your mother now, I would think,' Clementine observed, drawing Madeline back from her wool-gathering. 'Mother-in-law and step-grandmother, both.'

'At least Grandfather took more time in marrying than we did.' Madeline pressed her hand to her stomach.

'Neither of us had much choice about it, yet I do not regret a thing.'

Her cousin cast a glance at the rail.

'Clemmie? Are you ill?' Just looking at her made Madeline feel worse.

'No. I would not call it ill, quite.'

'Seasick?'

Her vibrant red curls caught the glitter of noon sunshine when she shook her head. 'Not that either. And you? Are you ill?'

'I suspect that I have the same condition as you do.'

Clementine winked, smiled. 'Cousin, would you like to join me at the rail for a bit of…relief… I suppose one must call it?'

'The Captain has only now come on deck. We have time.'

Side by side they strolled to the rail, glanced about to see if anyone was close by.

There was another poor soul seeking relief, but he was a good distance off and clearly his stomach would settle once the ship docked.

Clementine nodded. Madeline shrugged.

When they finished doing what Mother Nature required of them, they turned to look at each other. Madeline laughed and Clementine gave her a great hug.

'That ought to keep us through the ceremony, I expect,' her cousin declared.

'Does Heath know?'

'Not yet. And Rees?'

'He assumes I have seasickness again.'

Madeline spotted Grandfather coming out of his stateroom with Rees at the same moment Mother came out of hers, laughing and chatting with Bethany.

'This has all worked out rather well for Grandfather,' Clementine observed. 'Both of us wed to nobility and now a Dowager Viscountess of his own. Does she keep that title when she marries Grandfather? I wonder. I've forgotten most of Grandfather's notes on the subject.'

'She does, indeed. I suspect Grandfather is delirious over it.

'We ought to tell them,' Madeline said, watching their husbands coming to collect them for the ceremony.

'Together or separately?'

'Some of both, I think. You stay here and I'll go about twenty feet that way.'

'The ceremony will start in five minutes,' Rees said, taking her hand and placing it in the crook of his arm.

'That should be enough time,' Clementine said with a wink.

'Enough time for what?' Heath asked.

Clementine did not answer, but led her husband down the rail a bit.

'How many children do you want, Heath?' she heard her cousin ask.

'I don't know, but I'm sure you have a number in mind. Have you come across some more orphans?'

'Not an orphan and it's only the one.'

Rees grinned at them while Madeline led him in the other direction. 'What amazingly good news! And to get it on the wedding day.'

She stopped walking. Already her stomach was in revolt. She could only hope the ceremony would be a quick one.

'I know that look. Would you like to rest in the state-room? I ought to have kept the ivy pot.'

It was a lucky thing he had not, she might wallop him with it for making such a joke, but then, she would rather kiss him. Which, of course, was what had led her to be feeling as she was.

'You do not know this look, Rees.'

'Ah, but I do. I have seen it—'

'Perhaps you have, but you have not seen it on me.'

'Have I not?' All of a sudden, his smile flashed up on one side as the knowledge of what she was saying became clear to him.

He enfolded her in a hug, swaying.

'If you rock me like that, you will be sorry.'

'I will never be sorry. What was it we said in the garden the night of the ball?'

'Love was a great miracle.'

'Yes, and so it goes on, my angel. Miracle upon miracle.'

* * * * *

*If you enjoyed this book, why not check out
these other great reads by
Carol Arens*

The Rancher's Inconvenient Bride
A Ranch to Call Home
A Texas Christmas Reunion
The Earl's American Heiress